The Grievers' Group

by

Richard Wiley

For Penny —
warmly,

Books by Richard Wiley

Tacoma Stories
Bob Stevenson
The Book of Important Moments
Commodore Perry's Minstrel Show
Ahmed's Revenge
Indigo
Festival for Three Thousand Maidens
Fools' Gold
Soldiers in Hiding

STAY THIRSTY PRESS

An Imprint of Stay Thirsty Publishing

A Division of

STAY THIRSTY MEDIA, INC.

staythirstypublishing.com

For Sebastiana Wiley

The Grievers' Group

by

Richard Wiley

Everyone can master a grief but he that has it.

-- William Shakespeare

No one ever told me that grief was so much like fear.

-- C.S. Lewis

Part One

1.

Cornelius

It started when I won a ten dollar blackjack bet at Mandalay Bay casino and let my winnings ride, my eyes on my cards, but flitting occasionally to the only other player at the table, a beautiful woman in her forties, who sat down just after I did and ordered a Paloma when the cocktail waitress came by. It was four o'clock on a sunny December afternoon, but low-lying clouds filled my heart.

"What's a Paloma?" I asked the woman.

"Tequila and grapefruit juice," she said, "it's an underrated drink."

When the cocktail waitress lingered, I ordered one, too.

"Paloma was the name of one of Picasso's daughters. Her mother was Françoise Gilot, who later married Jonas Salk," I said.

Showing off such random knowledge had once been common with me, though lately I'd kept it to myself. I won my second bet, and when I also let the forty dollars ride I soon had eight ten-dollar chips in front of me.

"Beginner's luck," I told the dealer, a woman whose nameplate said "Louise."

"Are you betting the whole eighty dollars?" the Paloma woman asked.

"Why not? If I lose I'm out ten bucks...probably be the

cost of a drink at the bar."

I pantomimed raising a drink to her, since our Palomas hadn't come yet.

"Salud," she said, raising her invisible drink, too.

Louise dealt me two aces so I split them. I pulled four twenties from my wallet to cover the split, then drew a black-jack on one hand and a nine on the other, winning both and coming away with $360, since a blackjack pays one and a half times a person's bet.

"Wow," the Paloma woman said.

That was when it actually started, for "wow," spoken calmly and without inflection like that, had been a common expression of Yuki, my late wife.

"Put those twenties back in your wallet," the woman said. "That way you'll never be risking more than your original ten," but by then Louise had turned my extra twenties into chips, so I left everything where it was, in a fit of what Yuki would have called my "passive braggadocio."

But I won again, mounting a total of seven hundred and twenty dollars in just about no time. The clouds in my heart began to lift.

"Stop now," said the woman. "Take your wife out to dinner and to a show."

Our drinks had come by then so we drank from them.

When Louise's shift ended I took a ten dollar chip off my stack and tipped her with it. Considering how much I'd won it was a paltry tip. My $720 was now $710.

"Seriously, stop," said the Paloma woman, "you get a new dealer around here and things can go downhill fast."

But our new dealer was a smiling young man named Pat, who said, "No downhill with me, lady. I bring everyone luck 'cause it's Saint Patrick's Day!"

It was not, of course. The reason I was even in Las Vegas was to celebrate my granddaughter, Phoebe's, fourteenth birthday, December 6, 2019, the day before Pearl Harbor Day. Phoebe's mom, my daughter, Emi, was with us, both of them down at the Mandalay Bay pool.

When Pat pointed to his nameplate the Paloma woman rolled her eyes. "How much chutzpah does that take to call yourself Saint Patrick?" she asked.

When she said that her name was Natalie, I told her mine was Cornelius.

A pit boss came by to see what was holding up the action, so I said "Let it ride, Pat," in order to show a little chutzpah of my own.

This time I got a queen and an eight, as did Natalie, who was betting ten dollars per hand. Pat's visible card, his 'up' card, as they say, was a six, his hole card a ten, so he had to take a hit - that was the rule, dealers had to hit sixteen and stand on seventeen. When he busted with a king, Natalie won ten bucks, while I now had $1420 in front of me. I sat up straighter on my stool. "Six bets and look where I am," I said. "I could buy Phoebe a laptop and a phone."

I told them about Phoebe's birthday and that she was the love of my life since my wife died. We had scattered half of Yuki's ashes on Puget Sound only three months earlier - my promise being that I would eventually take the other half back to Japan - so it felt wrong to bring her death up casually. What was worse, Natalie moved to the seat beside me.

"Let it ride again, Pat," I said.

This time Pat dealt me a blackjack, the king and the ace of hearts, turning my $1420 into $3550. Natalie said, "You want another Paloma, Cornelius? I'm having one."

The casino was fairly empty, with only two other blackjack tables open. Even so, a handful of people formed a half circle around us, like the choir in a very small church.

"All in again, Pat," I said. I also agreed to a second Paloma.

Pat drew our cards from an eight-deck boot, so he hadn't had to shuffle since taking over from Louise. This time he dealt me a four and a five, Natalie two queens, and himself a jack for his 'up' card. When I asked for a hit I got a two, took another hit and got an eight, and stood on nineteen. Natalie stood on her queens, and Pat's hole card was an eight, so I beat him by one and got seven thousand one hundred dollars worth of chips. When the pit boss came to speak in Pat's ear, Pat said, "The limit at this table is five thousand dollars, sir. If you want to keep this up you have to go to the high rollers' room."

"I'd like to bet it all again," I said, "but only if I can stay here."

The pit boss went to his station and picked up a phone. I looked at the ceiling for cameras, supposing that whoever he was talking to would like to get a better look at me.

"I'm happy to say we're lifting the limit," he said, when he came back.

This time Pat dealt me two tens, Natalie two nines, and himself two jacks, so Natalie lost while Pat and I tied. A "push," they call it. But I won the next hand.

"Wow," Natalie said again. "Two times seventy-one hundred is fourteen thousand two hundred bucks. Quit now, honey, don't press your luck."

When our second round of Palomas came, the waitress

put Natalie's under a fresh coaster but Natalie told her to leave mine alone, that no changes were possible since luck was a fickle mistress.

"Do you live in Las Vegas?" I asked her. "Something tells me you're a local."

I didn't care where she lived, but I had to bring the regular world back in. A half hour earlier I was down by the pool with Phoebe and Emi. I told them I was going to my room for a nap, but wandered over to the blackjack tables and now I was involved in this amazing thing.

"I am indeed," Natalie said. "I came here to meet someone."

"Sir, are you betting?" asked Pat.

"All in again, Pat," I said.

Natalie bet again, too. When I got another blackjack the choir behind us said "Ah," for I had won thirty-five thousand five hundred dollars.

"Can you tell me how taxes work on winnings like this?" I asked Pat. "If I cash in now, will the casino take out Uncle Sam's cut?"

"Not on table games," he said. "You handle that yourself later on."

"One more time, then, Patrick," I said. "Let's see what's what."

Such joviality was deeply unlike the man who used it, even before Yuki's death.

Pat dealt me a seven and an eight. This time Natalie got a blackjack, and Pat's 'up' card was a six. It meant that no matter what his hole card was he had to take a hit, while I could take one or not, with about equal chances of winning or losing. It was my first hard decision but I made it quickly, holding on fifteen. Pat's hole card was another six, followed by a three, and then a seven, busting him at twenty-two.

Natalie took a pen from her bag, wrote "$71,000" on her new coaster, and pushed it into my line of vision.

On the next hand I got two more aces, but didn't have another seventy-one grand, so I could hardly split them. Natalie got a king and a nine. Pat's 'up' card was a seven. My aces could be two or twelve, so I took a hit, got an eight and stayed on twenty. Natalie stayed on nineteen. Pat's hole card was a seven and he hit it with the jack of spades.

"Busted!" said the pit boss, whose nameplate said "Frankie C."

Natalie drew a line through "$71,000" on the coaster, writing "$142,000" below it.

"Today's my granddaughter's fourteenth birthday and this will be my fourteenth hand, if I count the push," I said.

When I looked at Natalie's coaster I also saw her legs below the edge of the table, as thin and shapely as Yuki's had been.

"Pat, we're going for it," I said. "One last hand."

Pat drew the cards with the smooth stroke of a man petting a cat. My first card was a two, Natalie's a three. Pat gave himself his hole card, then dealt me an eight, Natalie another three, and himself, face up, an ace. The choir behind us "ahhed," while Pat looked at Natalie and me to see if we wanted "insurance," a way of saving ourselves if his hole card gave him blackjack. When we refused, he slid a corner of his hole card under a device that let him see it before flipping it over and ending this brave new world I had entered with the quick brutality of a sword thrust. He peeked, then looked at us. No ten or face card, so no blackjack for Pat.

My two and eight made ten, so I couldn't bust on the next card, which was the four of clubs. I now had fourteen and was in trouble. I couldn't stand on fourteen, everything I knew about the game told me that, and I was about to ask for a hit when Natalie placed a hand squarely in the center of my back. "It's Phoebe's fourteenth birthday, this is your fourteenth hand, and now you've got fourteen," she said.

The way she said Phoebe's name made me know, for a second, that Yuki had come back to inhabit this woman. So did the touch of her hand.

When I told Pat, "no more hits," Natalie split her threes, doubled her bet, got a ten and then an eight on her first hand, giving her twenty-one. She busted on her second hand, but had played both correctly so the blackjack gods wouldn't frown on us.

Pat turned his hole card over to let us see a second ace. His next card was a jack, giving him twelve, so any ten or face card would bust him, and anything else, save another ace or a two, would beat me. He did draw another ace, but then he drew a jack, making twenty-three.

Natalie pulled her coaster back to write $284,000 on it. A man who looked like a bodyguard and another man who looked like he owned the place came to our table. I found a five hundred dollar chip in my stack and pushed it across the table to Pat, who nodded but left it where it was.

"Are you staying with us, sir?" asked the man who looked like he owned the place. "If so we'd like to comp your room."

He looked at Natalie. "Have we met before?" he asked.

"I come here sometimes. I'm about to meet someone at Red Square," she said.

She pulled out a business card, tucked it in the pocket

of my shirt, then walked away. Pat, meanwhile, counted out twenty-eight $10,000 chips and placed them on the table by a few more chips of smaller denominations.

"Let's get you paid, Mr. MacLeish," said the man who looked like he owned the place.

I wanted to ask, but didn't, how he knew my name.

The impulse I did give in to was to turn and watch Natalie walk away.

*****

Cornelius MacLeish wrote the above description of his trip to Las Vegas for his North End grievers group in Tacoma, Washington. Since he "used to be" a writer - his current way of describing it - he had tried to put in what flourishes he thought might please the other members of the group without getting away from the facts as they occurred. But when he read it aloud just now he noticed that the others stared at their hands or at some spot in front of them. So whatever his intentions, he had no idea what they thought.

Þórdís Jakobsdóttir, their therapist, was the first to speak when he stopped.

"Well," she said, "we certainly got more than we bargained for."

Frank, the only other man in the group, said, "Corny, did you make all that up?"

The group wasn't large, only Cornelius, Frank, three women their age; Ruthie, Millicent, and Jane, plus a younger woman, LaVeronica, who hadn't shown up tonight. There was no rule that they had to live in the North End of Tacoma to join the group, but they met at Þórdís's house, and that happened to be where it was.

"No, I didn't make it up. That's exactly what happened," Cornelius said.

"Well, I liked 'It was four o'clock on a sunny December afternoon, but low-lying clouds filled my heart,'" said Jane "I feel like that every single day of my life."

Jane was a dour woman of seventy, an earlier prettiness determinedly fleeing her face.

"I liked the part where she put her hand on your arm," said Millicent. "Or, I'm sorry, maybe it was your back."

"No need to be sorry. We don't apologize here, except when I say that I'm sorry our time is up," said Þórdís. "Any last comments? This entire week belongs to Cornelius remember, he's up again on Wednesday and Friday, so we'll see what he has to say."

The idea of one client being "up" for an entire week, of having that kind of focus, was not the norm for grief groups, but an invention of Þórdís's mentor, Josefine Christophersen-Hemmingsen. She had said it avoided both random waves of emotional excess *and* monopolization.

"I bet we'll discover that there wasn't any Natalie, that he only wished there had been," said Jane. "My Giancarlo…"

"I'm sure your Giancarlo would have sat beside you at any blackjack table in any casino in the world," said Þórdís.

She hoped that wasn't too condescending, *nor* too Bogartish.

"Thanks for listening. I know I went on too long," Cornelius said. "The rest will be shorter, I promise."

He really had gone on too long. They were supposed to discuss their feelings in here, not listen to some retired writer's nearly impersonal essay.

Another group waited in Pórdís's living room, five kids not much older than Phoebe, each with an accompanying adult. Frank suggested that they go for a drink, but Cornelius had only come back from Las Vegas the night before and had stayed up late writing what he just read to them. Still, he didn't want to be rude, or discuss it in front of the others, so he said he had to use the bathroom first and would meet Frank outside. Frank had tried to jump off the Narrows Bridge after his wife died, but a passing motorist talked him down.

Cornelius stayed in the bathroom for a long few minutes and Frank wasn't there when he went outside. Ruthie, however, was leaning against her Porsche.

"Hey," he said. "Have you seen Frank?"

"He drove off in a huff," she said. "I did a bad thing, Cornelius. I told him I had a date with you for a drink."

Ruthie lost her husband, Ben, at about the same time that Cornelius lost Yuki. She'd gone out early on the morning of his funeral and gotten herself a pageboy haircut; "exactly" like the one Audrey Hepburn wore for most of her life.

"Why did you tell him that?" Cornelius asked.

"Oh, I don't know. He's been aggressive with me lately, calling me at night and such. At first I was nice to him because I thought it was an emergency or that a meeting had been cancelled, but it wasn't either of those things."

When Cornelius asked, somewhat guardedly, "Do you want me to talk to him?" Ruthie laughed and said, "I just wanted you to know about it since I used you as my excuse," then she got into the Porsche and drove off.

As Cornelius drove off, too, toward a supermarket, his check from Mandalay Bay for $280,000 rode beside him on the passenger seat, tucked inside an embossed envelope. He picked it up, put it in the glove compartment, and took out the supermarket's coupon offering two chinook salmon filets for the price of one. The regular price was twenty-five bucks a pound, making the two-for-one deal just okay, but Phoebe might come over - she was likely to whenever her parents fought - and Phoebe loved salmon.

Inside the supermarket Cornelius noticed a thin Asian woman with bobbed gray hair standing over by the fancy cheeses, and immediately decided that she was Yuki. When he guided his cart near her, however, he saw that she wasn't even Yuki's close doppelgänger. She felt him standing there, but when she turned a wary eye in his direction and saw his craggy face, she dropped her guard.

"Sorry," she said. "I get lost in thought in here."

He held up his salmon coupon to let her know where he was headed, then passed without speaking. Salmon wasn't the only thing he needed. Yogurt, fruit, and milk were on his list, plus bread and salad fixings. He looked back toward the woman and to his surprise found her right behind him.

"Hi again," she said.

"If you forget your coupon they can usually find you another one," he told her.

He reached into his pocket and pulled out Natalie's card. He carried it over to a nearby waste bin, dropped it in, and brushed his palms against each other.

"Washing your hands of something?" the woman asked. "I do that a lot these days."

Those were the words of the bereaved. They recognized each other like members of AA.

Cornelius picked up two salmon filets and hurried off to

finish his shopping.

Before he left the supermarket he retrieved Natalie's card.

2.

Þórdís

Þórdís Jakobsdóttir, the therapist, didn't have a PhD or an MA or an MS, nor even a BA or a BS degree. What she had was an *honorary* doctorate in therapy from the Chokkold Institute in Iceland, pronounced like it sounds - choke old - not "Choke hold" or "Cuckold," though people made jokes. Chokkold itself, however, was no joke, but an internationally renowned center for the study of grief and mourning. People came to study there from all over the world: scholars doing post-doc work, therapists learning new techniques, even the occasional medical doctor. Þórdís's own interest in it was long-lived, for her childhood home had been across a rutted alley from the Chokkold campus. Some of her earliest memories were of playing on its grounds, where she could listen to the conversations of students and faculty as they walked about or sat on benches. If the weather permitted, classroom windows were open, allowing Þórdís to scrunch beneath them in order to take in the lectures from start to finish. She supposed she was easily captured by grief because she was the happiest of children, with happy parents who lived busy lives. Grief was interesting to her because it was foreign, the case studies like portraits from another world, the one she remembered best having to do with a girl her age who lost both her parents in a fire. It moved her to tears and then to outright sobbing to hear what that girl went through, causing the lecturer, a woman from Denmark, to lean out the window, reach down and put a hand on Pórdís's head, then help her stand and climb through the window, where she could sit on the floor inside the classroom and listen to her heart's content.

Which she did for three years, until *her* parents were killed, not in a fire, but in a fishing boat accident. A few weeks after the accident that Danish lecturer, single and living in university housing, moved into the Jakobsdóttir home, where she raised Pórdís "the rest of the way," as they both liked to put it, and also, with Pórdís's permission, turned the Jakobsdóttir dining room into the same sort of therapy room that Pórdís later fashioned in her Tacoma house.

As time went by, not only did Pórdís and the lecturer, Josefine Christophersen-Hemmingsen, grow as close as a mother and daughter, but Josefine's star rose at Chokkold until for a brief couple of years she became its president - brief because of esophageal cancer, but long enough to bestow - a dying president's privilege - that honorary degree on Pórdís. So Pórdís became a doctor whether anyone liked it or not. Though, since no one *did* like it, nor, more to the point, respected it, she soon moved to the United States and took up residency in Tacoma. Why Tacoma, exactly, will be the subject of a Pórdís section later on.

At the Chokkold Institute bookstore, on her last day in the country, Pórdís bought a T-shirt that she still sometimes wore, its slogan, *"Chokkold's Got a Grip on Grief,"* festooned above a cartoon depiction of Josefine Christophersen-Hemmingsen wrestling and defeating a monster called "Despair."

Pórdís had a framed photo of her mentor on the wall of her dining room.

"My mom," she sometimes said.

She didn't think that that was in any way disrespectful to her birth mother...she simply thought of herself as having been lucky twice.

3.

Cornelius

Cornelius marinated his salmon in lemon juice and olive oil and made a salad. He would cook both fillets out on his deck whether Phoebe showed up or not, then listen to music or watch the news on television while he ate at his kitchen table. That was his routine, not interrupted since Yuki's death, except by the trip to Las Vegas and on his therapy nights when everything happened a little later.

So far it had been a mild winter, occasionally cold and gloomy, but with a few sailboats still venturing out onto Commencement Bay daily, and flotillas of them on Wednesdays. When he dug Natalie's card out of the trash at the supermarket it had smudges on it, like it landed on a glob of mayonnaise. To make matters worse, he'd put his thumb on a smudge, so now the card held a partial thumbprint - evidence against him, he couldn't help thinking, at a sanity hearing.

When his dinner was ready he turned his radio to a classical station, tonight devoted to an F minor Scarlatti piano sonata. Tomorrow, he had a private session with Þórdís, after which he would deposit his money in the bank. A man on the radio was talking about Scarlatti and also about what his audience would listen to next. The man's voice had the calm discernment that classical music DJs always seemed to have, a closeness that made Cornelius feel as if he were being spoken to by a friend.

"Mozart's clarinet quartet in A major is coming right up," the man said.

"What? I have to listen to four clarinets?" Cornelius asked his empty kitchen.

Phoebe would have laughed at the joke, if only to please him, but Phoebe hadn't shown up. So after he had his fill of salmon *and* Scarlatti, he went upstairs to work on the next installment of his Las Vegas story. That the writing came easy cheered him, since it hadn't come easy for a good long while. Sleep hadn't, either, but he went to bed at midnight and when next he looked at his clock it was six a.m., so that wasn't bad. Six solid hours. A postpartum record, if he could use "postpartum" for this situation.

When he dressed and went downstairs, he was surprised to find that not only hadn't he cleaned his grill but he hadn't even closed its lid, a thing made clear to him by a seagull standing on the nearby railing and plucking at bits of salmon skin. When he opened the deck door and shouted "git!" the seagull flew off.

This cleaning forgetfulness was unlike him - he'd been orderly since his days in the Marine Corps, a person who thrived on routine - but at least the kitchen was neat, the leftover salmon and salad stowed in the fridge. So he found a scraper, cleaned the grill, then got a broom and swept the kitchen and deck. After that he got his outdoor broom, went down into his backyard, and swept the granite slabs that meandered from the bottom of the deck to the chairs and table that sat under a weeping willow at the end of his yard.

His appointment with Pórdís was for nine o'clock. On the off chance that Phoebe might barge in for breakfast, he hung around until after she had to be in school, and still got to Þórdís's before the appointed hour. He could see her through her living room window, dancing around with a duster in her hands. It was like a scene from a cartoon musical, where the duster would soon take on a personality of its own.

Þórdís saw him in his car, put down the duster, and walked out onto her porch.

"Come in! No need to wait!" she called, so he got out of his car, walked up her steps, and followed her into the dining room. He listened for the dusting music, but her house was quiet.

Þórdís had coffee ready and poured him a cup. She sat where she always did, under a photo of her mother back in Iceland. He sat closer to her than he did during group. It made it easier to hear her when she spoke like that classical music DJ, as she did when they were alone.

"Were you satisfied with what you read last night?" she asked.

"No. I went on too long about each blackjack hand and I embellished too much, when I really wanted to talk about thinking Natalie *was* Yuki," he said. "She's everywhere, Dr. Jakobsdóttir, I even thought I saw her at the supermarket after I left here."

"Þórdís," Þórdís said, then, "Embellished too much how? I thought you were paying attention to detail. But let me ask you…the thing with Natalie writing numbers on a coaster. Did that really happen or did you embellish that?"

"It happened exactly as I wrote it."

"Which was how I understood it. I felt you were concentrating as much on her as on the blackjack hands. How her legs looked like Yuki's, how she said 'wow' without inflection, and the bets that *she* was making… You say you thought she might *be* Yuki, but I couldn't help wondering if you hoped she might turn into someone new in your life. And that reminds me. The thing with Natalie's card. Do you still have it?"

"I can assure you, I don't want anyone new in my life, but yes, I still have the card. I threw it away. Then I fished it back out of the trash."

Pórdís raised an eyebrow. He thought about mentioning the mayonnaise but said, instead, "If I tell you more about Natalie now I'll be stealing from tomorrow night."

"And I want to react with the others. Speaking of which, do you mind if I ask how you think the group is going? Normally I wouldn't ask such a thing, but an issue has come up."

Cornelius wondered if Ruthie had called her to complain about Frank.

"I hope it doesn't have to do with me," he said, knowing that it did not.

"As a matter of fact, it does have to do with you. One member told me that you and another member are meeting after our sessions. And though that's not against the rules, the person who told me was upset about it."

"And the upset person would be Frank."

"So you know already? Enough said then. Frank's feelings are his business. And what you do is yours."

"To be clear, I haven't met anyone for a drink, except for Frank himself once. I like things the way they are."

"Good," said Pórdís. "I like them this way, too."

For the first time since he started therapy, though he took them copiously, Cornelius opened his notebook to peek at his notes.

"You know, when it was his turn to be up, Frank said, 'The seeds of grief are planted when you give up part of yourself to make room for someone else. The other person does it, too, until you've made a new person called 'us.'"

"Yes," said Pórdís, "I remember that."

"Well, at the time, I thought it was nothing short of obvious, but now I think about it often. Yuki's death not only left me shipwrecked on the shoals of a singular misery, but it killed our 'us,' as well. It's two deaths, really, not one. I don't think I knew that, or at least I didn't think of it that way, before…I guess before Frank clued me in on it."

Though it was hardly noticeable to Pórdís, he had never been so open about what he felt, with her or anyone else.

"And sometimes more than two," she said. "Frank's comment wasn't only erudite but surprising, for a tendency among those who grieve is to focus on the hole in their own hearts, while failing to notice how others suffer over the same loss."

That wasn't what he meant. It wasn't what Frank meant, either. Was Pórdís purposefully misunderstanding him, in order to say that he had failed to notice the suffering of Emi and Phoebe? Or hadn't she been listening?

"I can understand your being surprised by Frank's erudition," he said.

"But I wasn't surprised by that. Frank has lots of erudition stored up, just like you have lots of ways of avoiding the question at hand."

What was the question at hand? How had this gone so quickly wrong?

"If the question at hand is whether I'm oblivious to the loss that Emi and Phoebe are also suffering, I don't think I am."

He waited but Pórdís stayed quiet, so he tried again. "If you mean that Emi and Phoebe weren't in the Las Vegas piece I read last night, it was only because of my phenomenal winning streak. They are in the next two parts."

"You keep asking if I mean this or that, when you know what I mean," she said.

But he didn't. He was lost again. He had the next installment of the Vegas story folded and stuck inside his notebook, so he pulled it out and shook it.

"Do you want me to read this to you now?" he asked.

"No, I just said I like to hear it when the others do."

"Look, as I told you, the trip to Vegas was to try to help all of us begin to heal. All of us, Dr. Jakobsdóttir, not just me."

"You did tell me that, but do you believe that grief has a half-life, and that therefore going to Vegas, or anyplace, actually, helps put it to rest ahead of time?"

"I don't know, *begin* to put it to rest at least, though I don't mean to imply that grieving for three months is too long. The others in our group, save Ruthie, lost their spouses a lot longer ago than that."

"They did, but you'd be surprised at the capacity some people have to keep grief alive," said Pórdís. "I've seen it go on for decades."

"Then can we agree that it's got no half-life, that there's no particular time that I can look forward to it ending, but also that letting it go on for decades doesn't help?"

"I don't know what we can agree on, but I do know that it's not like circling a date on a calendar. It ends when it ends, it can neither be hurried nor extended. Or so I learned from her."

She cast a glance up at Josefine Christophersen-Hemmingsen, whom Cornelius thought looked puffy and cerebral, like the pictures he'd seen of Madame Curie.

"How long did your grief last after she died?" he asked. "Knowing that might give me a rule of thumb."

"Listen to you, nimbly finding another way to ask about grief's half-life. But okay, I can tell you that I didn't grieve for very long, because, like you with Yuki, her cancer gave me time to get ready. Except that, unlike you, I didn't have anyone else whose grief I had to take into consideration."

Cornelius still felt that, rather than getting to the bottom of things, they were circling around each other, playing a game. "Okay, I admit to not including Emi much, even in this new section, but Phoebe's all over the place, driving me crazy by *not* talking about her feelings."

Þórdís shrugged. "Some people talk, some don't. And some talk through their hats. Did you see the kids who were here last night, just arriving when you left?"

"Yep. Each with a parent. Were they here to mourn the loss of the other one?"

"Yes, though the loss usually came through divorce. I talk to them by themselves, the adults just bring them and then come take them home."

Cornelius was sure that she would ask if Phoebe might like to join them, but all she said was what she always did... that their time was up.

4.

LaVeronica

LaVeronica Williams, the woman who missed Cornelius's reading at the group session the night before, waited in her car outside Pórdís's house until she saw Cornelius leave. He was about the last person she wanted to see just now. She had been foolish in thinking she could join this group, that enough time had passed from the horrors of a dozen years ago for them to accept her and for her to accept them. She had seduced herself into joining because she liked Pórdís and because the other members were a generation older. She'd always felt, even before the horrors, that older folks were more understanding. Yet now she had to quit the group.

What were the horrors of a dozen years ago? She killed a man who invaded her house, and Cornelius's son-in-law, Donnie Cassavetes, had been the prosecuting attorney assigned to her case - a thing she realized before she joined the group, so how stupid could she be?

The story behind the killing was complex, but went like this: From the time she met the man she killed - Johnny Sylvester - back when she was in high school, he never gave her much thought except to know that he could have her whenever he wanted her. For years that was true, consensually, even after she married someone else - until she got pregnant with Dwayne, her now fourteen-year-old son. When she finally cut things off with Johnny "for good," as she put it at her trial, he didn't accept it, and one night when Dwayne's father was out of town, he came over late, right up onto her porch. He didn't knock but opened the door, "like Ulysses home from the sea…" - again, that was how she put it in court, for she supposed that a literary reference might win her some support with her all-white jury.

"You remember how when Ulysses came home from the Trojan Wars only his dog recognized him?" she had said from the stand. "Well, in my case, I was upstairs taking a bath, sunk down in the tub with music on, but I still heard him open the door, and do you think I thought, 'Oh oh, I'm not expecting anyone, I better see about this?' No, I didn't, because I knew it was Johnny, just like Ulysses' dog knew it was him."

"You had music on but you still heard him?" Donnie Cassavetes had asked.

He smiled at the jury, in a "Now I've got her," kind of way.

"Yeah, well, Ulysses's dog was blind and deaf but he still recognized his master," LaVeronica had said. "And what did Ulysses do in order not to be outed as he snuck in to kill his wife's wannabe lovers? He walked by that dog without even saying hello."

"Then what happened?" Donnie asked, leading her to an ill-timed joke.

"He thumped his tail and died," she said of the dog, before admitting that she had been sad in the bath, listening to Otis Redding and thinking about her life; that she got out of the tub, went to her bedroom to get a pistol, which she carried to the top of the stairs where Johnny was on his way up with a fixed expression on his face. She raised her pistol, told him to leave three times, and when he kept on coming, shot him in the forehead. She said she thought the pistol would be loud, but it blended into *Try a Little Tenderness*.

Donnie Cassavetes asked if she "even bothered" to cover herself before going for the gun, and she admitted that she had not.

When Johnny Sylvester tumbled down the stairs, she went into the bathroom to let the water out of the tub, then she got dressed, dragged Johnny through the kitchen and out the backdoor to her car in the garage, and went back in to get Dwayne from his crib. She put him in his car seat and drove around for half an hour with Johnny sitting beside her like he was sleeping, as Dwayne really was. She knew she had to leave him somewhere, but she didn't want to get on anyone's CCTV and didn't want to stay out much later, either, so she drove to the Chinese Reconciliation Park, lugged Johnny down to a nearby beach, and kept on going until she was up to her armpits in the bay. And then, while the air in his clothing still held him up, she went back to her car and got out of there. At home she put Dwayne to bed, threw her clothes in the dryer, and went to bed herself.

But since all this was known to everyone before she joined the grief group, what did any of it have to do with her not wanting to see Cornelius MacLeish a dozen years later at her therapist's house? Read a little more to find out.

As with Cornelius, Þórdís spotted LaVeronica through the window, so she went out onto her porch in order to invite her inside.

"I came to say I'm stopping therapy, so I won't be a minute," LaVeronica said when she got out of her car.

Þórdís's exuberance departed. "Stopping therapy? Why?"

"Because I'm younger than the others, the only person of color, and because they don't accept me as truly grieving over what I did."

Those were the reasons she had wanted to join, not why she was quitting.

"I know you're grieving," Pórdís said, "and it's my hope that they will all come to understand that the door to grief is wide enough to let everyone inside."

She pointed to her wide front door and smiled a welcoming smile, but this was a surprise. Pórdís did *not* want to lose LaVeronica.

LaVeronica followed her inside, allowed her to close the door and lead her into the dining room, where she took a look at Josefine Christophersen-Hemmingsen.

"What would she think if she knew you were coddling a murderer?" she asked.

"You aren't a murderer. You were convicted of manslaughter by a jury of your peers."

"Well, it was a jury, anyway, but more like your peers than mine."

"Not unless they were Icelanders," said Pórdís. "Listen now, everyone has a story, and everyone's story is complex, as you'll find out if you stick around. So far, you've only heard Frank. You even missed the first of Cornelius's sessions last night, and, let me tell you, he has a whale of a tale to tell."

"I saw him just now, but he ran off before I could apologize," LaVeronica said.

"Apologize tomorrow. Come on, don't quit. You don't strike me as that selfish."

"My son goes to school with Cornelius's granddaughter."

That was enough. Too much, probably, for she had *promised* Dwayne she would keep him out of this, keep their home life private.

"There was something in Cornelius's session that I'd like to tell you about, if you say you're not quitting," Pórdís said.

"Meaning you won't tell me if I quit? Neat trick."

"It *is* a neat trick, and it puts you and Cornelius together in a way that excludes the others."

They were already together in a way that excluded the others, but LaVeronica had to stand her ground. She had come to quit without giving the reason, not to get talked into staying.

"How about this?" Pórdís said. "Hang in just through Cornelius's next two sessions and if you still want to quit after that I won't think of it as selfish."

LaVeronica nearly said, "What do I care what you think?" but, for unclear reasons she wanted this woman's good opinion of her. And two more nights was only until Friday.

"Okay, but I'm quitting after that," she said. "Now what's the big deal about Cornelius session last night?"

"It's something you told me during our last private session, but Cornelius brought it into the open, and it's that, like you with Johnny Sylvester, he gets visits from his dead wife's ghost. We call that 'after death communication' in the trade. A.D.C., for short."

"He told you all that? Did they think he was nuts?"

"I think most of them thought it was a metaphor for how much he misses her."

"I hope this isn't your way of saying that I got a visit from Johnny because I miss him! And it was only once! I also hope you didn't mention me last night."

"Of course not. And it's not my way of telling you any-thing, except what Cornelius said. He thinks she came to help him win a lot of money in Las Vegas."

As she spoke, Pórdís realized that Cornelius had told her that in private, not in last night's session. Oh, she was begin-ning to lose track of things! She had to take better notes!

"Good grief! Johnny's ghost comes shrieking out of my cupboard *one* time and you equate it to Cornelius's wife com-ing back to help him win money? How much did he win?"

"Two-hundred and eighty grand."

"Holy shit, Dr. J! That's a ghost I could live with!"

Just as Pórdís didn't think that seeing ghosts, whether once or a dozen times, was something to joke about, LaVeronica didn't think that she should be jovial at a time like this. But neither of them said anything more, except when Pórdís said she hoped she would see LaVeronica tomorrow night.

Once back in her car LaVeronica drove off quickly, but then stopped a couple of blocks away to gain control over herself. She could *not* have imagined before going in there that she would fail to quit the group. Her mind had been made up. And Dwayne waited for her at home for whatever news she could give him! Oh, good lord! The truth about this North End grievers club was that she got a lot more out of it than she expected, and had been looking forward to hearing Cornelius last night. But then yesterday morning, as she was standing in her kitchen drinking coffee, what did she see out her window, but a girl climbing down her apple tree! Down the tree! From Dwayne's room! She rushed out and grabbed the girl, pulled her into the house, and ran upstairs to drag Dwayne from his bed, his horrible boxer shorts half-way down around his butt. She then sat them both down for a half an hour of her screaming bloody murder and them swearing that nothing happened, that they had only pretended to do it to see what it felt like.

"Pretended to do it? Ha!"

It wasn't until she laughed at them, that she recognized the girl as Phoebe Cassavetes, the daughter of the son of a bitch who prosecuted her *and* the granddaughter of Cornelius MacLeish, her fellow North End griever. Oh, what terrible coincidences towns like Tacoma continually served up! But she kept on haranguing them until she brought them to tears, gaining promises from both that they would *never* do it again! Fourteen years old! And Phoebe only just turned that age a couple of days before. Pretending to do it! God in his lonely heaven! Once she gained their promises, she promised them, in turn, that she would not tell Phoebe's parents or her grandpa. She regretted that immediately, it was an unworthy promise. but she made it and she had to keep it. So she skipped Cornelius' session because she didn't want to have to face him. The idea of wholly quitting the group only occurred to her this morning, when she hadn't been able to sleep and got up before six to go get an axe from her garage so she could chop the apple tree down as soon as it grew late enough not to anger the neighbors with the noise. She put the axe beneath the tree and was just heading back inside when she looked up and saw, wonder of wonders, Phoebe's bare legs and round brown bottom emerge from Dwayne's window *again!* She froze, but when Dwayne's head and shoulders appeared in the window, too, to throw parting kisses to his beloved, and when he saw her standing there with the axe back in her hands, he screamed "No Mom, no!" thinking, of course, that she was waiting to chop Phoebe with it.

And why would he not? He knew her past.

When she caught them the first morning, after her bout of screaming she took them to school, with Phoebe assuring her that her parents thought she was staying at her grandpa's house and so they wouldn't miss her. *This* morning, though, she told them the story of when *she* was fourteen-years old and first met Johnny Sylvester. She terrified them with a litany of the sexually transmitted diseases Johnny gave her, and then - never mind her promise - she made Phoebe call her mother and tell her what happened. Phoebe cried and her mother cried and then LaVeronica took the phone and conflated Monday and Tuesday's tree climbing into only Tuesday's. Phoebe's mother came over, grabbed her daughter and roared off again, just before LaVeronica arrived at Pórdís's house.

"Ah love!" she said now, and then she laughed a little bit before driving home.

5.

Phoebe

After depositing his check in the bank, Cornelius drove down
to the waterfront for an hour's walk along Ruston Way, then
he stopped at the Grand Cinema up on Fawcett Street for
a midday showing of the 1963 Kurosawa classic "High and
Low," in which a wealthy executive struggles to gain control
of a women's shoe company. During the struggle the executive receives a phone call from someone claiming to have
kidnapped his son, so the executive stops everything in order
to pay the ransom. But the call is dismissed as a prank when
his son comes nonchalantly in from playing outside. His son's
playmate, however, the child of the executive's chauffeur, is
missing. In another phone call the kidnapper admits his mistake but still demands the ransom, forcing the executive to
decide whether or not to save a child who isn't his own. After
a night's contemplation he announces that he will not pay the
ransom, explaining that doing so would mean the loss of his
company. Finally, however, under pressure from his wife and
the groveling chauffeur, he changes his mind and, by movie's
end, becomes a better man because of it.

A story with a moral. A story with personal ethics at its
heart.

By the time Cornelius got home, school was out and he
hoped to find Phoebe sitting in his kitchen eating a sandwich.

But the kitchen was as empty as it had been that morning. Out beneath his willow tree, however, a woman sat in one of his lawn chairs. This time she looked like the actress who played the shoe company executive's wife in that movie. He ran to his breakfast nook window in time to see her morph into Yuki, the woman who had played *his* wife, and then turn to smoke and rise up into the tree. He slumped down into a chair. "I can't go on like this," he said, before noticing, across the table from him, a plate with breadcrumbs and bits of salmon on it.

"Phoebe!" he shouted, "come out here right now!"

"No!" said Phoebe's voice.

It came from the pantry on the kitchen's far side.

Cornelius stood and carried her plate to the sink. "You left this on the table so I would know you were here," he said.

"No I didn't! I left it there by mistake! And I am never coming out of here again!"

"Well, there's food in the pantry so I guess you'll survive," he said. "Do you want me to bring you a can opener?"

"Don't patronize me, Grandpa! You know how I hate that!"

He rinsed off her plate, put it in the dishwasher, then pulled a baguette from the breadbasket, opened the fridge and took out the mayonnaise and salmon. "I'm having a sandwich, too," he said. "Do you want another one?"

He was used to dealing with Phoebe's terrible fights with her parents, but hiding in his pantry was a new one.

"No, I don't want another sandwich, I want another life! I wish we'd stayed in Las Vegas. I could hang out on that beach instead of being back up here with all this heartache. Why did you make us come back?"

"I didn't make us come back, Phoebs, you did that."

"I know," she said, "and I shouldn't have."

Cornelius spread some mayo on the baguette, filled it with salmon, cut a lemon, squeezed some of its juice onto his sandwich, and carried it over to the table. Then he went back to the sink to wash his hands.

"You should wash your hands *before* you make your stupid sandwich, Grandpa. Didn't Grandma teach you anything when she was alive?"

The pantry door was open a crack with Phoebe peeking out.

"I did, but I wanted to wash them again, to get the smell of salmon off of them."

When he took a bite of his sandwich things felt normal for a minute. Phoebe was in his pantry, maybe, but the sandwich was good.

"Mom hit me and I would have hit her back if Dad hadn't gotten in the way," Phoebe said. "My mother is a beast."

"Your mother hit you? When did you get here? Did you come right after school?"

"Oh, come on, Grandpa, don't act so clueless. I know someone told you."

"Someone told me what? And you know I have to call them, let them know you're safe."

The pantry door swung all the way open and Phoebe came over to the table. He thought she was going to cry, but she ate part of his sandwich instead. "You can tell them I'm here, but you can't say anything about Dwayne. Tell them if they try to come and get me I'll take off again, and then hang up."

"Okay," he said, then he called Emi's phone before she could lay down any more conditions. Emi answered in half a ring. "She's here but if you try to come get her she's taking off again," he said. "I have to hang up now. That's the deal we made."

Emi was in the middle of demanding he put Phoebe on the phone when he held up his part of the bargain.

"Not bad, Grandpa, but Grandma wouldn't have said anything about *having to* hang up, she'd just have done it."

"Grandma was a better accomplice than me, huh? You know, Phoebs, I still see her often and it's driving me a little bit nuts."

Phoebe knew about his grief group. She called them "the Mopesters." She said that her grandmother would not have joined such a group if he died first, but she also called after every session to ask him how it went. Except she hadn't called last night.

"Yeah, well, consider yourself lucky," she said. "Cause I could use a visit from her right now. She was a better accomplice than you and a better listener, too. You listen for a little while, but then you only pretend to, Grandpa."

"That's not true. Name one time when I have only pretended to listen."

"Last Thursday night in Las Vegas. I wanted to tell you something huge, but all you did was try to make me to watch some dufus movie. And when Mom came in - the very person you knew I *didn't* want to talk to - you bolted from our room like a crook. Grandma would have told Mom to give us a minute, but that was beyond you."

"Well, I'm all ears now. You can tell me anything."

"Okay, here's the deal, and if you really don't know about

it yet don't get mad. I snuck into Dwayne's house last night. Dwayne's got an apple tree outside his bedroom window and I climbed up it."

"If you think Grandma would have been okay with that, think again," he said.

"She might not have been okay with it, but she would have understood it. She knew better than anyone that times have changed since she was a kid."

To his amazement, Cornelius managed to ask a calm question. "Was last night the first time you climbed Dwayne's tree?"

"No, I climbed it the night before last, too. And a couple of times before we went to Las Vegas."

He needed to truly understand his granddaughter now. Pretense wouldn't do.

"Okay, I was going to say that I'd fix it so you could stay here for a couple of days," he said, "but we better see what explosions come from your house first."

"You're not going to freak out yourself?"

"I'm trying not to."

You know what's weird, Grandpa, if you're really not freaking out? I can do sex without much trouble, but I have a hard time talking about it. Does that make sense? When Mrs. Williams forced us to talk about it this morning I thought I was going to die."

Oh, Christ! "Mrs. Williams? The one who's in my grief group? She's Dwayne's mom?"

"You know very well whose mom she is. I've known Dwayne since kindergarten."

She stood back up in order to look out the window, paused then said, "Tell me who were you talking to before you knew

I was here. And don't try saying you were on your phone."

"I was talking to Grandma. I saw her outside. I told you, she's driving me nuts."

"Are you making that up?"

"No, it's why I joined those North End grievers in the first place."

"Not because you miss Grandma but because you see her ghost?"

"Maybe I keep seeing her because I miss her. I'm not sure yet."

"Well, I don't think that's it. I think you're seeing her because you've got Parkinson's disease. There's a TV ad about a guy who not only sees his dead wife, but also his dead dog."

"I don't have Parkinson's disease, Phoebe. I had a physical a month after Grandma died. The only thing I've got is high cholesterol and the old man's condition of having to pee in the middle of the night."

"You don't have to tell me that, I hear you traipsing down the hall whenever I stay over. But I have unfinished business with Grandma, too, so if it's not Parkinson's disease, how come I don't get to see her?"

"I'll ask her that the next time she shows up."

"What does Jacob's daughter say about it? Or any of the other Mopesters?"

"I haven't explicitly mentioned it to them. I almost have and I will tomorrow night. Jacob's daughter only listens and asks questions."

"Yeah," said Phoebe, "like psychiatrists always do on TV."

"Yes, exactly like that. Now answer me truthfully. Did you make up that thing about climbing Dwayne's tree so your mom and dad would stop fighting? Did you really do it, or are you saying all of this to shock us?"

"Hardly! Here's the whole story of my sex life, Grandpa. We did it a few times before we went to Las Vegas, in his room and in the tangly woods behind Garfield Park after band practice, once the night before last and then last night. I wouldn't make up a thing like that. I wouldn't do it, either, if I didn't love Dwayne. What kind of girl do you think I am?"

He thought that for a girl who had trouble talking about sex, she was doing a pretty good job of it. But he couldn't bear to hear more.

"You know what I could do now if you were interested. I could read you what I wrote for my grief group tomorrow night, about me thinking I saw Grandma in Las Vegas. "It would give me a chance to fix whatever's wrong with it, and I'd also be telling you something personal in exchange for all you just told me."

"Really, Grandpa! That would be fantastic."

"But I've got one condition and it's that you sit and listen. You can't interrupt."

It was a condition Phoebe had no chance of meeting, but she agreed right away.

6.

Þórdís

It had been a long day for Þórdís, too. She had four private sessions, two in the morning, with the visit from LaVeronica so messing her up that she wasn't ready for her third session after lunch, which she ate in her dining room so she could talk things over with Josefine Christophersen-Hemmingsen. In this case she didn't talk to a ghost, just a picture. But she did so daily, and she got a lot out of it.

"Ruthie, the Porsche lady, is coming after I finish this herring, but I would really like to know what you think of this LaVeronica thing," she said. "What you would have told her if you were her therapist?"

Þórdís gave Josefine time to reply, then said, "Yes, I know, I have to learn to withhold judgement better, even though you taught me that well in Reykjavik."

She picked up her herring plate and carried it into the kitchen, much like Cornelius had with the salmon plates at his house. Cornelius was the griever she was most drawn to. She readily admitted she had a thing for older men, though it was by no means connected with the "Daddy issues" that Americans liked to talk so much about. No, what she liked about them was their world-weary calmness, plus the sexual insecurity that came with diminished blood flow. Still, she hadn't had a lover of any age since just after settling in Tacoma, a place she thought at first would be under the radar of the licensing bureaus for therapists. Why only "at first?" Because, as Josefine told her through the croak and wheeze of her esophageal cancer, sooner or later her ruse would catch up with her. She also urged her to go to Denmark where she still had connections who could help Pórdís normalize. But during Josefine's illness Pórdís got involved with Lars Larson, a Tacoman who came to Iceland in search of his family roots, never mind that his patronymic spoke of Sweden, not Iceland nor Denmark. Pórdís came to Tacoma with Lars, where her enthusiasm for him soon departed. That Lars still sailed around her like a yacht in a love regatta was his problem, she tried to think, though affection for him sometimes held sway over pragmatism late at night. Not that she called him, but if he came over unannounced on one of those nights, à la Johnny Sylvester…suffice it to say that she would not shoot him.

Pórdís went to her bathroom to brush her hair and teeth, and then into her office to get her "Ruthie Segal" file. Ruthie's particulars were these: Her late husband, Ben, had been the owner of a roofing company with territory that extended south to Vancouver, north to Everett, and east over the Cascade Mountains to Yakima. He'd made a fortune - thus the Porsche and the fancy house on American Lake. Ruthie and Ben were married for forty-five years and Ruthie was just now facing the fact that she had to start living as herself, and not as Ben's wife. Or, better stated, she had to start remembering that there was a "Ruth" in the mix, renamed "Ruthie" by Ben in an attempt to ween her away from her conservative Jewish upbringing. That, at least, was what Ruthie was coming to believe, and what Pórdís encouraged during their sessions.

She was ready for her by the time Ruthie, or "Ruth," as she would try to remember to call her, showed up, tentative, shy, even apologetic… It made Pórdís want to shake her, saying "Come on, baby, get a life."

Ruthie drove her Porsche to the top of Pórdís's driveway, three feet away from the door of her garage. Pórdís watched through her kitchen window as she got out of the car to inspect its front, back, and both sides. The car was only a few months older than Ruthie's widowhood, Ben having bought it as, of all things, a parting gift to himself. Maybe he thought that, like King Tut, he could drive off to his just rewards, or that Ruthie would turn their garage into a museum filled with all his various toys: his boat, his Harley, the Porsche. They were what Ruthie call Ben's "getaway" toys, but now that both their children, Rachel and Yehudi, were grown and gone, who was there to get away from but her, she asked Pórdís last time.

Today she locked the car and walked toward the front of Pórdís's house.

7.

Cornelius

Phoebe tucked her feet under her, love for Dwayne written all over her face.

"You need to know a couple of things before I start," Cornelius said. "First, there was this woman named Natalie who sat beside me at the blackjack table. She's the one I started thinking was your grandma."

"Was she shimmering like a regular ghost? Did she look like Grandma? What?"

"Neither. It was just a feeling I got. But I've seen others whom I thought were Grandma when they weren't, too, so we have to take it with a grain of salt."

"Okay," said Phoebe, "What else do I need to know?"

There *had* been something else, but he'd forgotten it.

"I'll tell you as I go along," he said.

"You know, Grandpa, forgetting what you were about to say is another symptom of Parkinson's disease. They've got a drug for that, too."

When he said, "How about zipping it?" Phoebe put a finger up and ran it across her lips, so Cornelius read, *"When we got to an office behind the cashier's cage, the tough-looking guy laid my chips out and counted them again - $283,500, all of my winnings minus that tip."*

"There was a tough-looking guy? Is that what you forgot to tell me?"

"There was a tough-looking guy and a guy who looked like he owned the place. But, no, that wasn't what I forgot to tell you."

"My daughter and granddaughter are down at the pool," I said. "Could someone call them? I left my phone in my room."

"We call it 'the beach,'" said the guy who looked like he owned the place, while the tough-looking guy opened the door and left again."

"Oh!" said Phoebe. "The man who came to get us is the tough-looking guy! He's Korean, Grandpa, and his name is Mr. Shim."

"Good to know," Cornelius said. "We'll send him a card at Christmas."

"Thanks for raising the table limit," I said when we were alone. "I've never been treated like a high roller before."

"Well, two-hundred and eighty grand is certainly high-rolling, but - and no offense - it's high rolling on its lowest floor," said the man. "There's an Australian comes in here who bets a million a night." He smiled and added, "We comp his room and we'd like to comp yours."

"High rolling's lowest floor is better than low rolling's highest, I suspect," I said.

It was a good-enough line to make the man laugh, open a cabinet filled with bottles, and ask me if I wanted a drink.

"How about a beer?" I said.

"There's no beer here but I can get you one," he said.

"When I said I'd like a pale ale and he left the office, I pulled Natalie's card from my pocket and thought about calling her from the phone on his desk. The card said Natalie Simone in a dark red font."

"Finally, we are getting to Natalie! All that stuff about high rollers and what kind of beer you want was making my eyes glaze over, Grandpa. But you were thinking of calling Natalie? You liked this woman, huh? That means that you still know what love is. Mom and Dad don't."

"I didn't like her, Phoebs, I was trying to get to the bottom of the Grandma thing."

"Yeah? Well, that's not what it sounds like."

The man came back with two beers, followed by the tough looking guy who said that Emi and Phoebe wanted to get dressed first. When I asked him if he told them about my winnings, he said that he had not.

"So the Mopesters are gonna know my name?" Phoebe asked. "Will you tell them that I am grieving, too, that it's not just you who misses Grandma?"

"They already know that you are grieving, too," Cornelius said, though, after his private session with Pórdís that morning, he wasn't quite sure.

"I hope you don't mind that I also brought a beer for myself," said the owner-guy. "I never drink on the job but the idea of a beer right now… Sometimes you don't know what you want till someone else wants it - do you agree Mr. MacLeish?"

This marked the second time he'd used my name, so I asked how he knew it.

"When you started winning we looked you up, but we aren't just socializing here. Before we can cut your check I have to ask about the woman at your table. Did you know her previously?"

He opened both beers and gave me one. Did I know her previously? I couldn't very well say that the spirit of my dead wife had come down to light on her shoulder.

"Oh god, Grandpa, it's a good thing you didn't say that! He might not have given you your money on the grounds that you were nuts!"

"Of course I didn't know her. Go ask her if you want to," I said. "She's only over at Red Square."

"Red Square's that place with Lenin's statue in front of it

with his head cut off."

This time Phoebe was talking to herself. They had stopped to look at the statue when walking around the hotel.

"Well, there's the rub, she isn't over at Red Square," he said. "We have her on a security camera passing it by."

Before I could say anything more someone knocked on the door. When the tough guy opened it, it wasn't Emi and Phoebe, but the pit boss, Frankie C.

"People sometimes do win thirteen hands in a row, Mr. MacLeish, but no one let's his bet ride thirteen times. So let's just hear what Frankie has to say."

"The lady was doing a bit of do-si-do on you, Mr. MacLeish," said Frankie. "That means she was working you for later on."

"What else, Frankie?" asked the owner-guy.

"What else is that usually some dufus gets himself hooked on her, but this time, with all that winning, things got out of hand...so she didn't have a chance to work her magic on you," said Frankie C.

"That means you think Mr. MacLeish's winnings were legit?" the owner asked.

"As legitimate as my two kids. I've never seen anything like it."

The fist that had been gripping my heart eased up.

"Okay, a check for two hundred eighty-three thousand five hundred dollars will be here momentarily. The clumsiness of the last half hour is not something we strive for, Mr. MacLeish. I hope you will accept my apologies, and anything you want in this hotel is comped, whether you leave on Sunday or accept my invitation to stay longer with us."

Had we only been in that office for a half an hour? I felt like I'd been there since the sun came up."

Cornelius put his papers down and looked at Phoebe.

"It's not exactly bad, Grandpa, but it's got a ton of extra stuff that you don't need to tell the Mopesters. And it hardly mentions what's important."

"My grief? Grandma's ghost?"

"Yeah, get *that* down on paper. If I had to write about what *I'm* going through I think I'd pay a lot more attention to Dwayne than to playing cards with someone."

"What *are* you going through, honey, you haven't told me yet."

"Never mind that for a second, are you done?"

"I have more but it gets pretty crazy. I thought maybe reading this would get them ready for the crazier stuff on Friday."

Read them the crazy stuff tomorrow," said Phoebe. "Forget this part."

After that they sat in silence. If Phoebe had to write about what she's going through with Dwayne, Cornelius realized, he had no idea on earth what she would say. He had to find a way to talk to this girl.

When she finally said, "Okay, I'm going upstairs to study algebra," he asked, "Dwayne's in that class, too?"

"Dwayne's in all my classes and we get exactly the same grades. We are kindred spirits, Grandpa. I will *never* love anyone else."

"I guess you're lucky you found each other so early then," Cornelius said.

8.

Ruthie

Þórdís made it to her porch by the time Ruthie got there.

"Hey," she said, "Come up. Come in."

"I hope you don't mind that I parked by your garage," said Ruthie. "When I left that stupid car on the street last time, I worried about it all session long."

She wanted a response, a dismissive laugh or a smile, but Þórdís only waited until she came up onto the porch before leading her into the house and closing the door.

"Go on into the dining room," she said. "I'll get my notes from my office."

Her notes were on the counter in her kitchen, below the window through which she watched Ruthie park her car, but she wanted time to center herself. When she circled around and got them, and came into the dining room, Ruthie was sitting where she usually sat.

"How are your children?" Þórdís asked. "Rachel and Yehudi, right?"

"Oh, they're the same. One of them loves me and the other doesn't. So I call the one who doesn't every day."

Both women laughed.

"That would be Yehudi, if I remember correctly," said Þórdís. "The boy who thinks the car outside belongs to him? The one with the African American wife?"

"That would be him. He wants to be the fanciest man at

the synagogue with that car, while Rachel wants to be the humblest woman, going everywhere on foot or taking the bus. So I drive the car to services in order to piss them both off."

"Are you back to attending services regularly now that Ben is gone?"

"Yes," said Ruthie. "I'm not surprised that Rachel sits with me, despite the car, but I'm still trying to figure out what's up with Yehudi. He's been an atheist since the day after his bar mitzvah - it would have been before if he didn't want the gifts so much. Or so I thought. Lately, though, he's been sitting with Rachel and me and even bringing Bess. At first I thought it was about the car again, but Rachel says Yehudi only staked a claim to atheism to please his dad. So we'll see, I guess. But it sure lets me know how much I never knew my son."

Pórdís met both of Ruthie's children, and Yehudi's wife, too, when she went to Ruthie's house on the last day of Ben's shiva. Ruthie wasn't her client then. Pórdís went with Millicent, one of Ruthie's oldest friends, after Millicent said that Ruthie asked about joining the group. So in a way she'd gone to the shiva to scare up business, though American Lake was quite a long way from Tacoma's North End.

"Well, other than with Yehudi and Rachel, how have you been coping lately? Any more staying in bed all day long? Any more pills?"

"Nope. I'm up with the chickens, walk two miles before breakfast, and I don't turn on the television either, except to hear the news at noon and again at six o'clock. What I do in between times is ride around in one or another of Ben's toys, the car and the boat...I don't know how to ride the Harley yet."

"You take the boat out onto the lake? Do you fish?"

Fishing had been Þórdís's all-time favorite pastime back in Iceland. It was only by freakish luck that she hadn't been with her parents on the day of their fatal accident. The freakish luck was that she had a cold.

"I fish like a maniac," said Ruthie. "Rainbow trout, largemouth bass, smallmouth bass, cutthroat trout, rock bass… I'm partial to either kind of trout. They aren't kosher if I catch them and bring them home and eat them, but I do it anyway, every Sunday. Ben used to tow his boat to Steilacoom during fishing season, launch it into Puget Sound where he might catch salmon. On the lake, though, fishing is allowed all year long."

"What did he use to tow the boat to Steilacoom? Surely not the Porsche?"

"He used our Ford 150. Even at home I pull the boat around to our launch with that truck. It's a thirty-second drive from my garage, but I nevertheless think I'm the real me when I'm driving that truck, and the fake me when I'm in the Porsche."

Ruthie noticed the change in Þórdís when fishing came up. It was slight, like watching the lips of a tulip at the beginning of its blossom, but she saw it, and said, "You know, if you like to fish, I'd be glad if you would join me one of these Sundays."

"Really?" said Þórdís. "My parents used to take me to Lake Thingvallavatn."

"Let's do it, then," said Ruthie. "And American Lake is easier to say."

She pointed at the photo of Josefine Christophersen-Hemmingsen. "She doesn't look like someone who'd take you fishing, but that just proves that my cluelessness with my own family extends to others, too."

Now would be a great time for Pórdís to admit that Josefine was her mentor, that her mother and father had gone down with their boat, not on Lake Thingvallavatn, but off the coast of Reykjavik. But all she said was, "you can't tell what a person's like by looking at a picture."

"No, of course not, I didn't mean to give offense. I really do have foot in mouth disease, as Ben was kind enough to tell me," Ruthie said.

"I'm not offended," said Pórdís. "And Josefine wouldn't be, either, if she were here. It's true that she doesn't look like someone who would fish, and let me also say that Ben and that thing about foot in mouth disease doesn't only seem unkind. It also seems untrue."

"Yes, well, do you know what else Ben used to tell me all the time? That I used the wrong words for things, that I said 'miffed' when I thought a thing was funny, and that I used 'canard' once when I meant canary. Back at the beginning of our marriage he even claimed I said something was 'horny' when I meant 'corny.' But that wasn't true! Can you imagine someone thinking 'horny' meant 'corny?' Listen, I'm not kidding about fishing, though. Please know that if you come there'll be no free therapy expected. Just a couple of women looking to catch and eat some trout."

"It's a deal," said Pórdís. "I haven't been fishing since I got here."

Ruthie nodded, like that settled things.

After that they talked about what a prick Ben could be until Ruthie's time was up.

9.

Cornelius

When Cornelius woke up the next morning, Phoebe was gone. She left a note saying that Dwayne had found a way to text her during the night and she was meeting him at the Harvester before they went to school. Cornelius hoped he'd have an open day, with time to think about what he would to tell his fellow grievers that night, but now what should he do? Drive to the Harvester? Call Emi?

He managed to stave off both impulses - and trust the kid a little bit - by making himself an omelette with tomatoes and cheese and the last bit of salmon. He took the omelette to his deck, where it was cold and drizzling, but dry enough to sit. The table and chairs down beneath his willow tree, however, were soaked and looked forlorn. So much so that seeing them, ignored since Yuki's death, made him leave his omelette to take them into the basement and dry them off. He would warm the omelette up when he got back.

Their house had a side door with stairs leading up to the kitchen and down to the basement, so he picked up the table and carried it there, then went back for the chairs. Since he held them against his body, his sweatshirt and jeans soon got as wet as they were, and the side door was locked, so he had to go back up the outside staircase and through his kitchen to unlock it. In the kitchen he stripped off his wet clothes and poured himself another cup of coffee. And just as he was about to find his omelette again the doorbell rang. To get dry clothing he had to walk past the front door's glass panels and climb the stairs to his bedroom. He wasn't expecting anyone, so he waited for whoever it was to go away. But soon a man's voice said, "I know your in there, Cornelius, your car is in the driveway."

It wasn't a voice Cornelius recognized. "I'm busy!" he shouted. "Go away!"

He tiptoed over to where he could see the man's shadow.

"Okay fine," the man said. "If I need someone, I guess it ain't you *or* Ruthie."

Cornelius went into the hallway and opened the door to a downtrodden Frank, about as forlorn looking as his table and chairs. The North End grievers all had each other's phone numbers, but he didn't remember giving anyone his address.

"Frank," he said, "I was outside and got wet. Go in the living room while I get dressed."

"Ruthie came to her door in a bathrobe," Frank said. "She let me know that if I ever darkened it again she'd report me to Pórdís."

"Just come in," said Cornelius. "There's coffee in the kitchen."

"Coffee's for the living, and you are looking at a dead man," Frank said.

Cornelius pulled him inside and closed the door. "Coffee's for anyone who wants it," he said. "How do you take yours?"

"Two sugars and about one-third milk," said Frank. "But then you got to heat it up again…that much milk makes it cold."

"Just let me get some clothes on first."

Cornelius went upstairs, found pants and a sweater in his closet and put them on with a dry pair of socks. When he got back downstairs Frank was where he'd left him, so he led him into the kitchen and made his coffee the way he wanted it.

"You don't know who your friends are till you knock on their door," Frank said.

"Maybe Ruthie thought you wanted more than friendship, Frank. Word on the street is that might be the case."

"Yeah, well, when you're wrong you're wrong. It don't matter now, though, cause this here coffee's my last supper. I want you to drive me out to the Narrows Bridge after I drink it, so I can jump off the goddamn thing. That way my truck won't disrupt the traffic. Do that and you can have the truck, I'll sign the title over to you right now."

"There's a toll on the bridge so I'm gonna want six bucks, too," Cornelius said.

"Ha ha," said Frank.

"What happened since last night that makes you want to jump off a bridge? And if you really do jump, you're going to set Ruthie's progress back six months. She may not want you knocking on her door, but think how she'll feel when she hears you killed yourself because of it. Plus, our group has a fine dynamic, which you're a big part of, Frank. Just the other day Ruthie told me so."

"She did not! If you hit on her she'd be fine with it."

Cornelius wanted to ask what Doris, Frank's late wife, would think if she heard him talking like that, but he said, instead, "Ruthie's grieving, too. Try helping someone else and maybe you won't be so miserable. I'm trying that, and I'm finding a little relief."

"Yeah? Who you tryin' to help, Ruthie or Millicent?"

"Just someone in my family, but you have children. Think about them."

"Beatrice and Bucky, yeah," said Frank. "Bea's a CPA and Buck's an actual pitching scout for the Mariners. Bea lives in Bellevue and Bucky on Capitol Hill. I'm supposed to go to dinner at his house tomorrow night and Bea's on Saturday. They invite me every week but they don't like me, Corny. They do it out of a sense of obligation."

"Nothing wrong with a sense of obligation. Why not cut everyone some slack?"

"Do you really think me jumpin' would set Ruthie back?"

"Of course it would. It would set all of us back, Frank, you know that!"

"Ha!" said Frank. "You might be right."

"It's settled then. Now, go home and clean your house or take a nap. I'll see you at Þórdís's house this evening."

"You know, if we had known each other when Doris and Yuki were alive we could have been friends, meetin' up for dinner and such. Show me a picture of Yuki, will you. And I'll bring one of Doris tonight."

Good god, if Cornelius actually showed Frank a picture of Yuki, her ghost might come and knock it out of his hands. But Frank was watching him warily, so he told him to wait while he went upstairs to get one.

In a frame on a table in the guest room was a photo of the 1930s singer, Ruth Etting, whom, for a time, Yuki and Cornelius had both loved. He grabbed it and took it downstairs.

"She was fond of this one," he said. "It was taken at a costume party we went to one time. Everyone was supposed to dress as a character from literature."

Frank took a long close look at the picture. Surely he

didn't know Ruth Etting. Cornelius thought he'd say that she didn't look Asian, but he asked, instead, "Who'd she go as, Madam Butterfly?"

"As 'Bernice,' from the Fitzgerald short story, 'Bernice Bobs Her Hair.'"

"I'm gonna find that story and read it," Frank said.

He held onto the Ruth Etting photo while Cornelius walked him back into the hallway, opened the door, and pushed him out onto the porch.

"See you tonight," he said. "I'm 'up' again, you know, so please be kind."

He pulled the picture out of Frank's hands.

Frank patted his shoulder and headed down to his truck.

*****

Three hours later, after Cornelius stowed his table and chairs, finished his omelette, and was back working on his presentation for that night, the doorbell rang again. This time his son-in-law, Donnie Cassavetes, stood there with a very long face and his hat in his hands. Cornelius instantly knew that something had happened to Phoebe.

"Cornelius, do you know a man named Francis Blessing?" Donnie asked him.

"I don't think so, Donnie, who's that?"

"Did a Francis Blessing not visit you today? They found his truck at a pull-off by the Narrows Bridge. Your name was on a paper on its front seat. The cop who got there first knew of our connection and called me as a courtesy. And do you also know someone named Jane? She was on the paper, too, but without a surname."

Cornelius slumped against his doorframe, but was able to tell Donnie that Frank was in his grief group, and that he had come over earlier to ask him to drive him to the bridge. He told him the names of Frank's children. He told him everything just the way it happened, except for the part about the Ruth Etting picture.

"Would you mind going up to Tacoma General? Believe it or not, the guy survived, and he's asking for you. They're deciding now whether to charge him or not."

"Frank's alive?"

"Alive and apparently stunned by that fact," said Donnie.

10.

Millicent

Millicent scheduled her private session with Pórdís for late that day, with the idea that she would hang around until the meeting started at seven. She understood that this was a one-off, that hereafter her private sessions would conform to the workday, giving Pórdís time to eat, reflect, and get ready for the group. Today, however, because she had to take her daughter and her son-in-law to the airport to catch a flight back to England, Pórdís allowed the late session.

Millicent got there at five-thirty. When Pórdís saw her from her window she opened the door and went out onto her porch, like she had with the others yesterday.

Millicent wasn't as pretty as Ruthie, nor dreamy like Jane, but she was the absolute champ of older-woman sexiness, with the lithe body of a woman twenty years younger, and a conservative use of makeup, highlighting only her round blue eyes. Her shoulder-length, light brown, hair had no gray in it, yet no sense, either, that it had been dyed. It simply swayed to rhythms of her walk, like it had since she was a girl.

"So you got them off okay?" Pórdís asked. "Good-bye Milly and Phillip?"

"Good-bye and good riddance as far as Philip is concerned," Millicent said. "Do you know what Jonathan and I used to call him back in the day?"

"Phillip Pirrip," said Pórdís. "A name you snagged from Dickens, you said."

"Right. I need to remember what I already told you."

Once inside, Millicent sat beneath the Josefine Christophersen-Hemmingsen photo.

"What do you think now that she's gone, Millicent? Was having Milly around helpful? Did she keep your loneliness at bay?"

"She kept me talking, if that's what you mean. But I don't call it loneliness, what I've been feeling since Jonathan died."

Pórdís looked at her notes. "You called it loneliness last time. Loneliness and…it's hard for me to read my writing."

She turned her notebook so Millicent could see a scribbled word that began with 's.'

"'Solitude,'" said Millicent, "which, I told you, is loneliness stood on its head."

"I'm sorry?" asked Pórdís.

"If you want it it's solitude, if you don't, it's loneliness. Yet objectively speaking, they're the same thing."

"I see," said Pórdís. "So, you think it's a matter of deciding whether to embrace the solitude or be battered by the loneliness?"

"Greatly so, yes. I'm English, and inclined to give credence to a stiff-upper-lip."

"I can understand that when the Germans are bombing London, but when sitting alone at home after the death of one's spouse? Also then?"

"Even more so, arguably. With the bombings you've got others to huddle up with, but with this you've only got yourself."

That all sounded abject, and more self-pitying than Millicent intended. Having Milly leave had put her in a mood, never mind that she also got rid of Phillip.

"I'm sorry," she said. "I get this way when Milly leaves. So much so that it's almost better if she doesn't come. And this time along came Phillip, when I'd been told he wouldn't be able to get away."

"What does Philip do again?" asked Pórdís.

"He's a cardiologist, deals with affairs of the heart of an entirely different sort. When Jonathan was alive his visits were bearable because the two of them would go off together, but this time he stood around with his mouth open, like I was one of his terminal patients and he didn't know what to say. Do medical schools teach a course in 'stupid bedside manner?' Because it seems ubiquitous, and Phillip has it in spades."

"I'm the wrong person to ask. At Chokkold good end-of-life care was as important as good grief."

Pórdís laughed and nodded up at Josefine Christophersen-Hemmingsen; a habit she should try to break.

"You know, Milly looked up your institute when she was fooling around online. Your mother… You never told us what a prominent role she played."

Nothing in Millicent's manner said that Milly had dug down deeply enough to see that Pórdís wasn't listed among Chokkold's regular graduates. But could this be the moment Pórdís feared? "They made her president a couple of years before she died. Chokkold practiced what it preached by giving her that honor even though her cancer was stage four."

"You'll remember, I think, that Milly's a psychiatrist, and when I told her about our group she had all kinds of questions."

'Here it comes,' thought Þórdís, but she said only, "You should have brought her to one of our sessions. I'd have been glad to meet her, and we all might have benefited from her perspective. Especially regarding what Cornelius read last night."

"Ha!" said Millicent. "If she had been here she'd have wanted to prescribe him drugs. Milly isn't one for flights of fancy."

"You know, Millicent, you're describing her now, about like you described Phillip. Yet earlier I got the feeling she was your kindred spirit, the only lifejacket that you allowed yourself when bouncing around in the heavy sea of your grief."

"Sheesh. You're confusing me with someone else. I don't speak so fancifully."

"Well the metaphor is mine, but the truth behind it is all over my notes. You're on the phone with Milly daily, on WhatsApp or whatever with her…"

"What else am I supposed to do? She's the only family I've got. But you're right in sensing that she's turning into Phillip, little by little showing nothing but her analytical side. She didn't even want to go to the cemetery to visit her dad."

"She didn't? But isn't this her first time here since he died?"

"She was here *when* he died, but it's the first time since then. Don't get me wrong, she went to the cemetery, but only after a good old English nudging from Philip."

"Of all people," Þórdís said.

She was beginning to think that she was in the clear regarding Chokkold, when Millicent said, "We couldn't find you on there, Þórdís. Was your name the same as your mom's back then? Because there's a Þórdís Christophersen-Hemmingsen, but no Þórdís Jakobsdóttir. There's also a picture of someone who looks like you at the ceremony where she got sworn in as president."

"I always hated that picture," said Þórdís. "And for my courses I did use her name, in order to get the fee waved."

She was certain Millicent would say more, but Millicent's interests lay elsewhere.

"What happened to Mr. Jakobsdóttir?" she asked. "Did she divorce him?"

"Mr. Jakobsdóttir died in a boating accident when I was twelve years old... Mrs. Jakobsdóttir died then, too," said Þórdís.

She then told Millicent about wandering the Chokkold campus under the weight of her own unbearable grief, of sitting beneath the window of Josefine's classroom and how Josefine lifted her through that window and into the beginnings of the life she led now. She said that calling Josefine "Mom," was not so much a falsehood as an homage, since she had mothered her through the second half of her childhood. She had to remember to clear that up with Ruthie, too, when they met to go fishing.

Millicent listened like she was the therapist and a longtime patient was finally having a breakthrough. Þórdís made no mention of how she attained the degree, for she believed that its "honorary" designation made it *dis*honorable in the eyes, not only of the therapy world, but of therapy's vast clientele.

"That's the most touching orphan story I have ever heard," Millicent said. "Listen, Þórdís, it would give you more 'street cred' if you shared that with the rest of our group."

"I will," Þórdís said, "but our sessions are supposed to be

about you all, not me."

Neither of them mentioned that that hadn't been true of *this* session when Pórdís also said, a few minutes later, that Millicent's fellow grievers were about to arrive.

11.

Frank

Cornelius hadn't been to Tacoma General Hospital in years and he couldn't find his way around. When he gave a receptionist Frank's name, however, she told him what ward to go to, exactly how to get there, and that Frank was in police custody. At the door to Frank's room he found a young policewoman.

"I'm here to see Francis Blessing," he told her. "Donnie Cassavetes sent me."

The policewoman found Cornelius's name on her clipboard and sent him into a room with two beds. The one nearest the door held someone wrapped in casts and bandages, like the 'soldier in white' in Catch-22. Frank was in the second bed, staring at a silent television.

"Did you break any bones? What did it feel like? Have they told you how long they'll keep you here yet?" Cornelius asked.

He had read that people should act normally around suicide survivors.

"They say I can go home this afternoon if I promise to see a psychiatrist. *You* have to promise not to tell the group, though. I don't want sympathy from the likes of Ruthie, Corny."

"What about Þórdís? Did you say that she was your psychiatrist?"

"Yes, but I guess they mean a regular doctor who studied about mental illness."

"That's pretty much what it means everywhere," Cornelius said.

Frank turned toward the room's only window to look out at the rain. He said, "I told you what I was gonna do, but you didn't believe me."

"I should have believed you. I should have called the others in our group. That's the reason we exchanged phone numbers, for emergencies like this," said Cornelius.

"Yet you didn't because you don't take me seriously. What's life about if a man don't make a greater effort than you did to stop a friend from jumpin' off a bridge?"

Before Cornelius could respond, Jane walked in with her hands in her pockets.

"I want you to know that *I'd* have stopped you, even if I had to use my body," she said.

Despite everything, Frank gave her a lascivious look.

"You two are okay, but I don't want the others knowing about this," he said. "Not Pórdís now that she can't be my psychiatrist, nor Millicent, and especially not Ruthie nor Veronica."

Jane couldn't help sighing, though she knew that they were supposed to act normally, too. "It's four o'clock, Frank. They told me outside that we could help you dress and get you out of here if we vouched that you've got somewhere to go and someone to stay with," she said. "Should we call Beatrice or Bucky?"

"Hell no, I don't want them knowin' about it either! But I got a place to stay called 'my house.' I'm fine by myself, unless you want to come over and help me out, Janie."

When Jane only stared at him, he said, "Okay, I'll call Bea, but then I'm goin' to listen to the rest of your Vegas story, Cornelius, right on schedule. So I will know if either of you blabbed to the group. Is that a deal or not?"

"Of course it's not. You can't jump off a bridge and then sit and listen to someone else's grief story," Cornelius said. "It's against the natural order of things."

"I agree," said Jane, "you should stay home," but Frank told them that they had to think of it the other way around.

"I jumped off the Narrows Bridge and survived! I knew before I hit the water that I made a mistake, so I screamed 'God help me!' and now here I am sittin' up in bed and talkin' about it! I mean, it's rarer'n you winning all that dough in Vegas, Corny! I do owe a debt to a guy at Salmon Beach, though, who saw me floating by and called the police."

"You know, the guy the cops called, the man who saw to it that Jane and I both came over here, is also my son-in-law," Cornelius said. "What are the chances of that?"

Frank looked at him meanly. "You always gotta one-up a man, don't you?" he said. "You ought to work on stoppin' that, Cornelius."

12.

Cornelius's Vegas Story
Part Two

"Before we begin I want to thank Cornelius for the full-throated rendition of what happened to him in Las Vegas last time," said Pórdís. "Tonight is a continuance of that and I hope the rest of us will feel free to support him."

She hoped that Cornelius understood "full-throated" to mean "too long," and that the others knew "feel free to support him" meant "don't be afraid to interrupt." She'd had less than half an hour to prepare after her session with Millicent, while Millicent stayed in the dining room, kicking her leg and reading something on her iPad.

Pórdís felt something odd in the air and was sure it had to do with her diploma, for Frank was grinning like a crazy man and Cornelius pulled out his papers and started reading with no preamble at all, just as soon as they were seated.

"Emi and Phoebe screamed when they heard about my winnings. They pranced between our rooms and had a pillow fight on my bed. It was a first moment of forgetting for them, too, since the passing of their mom and grandma. That money could stave off grief had not occurred to me before, but for a moment grief was staved.

"Why, that's pure lovely!" said Frank. "'For a moment grief was staved!' Holy mother, that's a good one, Corny! Lemme write that down."

Pórdís and Jane both glared at him, but his look was as sincere as a dog's. And for the first time ever he took out a notebook of his own and started scribbling.

Phoebe had sunburned shoulders from hanging out at the beach, but put on a thinly-strapped blue dress for our foray out to dinner. We were going to Picasso at Bellagio, our reservations made for us before I came upstairs. Emi wore a similar dress, but shorter. Our Vegas trip was as much to give her a break from an unhappy marriage as to celebrate Phoebe's birthday and gain a little distance from our grief.

Pórdís interrupted. "Sorry, but good rule is to keep the personal situations of people not in our group out of our discussions."

Cornelius could see why that was necessary, and nodded. He thought of seeing Donnie that afternoon, and knew he wouldn't like it.

Our plan was to eat a fancy dinner then catch the evening's final performance of "O," which we also just bought tickets for. I wore a light suit with Natalie's business card tucked in its breast pocket. We got to Bellagio easily, stood in line at Picasso, were led to our table past original works by the artist, himself, then listened while a waiter explained the menu. I couldn't help thinking of Paloma Picasso and Françoise Gilot, married later to Jonas Salk.

"There it is again, damned good writing!" said Frank. "We're lucky to have Cornelius in our group, ain't we everybody? He's the Picasso of grief writing! The Jonas Salk of the grief vaccine!"

Frank looked like he was about to implode, but the others agreed that they were lucky to have Cornelius.

Emi said the food was fabulous, its presentation like a painting on a plate, but I hardly tasted it. When dinner was over and Phoebe wanted to browse through the fancy shops, I said I'd go look at the Dale

Chihuly lotus-petal ceiling above the registration desk, and would find them before "O". I wanted to call Natalie from under the lotuses, but just as I passed a piano bar the woman herself stepped out from behind an artificial palm.

"I hope you don't mind that I followed you," she said.

"Shit on a holy shingle, of course he didn't mind!" said Frank. "You shouldn't have minded, either, Ruthie, when I stopped by at your house!"

Ruthie stood up, but then sat back down when Þórdís said, "Tonight belongs to Cornelius. Please don't make me say that again, Frank."

Natalie wore a small black dress, a Ferrari of a dress compared to Phoebe and Emi's Fords, and her hair was pinned against her scalp. That I had been about to call her seemed absurd by then.

"It's good to realize the absurdity of something before the fact instead of after it," said Millicent.

"It truly is, Mills," said Frank, "but you heard Þórdís, don't interrupt the man."

"I don't mind, but I've got 'O' to go to. I just came out here to take a look at the famous ceiling," I said.

"No you didn't," she said. "You came out here to call me."

She pulled a large silver phone out of a small black bag and asked, "If I had waited another minute to show myself would you still be able to blame the ceiling? That ceiling, by the way, is about the only Chihuly I like. Otherwise, I think his work is garish."

"Hold on now!" said Frank. "I know we're not suppose to interrupt, but good golly, Miss Molly! Everyone knows Chihuly's fabulous!"

"I don't know that," said Millicent. "I agree with Natalie."

"Me, too," said Ruthie, while Jane said, "Well, I agree with Frank!"

It was just then, when they were about to fall to arguing about Chihuly, that LaVeronica arrived. "Sorry to be late," she said. "Family issues, what did I miss?"

Cornelius said that she hadn't missed much, but he was far more interested in her family issues than his own Las Vegas story. When LaVeronica sat down and Pórdís nodded at him, however, what could he do but push ahead?

"I pulled out my phone, too, along with her card, as if somehow calling her would prove her wrong. When her phone rang we both stood listening to the first few bars of Beethoven's sonata for violin and piano, the "spring" sonata, the very one that Yuki had asked for when 'spring,' for her would never come again."

"That just proves that you're a goddamned showoff!" said Frank. "No one knows a piece of classical music by its actual name!"

"Instead of answering her phone, Natalie stepped away with each bar of Beethoven, until she'd walked beneath Chihuly's ceiling and out Bellagio's front door. When the ringing stopped and her message came on I heard her say, "This is all beyond me, too, and we have to get to the bottom of it. Come to Anthem Country Club tonight. Don't worry about the time. I will leave your name with the guards."

When Cornelius stopped, to see if he could gauge what new torment his granddaughter might be going through from the way LaVeronica sat, everyone stayed silent. Until Pórdís said "Well, what stands out so far?"

"No question about it," said Frank. "What stands out is the woman don't know a thing about art!"

When Jane asked, "Since I'm not sure what stands out for me, may I repeat what I think I heard?" Pórdís said it was a good idea.

"Okay, this woman from the blackjack table shows up

where Cornelius is having dinner. She insists that he was about to call her, which he was, but he denies it. And then he calls her anyway and hears the same ringtone that his wife used on her phone."

"Not on her phone, it was the music she asked for on the day she died," Ruthie said.

"Plus she invited him to her house!" said Frank.

"Are we supposed to think of it as a coincidence, or believe that Yuki's spirit gave him a musical hint that she really was around?" asked LaVeronica.

She hoped this feeling she had, that she had to say something, didn't show. She should have stuck to her plan and quit that morning.

"It wasn't her spirit, it was her ghost, and I believe it wholeheartedly," said Ruthie.

"What's the difference between a spirit and a ghost?" asked Frank.

"One is visible and the other isn't," Millicent told him. "And all I see here is Natalie coming back to try to scam Cornelius out of his winnings if she can still pull it off."

"Then how do you explain the ringtone?" Jane asked. "I think Cornelius experienced a miracle, and Cornelius, if she's still coming to you, Yuki's ghost, don't discourage her! I think she's coming to make things right between you two."

"But things weren't wrong between us," Cornelius said.

"Well, if this all ended when she stepped out the Bellagio door, then Cornelius has some decisions to make; namely, what to believe regarding those moments that break the seal of our reality," Pórdís said.

"Hold on," said Millicent. "Frank's right for once. Natalie invited him to her house and we need to know if he went or not."

"Of course he went," said Frank. "No man can ignore an invitation like that."

"No, Frank, Cornelius would ignore it if he didn't think it was an invitation from Yuki," said Ruthie. "No one but you would think it was a booty call."

"We still have time to hear more, if it's not too long," said Pórdís. "Otherwise, you're up again on Friday, Cornelius."

"Are you kidding me?" said Ruthie. "We need to hear it now."

That made the others laugh, and it made Cornelius start reading again.

Like the meal at Picasso, "O" may have been wonderful, but I couldn't tell, for as the acrobatic divers dove, I dove, too, deeply into myself. My life with Yuki hadn't been perfect, but the rules we chose to live by were defined and loved by us both. Would I dishonor them now by believing that a woman nearly half her age had sat beside me at a blackjack table, helped me win nearly three hundred grand, then appeared again to tell me we had to get to the bottom of it? If I went to her house wouldn't I be dishonoring what Yuki and I had built?"

"That is the crux of the matter! How to go on with your life without denying the life you had!" cried Ruthie.

"That would be true even if it was a bootie call," Millicent said.

"O" ended at eleven, but when we got back to our hotel Emi said she wanted to play blackjack and asked me to take Phoebe to our rooms. Phoebe could watch a movie if she wanted to, while Emi would come up as soon as she lost the two hundred dollars she set aside for gambling, or won a thousand. Those were the rules she used to measure success... go broke or quintuple your investment. It was part of the reason her marriage was such a wreck.

He looked at Pórdís, fearing he'd gone too far again, but she was lost in thought.

We kept the door between our rooms open except when sleeping, so when Phoebe and I went into mine she flipped her shoes off then ran into the room she shared with her mom. When I followed her and said, "Let's see what movie would be age-appropriate," she said, "I already know there's porn, but Mom says it's not age-appropriate for anyone."

"*She's right, it's not, so how about we get some sleep?" I said.*

"You were trying to get rid of her. You didn't want to hear her problems."

LaVeronica's voice was as soft as it would have been were she talking to herself. Pórdís raised her head but Cornelius kept on reading, since he was about to prove LaVeronica's point.

"You can go to bed if you want to. I'll flip channels," Phoebe said.

Phoebe was a responsible girl - she would do what she said she'd do - but was I capable of going to my room, pretending to sleep, and then slipping out?

"How long do you think your mom will be?" I asked.

"If you want to know the truth, Mom's not down there trying to win money, she's down there so she can funk out about Dad without having to pretend she's not," Phoebe said. "Let me ask you, Grandpa. Do you think they're really getting a divorce?"

Cornelius stopped. He hadn't realized just how deep a violation of his family's privacy his story was.

"This is longer than I thought. Maybe we could talk more about it on Friday," he said.

"Yes, Friday works," said Pórdís.

13.

Phoebe and Dwayne

Cornelius was tired when he left Þórdís's house, but he was also hungry, so he stopped at the Frisco Freeze for a cheeseburger on his way home, hoping that, since it was late, there wouldn't be a line. He had loved the Frisco Freeze since he was a kid, but their burgers were slow cooked and he didn't want to wait tonight.

There was no line so he got out of his car, ordered his burger, then got back into his car until his number was called. He and Yuki did this occasionally over the years, and once, shortly before her death, a friend came up to her window to wish her well in her cancer battle. The friend delivered his condolences awkwardly then disappeared into the night. And now Cornelius sat waiting for his burger alone.

He hurried home with his food when it was ready, but rather than park in the driveway he drove around to the alley to put his car in the garage. He wanted to appear to be gone in the morning. He didn't want another interruption like Frank's.

He left his engine running while he got out to open the garage's ancient cupboard style doors. There had never been a lock on these doors, only a sturdy stick stuck down through the loop in the hasp. He noticed right away that the stick was gone and the hasp flap pulled free. It was a small thing, but it made him wary enough to open one door quickly, lest some thief be in there trying to steal his worthless things.

The garage hadn't had an overhead light in years, but now two large Japanese paper lanterns hung, one over each of its ceiling beams, their cords leading down to electric outlets on opposing walls. The diffused light from the lanterns illuminated Cornelius's tarpaulin in the center of the garage floor, on top of which one of Yuki's best futons lay half open and half covering two writhing bodies, limbs entwined. They hadn't sensed the door opening, so busy were they with their coitus, accompanied by *Tired of Being Alone,* of all damned things, a song from Cornelius's CD collection. Cornelius hadn't heard the song before opening the door, so he stood in shock for a second, but he didn't afford the lovers that same courtesy. Rather, he shouted "Phoebe!" causing the writhing body on top to leap from the one on the bottom like the space shuttle leaving its booster rocket. Phoebe turned in midair, grabbed her grandmother's yukata, and ran from the garage, Yuki's best *zori* clinging to her feet like flip flops at the beach.

Al Green started into *I Stand Accused,* before Dwayne jumped up, too, and tried to run after Phoebe, his pants still down around his knees. He stumbled and then tumbled onto the alley's slick wet gravel, scrapping and bloodying his hands and elbows. "Mr. MacLeish!" he cried. "I love Phoebe and she loves me!"

"Get up and call your mother," said Cornelius.

Dwayne climbed to his feet and pulled his pants up, but then he took off out of the alley, shouting Phoebe's name. Cornelius took his own phone out and called LaVeronica, whom he'd just avoided talking to at Pórdís's house. "Hi," said her voicemail, "if I'm not answering you've got me at a bad time, but don't leave a message unless it's an emergency."

"It *is* an emergency! I just found Dwayne and Phoebe in my garage!" Cornelius shouted.

He hung up and turned to pick up Yuki's futon when his phone rang.

"Give me your address," LaVeronica said.

He did, then he folded the futon, unplugged and pulled down the lanterns, took everything to his car, and drove around to the front of his house again. Had he parked there in the first place he never would have known.

Once inside, he noticed traces of Dwayne's blood on his hands and on his cheeseburger bag, which he somehow had the wherewithal to bring. He was just about to go into the kitchen to wash when he glanced into his living room and saw, there on his coffee table, on the squares of his ever-present chessboard, sixteen large origami standing across from sixteen more, half of them folded from white paper, half from black. Yuki had taught Phoebe origami since she was old enough to ask about it, until Phoebe became better at it than her grandma. They had folded a bewilderment of real and mythical animals, in fact, hiding them in Yuki's hospital blankets until just a few days before she died. And now here those animals were, facing each other in the world's most complex game.

Cornelius went in to stand above the chessboard, and was still there when his doorbell rang. He could see LaVeronica through its glass, just like he'd seen Frank. When he opened the door she burst past him shouting "Dwayne!" then looked at him and said, "What happened to you? You're about to bleed onto your rug."

Cornelius pointed at the origami. "That is what they left for us," he said. "The blood belongs to your son."

While he told her what happened in his garage, LaVeronica picked up one of the origami.

"Okay, you've got to think clearly," she said, when he was done. "Did Phoebe say anything that would tell you where they went? Would she have gone home or to another kid? Did she have anyone besides Dwayne?"

She looked like she was asking the origami.

"She wouldn't go home. What about Dwayne? Do you know where he might go in a situation like this?"

When LaVeronica didn't answer, Cornelius found his phone and called Emi.

14.

Kenji Okada

Kenji Okada was a well-known artist who had a workshop in a warehouse on Jefferson Avenue, a few streets above the Tacoma campus of the University of Washington. The area had been blighted for decades, with bars and pawnshops along Pacific Avenue and the nation's first "needle exchange" program, single-handedly created on the corner of 13th and Commerce by a guy named Dave Purchase. But when the University of Washington came to town in the 90s things began to change, until now the area was busy and cool. The Washington State Historical Society took over Union Station, with the Tacoma Art Museum next to it, and the adjacent Museum of Glass, care of Dale Chihuly, earning the city a worldwide reputation.

Kenji Okada took a long-term lease on the second floor of the warehouse before all the changes, so he had 10,000 square feet of cheap space in which to make his art. Phoebe figured that he was about her grandmother's age, and that both of them left Japan when they were young enough to learn English well but too old to lose their accents. She didn't know how or when they met, but she had gone to Mr. Okada's studio with her grandmother a couple of times, and since her grandmother's death she went there alone, to grieve with him in tandem.

So that was where she took Dwayne when he caught up

with her.

They entered the studio through a downstairs side door that led to an old beige hallway with bent and rusted mailboxes hung along one wall. The mailboxes had cards in the slots at their fronts with names written on them.

"People don't really live here, but Mr. Okada says that this is art because it shows what's left of us after we die," Phoebe said.

"What?" asked Dwayne. "You mean the mailboxes?"

She imagined her grandmother's name on a mailbox, a secret address that only she knew.

Just as they were about to head up the stairs to Mr. Okada's actual studio, the man himself came down with more old mailboxes lining his arms. When he saw them he gave two to Phoebe and carried three over to the nearby wall. He then turned to Dwayne. Perhaps he'd overheard him.

"The challenge is not so much in building the mailboxes as in deciding what names to put on them, in making those who actually lived mingle with those who came from our collective imaginations," he said. "Look, here is Yoko Sugiyama next to Henry Jekyll next to Deacon Brodie. Whether real or imagined, each lived a dual life."

Though he had no idea who those people were, Dwayne nodded, instantly taken with the idea. "I do that with rap," he said. "I make up a bunch of stuff then add Frederic Douglass or Denzel Washington!"

"He does!" said Phoebe, but Mr. Okada only told them to follow him upstairs.

More mailboxes lined the stairwell but at the top a final mailbox had Kenji Okada's own name written on it.

"Does that mean he gets his mail here or is it art, too?"

Dwayne asked Phoebe.

Inside, the studio was sectioned-off; one part for painting, another for sculpture, a third for carpentry and installations... In a mammoth frame that took up half a wall was a photograph of Kenji Okada's most famous work, dozens of ectomorphic Giacometti men, broken and strewn across a pink plywood floor. In a corner below that photo was an alcove with a tatami floor and a low table with a teapot.

"Go in there," he said, then he busied himself with more mailboxes.

Dwayne didn't want to go into the alcove, he wanted to look around, but Phoebe said they had to do what they were told. In the alcove were *zabuton*, comfortable square cushions placed around the table. When Phoebe sat down Dwayne did, too. There were teacups and there was tea, but they were afraid to help themselves.

"This is so cool!" Dwayne whispered. "How come you didn't bring me here before? Or even mention him to me when we told each other everything about our lives?"

"He was my grandma's friend and I guess I didn't mention him because there is more to 'everything' than we can stick into a couple of nights of talking," said Phoebe.

Maybe so, but Dwayne believed that he had bled his heart out. He scooted over closer to whisper a question that only just occurred to him but had been nagging Phoebe since her grandmother's death. "Were they in love like we are?"

A vision of her grandpa reading to her from his Mopester presentation came into Phoebe's head, diving down to wound her heart. "They can't have been!" she said. "Or I don't know. Whenever I was around they spoke Japanese, so I couldn't understand what they said."

She leaned over and kissed Dwayne, to keep him from asking any more questions, but when Kenji Okada came into the alcove and sat down next to her she stopped in mid-kiss and wiped her mouth. And then she turned to glare at the man. "Do you see Grandma's ghost? She's been haunting Grandpa, has she also been haunting you?"

He had brought a huge sketchpad with him into the alcove, and stood it on the table. Instead of answering Phoebe, he opened it to reveal a drawing of her grandmother. She wore a white kimono with yellow cranes flying across its shoulders. Her hair was down and she held a paper umbrella.

"Oh, she was so beautiful," said Phoebe.

"Did you love her, too?" asked Dwayne, but Mr. Okada only asked, in turn, "What do you see here young man?"

Dwayne was terrified of giving the wrong answer.

"Phoebe's grandma and an umbrella," he said.

"And what emotion do you see on her face?"

"That she's hiding something. I see that look on my mom's face all the time."

Dwayne reached out, nearly touching the umbrella. "She's carrying that so people will think she's relaxed, but she's not," he said.

This was why Phoebe loved him! She turned to Mr. Okada to see if he was in awe of Dwayne, too, but he only flipped to the next page of the sketchpad, revealing her grandmother again but in a much different pose. This time she was wearing the very yukata Phoebe grabbed when running away from her grandfather, and still wore now! Her grandma held a wooden bucket and her hair was wrapped in a towel, as if she was just coming out of the bath. Her feet were bare with the toes of one foot turned down. They seemed to be digging into the tatami.

When Phoebe looked at Mr. Okada again, this time he spoke to her.

"I drew these after she died," he said, then he closed the sketchbook, laid it on the tatami, and pushed it out of the alcove, as if to say, 'and that is all I'm going to say.'

When he turned back to them his posture had changed.

"Tell me what you two are doing here now," he said.

"We need a place to stay until we're old enough to get married," said Dwayne.

"And how old would that be?" asked Mr. Okada, before he pulled out his cellphone. "Who's calling whose parents first?" he said.

15.

Emi

After searching for Phoebe late into the night, Cornelius dragged himself home, fell asleep on his bed, then woke at 3 a.m. and got up to undress and get into it. When he moved to close his shades he could see that his willow tree, far from being barren, as it had been for weeks, had grown as bushy and busy with leaves as his head had been with worry before he fell asleep. He thought it was an optical illusion caused by the shadows from a neighboring house, until an aurora of blues and reds flashed out of the tree to dart across the yard, stopping just on the other side of his window. He had come to terms with Yuki's visits, but the face in the aurora wasn't hers. Rather, it was that of his own beloved grandmother, dead since 1958.

"Who are you?" he asked, in a very particular way.

Dead or alive, his grandmother would recognize the particularity of that question and answer by saying, *"Ask me who I was,"* for she had read "A Christmas Carol" to him dozens of times during his childhood, just as he had read it to Phoebe.

"Ask me who I was," she said, then she was gone like vision is when you close your eyes.

Cornelius woke again at six, got dressed and hurried down to make coffee. But when he went into his kitchen the coffee was ready and Emi sat out on his deck, her hands wrapped around a steaming mug of it. He got one for himself, grabbed a blanket from the back of a chair, and went out to join her. It was raining again and the yard below them looked swampy.

"I should reseed the grass or tear it all out and put in a lap pool," he said. "Your mom used to say that swimming was the best of the geriatric exercises."

"We have enough trouble keeping our heads above water without a lap pool," said Emi.

He sat down and threw the blanket across both their laps. He wanted news of Phoebe, of course, but he didn't want to ask. There'd been an ease between Emi and him that had continued through her first relationship with a hopeless druggie named Eric, her marriage to Donnie, even up to her mother's death. But the ease had recently left.

"Did you know she only started having periods six months ago, when these days the average age has dropped to twelve?" she asked.

"I did. Phoebe wanted your mom to buy her tampons, but I ended up buying them when your mom got too sick."

Emi shook beneath the blanket. "Do you understand how terribly I miss her? She was the one I talked to about every-thing."

Cornelius took her hand. *He* had been the one she more often talked to, but it hardly seemed necessary to point that out.

"We've been up all night, that's why I'm here so early," she said.

He chanced, "Who has been up all night? You and Don-nie and Phoebe?"

"All of us for half of it, then just Phoebe and me. She thinks she's in love with this Dwayne, Dad. Was I like that when I was her age?"

When Emi was Phoebe's age she tried to change her name to Amy, so she wouldn't have to spell it for people her whole life long. It had been Cornelius's idea to name her Emi, after a girl he knew in Kyoto back in 1972, but when he told her that she said she hated the Japanese part of her, that she wanted to be a 'full-fledged' American. A year later she ran off to San Francisco with Eric, the druggie, so when Cornelius gave her a cross-eyed look now she laughed.

"For the first time ever, after Donnie went to bed, I told Phoebe about Eric," she said. "I told her that I thought I loved him and would have killed you or mom if you tried to come between us. I also told her that in a month I discovered I was wrong, in far more ways than one."

"What did she say to that?"

"That she was nothing like me, Dwayne was nothing like Eric, and that she and Dwayne would never be apart again. And then can you guess what she said?"

"That she doesn't care what anyone thinks, I expect. Is she asleep now? Skipping school today?"

"Not on your life. I told her I was coming over here to set your mind at ease, and when I got home she had to be ready for me to drive her."

She looked at her phone. "In fact, I have to go. But listen, Dad, what she said next is the reason I came over instead of just calling you…it wasn't that she didn't care what anyone thinks, and I'm a little afraid to tell you what it was."

Emi took their coffee mugs inside, refilled her father's and brought it back out to him.

"Did it have something to do with Kenji Okada?" he asked.

He had tucked one end of the blanket around his feet, pulled the other end over his shoulders, and clasped the rest of it against his chest. He felt like a refugee sitting at the prow of a ship a century earlier, heading for his new life in America, his seedy backyard the swelling waters of the ocean after a storm.

Emi said it did have to do with Mr. Okada, then closed the front door on her way out.

16.

The Hob Nob and Agatha

Cornelius went to the Southern Kitchen for a breakfast of chicken fried steak - treating himself to a good bad breakfast was a thing he did when his mind was in turmoil - then he drove to Wright Park to walk it off. He had come to Wright Park for as long as he could remember. When he was four years old the very grandmother who flew to his window last night, brought him to its wading pool, but then refused to let him wade because of fear of polio. And, truth be told, he felt hobbled by something akin to polio now, since he had no idea of what went on between Yuki and Kenji Okada, and since he let Emi leave without telling him what Phoebe said.

He walked around the park at a fast pace, then slowed and walked around it again, finally ducking down to stand on the bridge that crossed its duck pond for some wildlife observation. His life was wilder, though, than anything he saw on the pond. As he was leaving the park, his mind on that wildness, who should he find leaning against his car, but Frank.

"We were sitting over at the Hob Nob and saw you," Frank said.

He pointed across the street to the Hob Nob Cafe.

"It's just me and Jane. I think you should come join us."

Cornelius was afraid *not* to join them, lest Frank go jump off the bridge again, so he followed Frank across the street and into the cafe, where Jane pushed a chair out for him.

"What you do is order yourself a Bloody Mary," she said. "They make them here with celery and olives, even salami and cheese, on toothpicks."

She pointed at two empty glasses. When Cornelius looked at Frank, Frank held up his palms, meaning both of the glasses were Jane's.

"It's too early for me. I just stopped in to say hello," he said.

"We were talking about how some people are what they appear to be and some are not," said Jane. She raised an empty glass and looked at Frank, like now was the time for him to say something true about himself.

"And we mentioned you just a second before we saw you," said Frank. "Jane thinks that means we conjured you."

"I didn't say that. I said that there were no coincidences. And let me tell you, running out to get you like he did, saved Franklin from a messy conversation."

"She also said she thinks you conjured Yuki's ghost. So conjurin' was our subject, mostly," Frank said. "Makes me think that Jane might have conjured Giancarlo."

Frank's eyes bored into Jane's, which, even after two Bloody Marys, looked sober.

"I remember you saying once that Giancarlo played the violin. Is that how he made his living?" Cornelius asked. "If so, my hat is off to him."

His hat would be off to any subject other than him conjuring Yuki.

"Lord no, Giancarlo was a hippie and a paint salesman. But his violin saw him through life's thicks and thins," Jane said.

"In the paint business there are a lot of those," said Frank.

"But Corny looks crestfallen, I think because he honors violin playin' more than he does sellin' paint, while I believe paint sellin' is God's work. So Giancarlo'd have a friend in me if he was still alive."

"I guess that means that you weighed the contributions you made in your life, and deemed them worthy before you jumped off that bridge," Jane said. "Would you care to enumerate them for us now, Frank? I'm sure we'd love to hear about what you did for a living."

There was so much heat at the table, so many undercurrents, that Cornelius couldn't help registering how contrary Jane's aggression was, to what they'd learned in one of Pórdís's first conversation with them, about how to deal with the suicidal.

Frank reached across the table to wrap both his hands around Jane's, but he looked at Cornelius. "Do you want a new version of me, too, Corny? Do you want to believe, like Janie here seems to, that jumpin' off that bridge put the skunk I was before I jumped in a cocoon, and pretty soon I'll be turning into a butterfly, free to give up all my secrets, and therefore live the rest of my life skunk free?"

Cornelius stood up. He had to get out of there, back to worries that plagued him before Frank appeared beside his car.

"I have all the hope in the world that you'll be free to live your life, Frank, and you can keep your secrets, as far as I'm concerned. But I've got miles to go before our session tonight. I'll see you both at Pórdís's house, I hope."

"Lemme walk you back to your car," Frank said, but Jane told him that if he knew what was good for him he would not get out of his chair again.

So Frank eased back, letting Cornelius leave the Hob Nob on his own.

*****

It may seem odd to have waited so long to mention that Cornelius had a cat who ran away on the day of Yuki's death and didn't come back until the morning they scattered half her ashes on Puget Sound. When she reappeared Cornelius took her to the basement for a bath, but when he came home after the ash scattering ceremony she was gone again, through an open window above the laundry.

Now, however, after he got home from those unnerving few minutes at the Hob Nob, she came limping across his backyard like a scurvy victim, like she, too, had come to America on that earlier-imagined refugee ship. She had been gone for a month this time, and he had given her up for dead.   Cornelius opened his deck door. "Agatha," he said.

When she heard her name, rather than taking off again, as he feared she might, she limped up the deck stairs, wet and miserable and still with a grief-stricken face. But she allowed him to pick her up and carry her inside, where he found both dry and wet cat food. When she didn't go near it he grabbed a dishtowel, sat down beside her on the floor and dried her off. She had a swollen eye and a mangled paw.

"It's a hard life without her but stay home now, Aggie, and we'll learn to love each other, okay?" he said.

He had to take her to the vet, but he couldn't say the word aloud, for she knew it and might once more try to escape. He would get her carrying case from the basement as soon as he could. In the meantime, he would let the vet know they were coming. Good! He had a plan!

When Agatha was dry and sniffing her food bowls he called the Jones Animal Hospital and told them his name, careful not to mention theirs or Agatha's. There were veterinary hospitals nearer his house these days, but this one had been in business for so long that Cornelius's parents took his dog there when he was a child.

"Sure," they said, "come in any time."

While he was on the phone he got a beep, and when he hung up he listened to a message. "Mr. MacLeish, it's LaVeronica Williams. Please call me back," it said.

Agatha ate a couple of bites of food, then came over and waited by his chair. When he picked her up again she purred a little against his chest.

"You need sleep, then we'll see if your appetite comes back," he said.

When he carried her upstairs she didn't fight. And this time he made sure that the windows to the room he shut her into were closed.

17.

LaVeronica

Though Cornelius had no desire to see anyone else after the Hob Nob, nor eat anything else after his chicken fried steak, he agreed to meet LaVeronica at Quickie Too, a vegan place on MLK, about halfway between his house and the vet where he had just taken Agatha. When he walked in and said, "I didn't know you were vegan," she told him that she wasn't, but that the food there was great. She ordered a meatless burger, he a vegan BLT. He would spend a half an hour with her and then go home. And he wouldn't come out again until the North End grievers' meeting that night.

"Okay listen," she said. "I know a couple of things and you know a couple of things, so I hope that we can talk about them, make life easier for us all."

One person he didn't want to make life easier for was her son. But he supposed that telling her that was a bad idea. So he asked, "What are the couple of things that you know?"

"Well, one, if you'll pardon my French, is that these two kids are fucking like minks. I caught them twice and you caught them once, and I hate to think of how many times they weren't caught, don't you?"

She paused, then said, "Now you tell me something."

He had a weird urge to tell her about Frank and Jane, but that, of course, wasn't what she was asking. And the truth was, he didn't know much about what she wanted to know.

Probably because he hadn't found a way to make Emi tell him.

"Phoebe says they'd rather die than be apart," he said.

"Then you must know why I called you rather than her parents."

That he *did* know - Donnie prosecuted her for shooting Johnny Sylvester.

"Because you and Donnie are on the outs. Did you see him when you went to get Dwayne at the art studio?"

"'On the outs' makes it sound like we were friends once, but that man's a horror, Mr. MacLeish. He knew everything about Johnny's death…knew I was within my rights to shoot him. But he chose to see what he might glean for himself from the situation. And no, I didn't see him when I went to get Dwayne."

"Okay, but why didn't you just call Emi?"

"I almost did but I changed my mind, called you in-stead."

When their food came she took a small bite of her burger, then said, "But now I don't think it was a good idea. What are you, a generation older than me? Is this what I've got to look forward to? Staring into the abyss with a bunch of strangers at a therapist's house?"

"What do you mean 'look forward to?'" he said. "You're doing it already."

"Maybe so, but not really. You all look at me like I'm from another planet."

"Phoebe used those very words to describe the way kids look at her at school. Maybe she got it from Dwayne who got it from you."

He didn't think he liked this woman and shoved his veggie

BLT away.

"Even if she did, that doesn't make it false. Have you truly never noticed what a couple of ducks out of water those two are? At their age I was that way, too, just a gangly black girl at a nearly all-white school. We didn't have social media back then, so at least if someone wanted to mock me they had to call my house. But these days…do you know what's happening to Phoebe and Dwayne online?"

He didn't and said so. He also said that if Emi knew about it she hadn't told him.

"I'm telling you now, and Phoebe's getting the worst of it. Have you ever heard of slut-shaming?"

A rage grew up in him like he hadn't felt since Emi ran off with Eric.

"Tell me the name of the person who called her that, I'll go kill him now!" he said.

LaVeronica's laugh was derisive. "Dwayne said the same thing, but he meant it, while you would only complain to the slut-shamer's parents… I'd do that, too, and where do you think it would get us?"

"I'll report it to whoever deals with these things at their school, too! They won't put up with something like that!"

LaVeronica let out another, less derisive, laugh. "Listen again, man! I said I had a couple of things to tell you, and now you're gonna hear the other one. I've been going to the AME church a block or so down from where we're sitting right now. It's how I learned about this place. I went there as a kid, stopped for a few decades, but started again after I got out of prison. Dwayne has been going with me during these hard days. He's 'stocking up belief' for when the weather turns cold, he likes to say."

To his surprise, Cornelius liked that phrase, but all he said was, "Phoebe doesn't go to church, so I guess that's one difference between them."

"My, what you don't know about your granddaughter. Phoebe came to the AME with us twice. Granted, it was before this apple tree business and maybe I shouldn't have told you, but nobody said it was a secret. That's not what I'm getting to now, though, so pay attention please!"

Cornelius had been paying attention, but he sat up straighter in his chair.

"If you push a seed into the dirt out in your garden and you don't dig it up during its germinating time, you'll get a tomato or a rose or whatever it was you planted," she said. "And that's what's going on with our two kids…or so the slut-shamers say."

Now great swells of panic rose up in Cornelius. Germinating time? Tomato? What?

"It's why I asked you to meet me instead of calling anyone else," she said. "Because, I don't know about her mother, but if it's true, Phoebe's father is going to want to dig that garden up straight away, and I, a woman who's already taken one life, will not be party to taking another. Nor with letting that motherfucker decide, ever again, what goes on in my family."

Cornelius grabbed the edges of the table so he wouldn't fall off his chair.

"She's fourteen years old," he managed to say. "And what makes you think that I don't feel the same as Donnie? Or that Donnie even feels that way? He's Catholic."

"Because if your wife's ghost is telling you that there is life after death, then she's also saying that there's life before birth. And Catholic? Really? He sure doesn't act like one."

An earlier version of Cornelius - maybe only days earlier - might have made some glib comment. But now he only looked at the air between them, noticing its stillness. He couldn't hear the other diners nor the outside traffic noise, nor even Bob Marley, who'd been singing in the background all this time.

"Why do you think it's true, what they're saying about her online?"

"Because Phoebe made the mistake of telling one of them that her period was late."

When their check came LaVeronica grabbed it. Neither one of them had eaten their sandwiches, so she asked the waiter to box them up.

18.

Millicent

"Tonight was supposed to be the culmination of Cornelius's week, but he called to say he has a family emergency and can't make it," said Þórdís.

Jane sat next to Frank, as if his guardian, while Millicent and Ruthie sat across from them with their legs crossed. Þórdís said she'd received similar word from LaVeronica. She didn't say that LaVeronica tried to quit the group or that she talked her out of it.

"Well dang," said Frank. "I was lookin' forward to hearin' Corny's next chapter."

Though the others ignored him, Jane patted his knee.

"I spoke with Millicent after I got Cornelius's call, and she agreed to be up tonight, even with this short notice," Þórdís said. "So thank you, Millicent."

"Did he say what his family emergency was?" asked Ruthie.

"He did, but I can't share it. Maybe he will when he comes back."

Þórdís waited for other comments, then said, "Okay, Millicent."

Millicent had some papers ready and read from them.

"Jonathan, my ex-husband, was so difficult to live with…"

"He's your 'late' husband, dear, not your 'ex,'" said Frank.

"Jonathan, my late husband, was so difficult to live with that I left him twice, once to go to our daughter, Millie's, house in England, and once, I'm ashamed to say, to move in with another man. Both times I was gone for less than a month and when I came back things were better for a while. But Jonathan was a conspiracy theorist and would soon start in on one damned thing or another, until finally I told him I wanted a divorce."

When she glanced at Pórdís, Pórdís bobbed her eyebrows in encouragement.

"After Jonathan got sick I put the divorce on hold, and when we heard he had six months to live…well, God forgive me, I thought I can take anything for that long."

When Ruthie started crying, Pórdís said, "I know you're not finished, Millicent, but let me ask…why did you return after the two times you left him?"

"Because I was a burden to Millie and I didn't love the other man," Millicent said.

"I wasn't asking why you left them, exactly, but why you returned to Jonathan."

"Maybe I didn't have anywhere else to go?"

"That appears to be a question," said Jane.

"When Jonathan was around I wanted to kill him, but when he wasn't around…I don't know. Millie had her own life and the other guy…"

"You heard Pórdís. Don't talk about them again, talk about yerself," said Frank.

Those words could have been spoken by the old Frank, except that his tone was softer, as if he were a friend advising Millicent privately. Millicent heard it and said, "Okay Frank, Jonathan was infuriating, yes, but he was also funnier than a crutch. We'd built our life on humor and I missed that part of it."

"I haven't heard anyone say 'funnier than a crutch,' since high school," said Ruthie. "It's de rigueur to say it differently these days."

She actually seemed to be waiting for Millicent to say it differently, so Jane asked, "You missed 'it,' the funny stuff? Or you missed 'him,' the funny guy?"

"It," Millicent said, "though I don't quite see the difference."

Her papers fell to the floor but she didn't retrieve them.

"Maybe there isn't one but try saying 'him,' just to see how it feels," said Pórdís.

"Oh god! I cheated on Jonathan, and not just with those two guys. But Jonathan didn't cheat! For all his dumb conspiracy theories, he was as loyal to me as my dog, Fathead, who died not long after Jonathan did. God how I miss him."

This time no one tried to clarify who she meant.

Pórdís picked up Millicent's papers. When Millicent wouldn't take them she placed them on her lap.

"Look," said Ruthie. "Can you try to separate your grief from your feelings of guilt about all those times you cheated?"

"I can answer that. She can't," Jane said. "Because guilt is a dead-end street, grief is a path with an end to it, and she doesn't know which one she wants yet."

"That's a good one, Janie," said Frank. "How'd you get to be so smart?"

"It wasn't 'all those times,' it was four," Millicent said, "but Jonathan kept forgiving me! There was nothing I could do that would make him *not* wrap his arms around me in his understanding way! Can you imagine how infuriating a thing like that can be?"

"I can, because I was that way with Ben," said Ruthie. "I was an absolute doormat when it came to that man."

Pórdís looked at Ruthie, asking her wordlessly not to change the subject.

"So Mills," said Frank, "you were waiting for Jonathan to stand up for himself, is that what you're sayin'?"

"No, I wasn't waiting for him to stand up for himself, Frank! I was waiting for him to die!" Millicent cried.

That shocked everyone save Jane, who said, quite pleasantly, "I understand that! So you could be a sad widow instead of a disloyal wife?"

"Yes! And that makes me a fraud! I am here under false pretenses!"

"No, you're not. Jane was trying to get you to substitute 'him' for 'it' a minute ago," said Pórdís "How about trying that now?"

Millicent read from her papers again. *"We built our life on humor over the years and I missed him! And I can't seem to navigate the world at all now.'"*

She put her papers back down. "'It…' 'him…' fuck it. Do you remember when Cornelius said it was four o'clock on a sunny afternoon but low-lying clouds filled his heart? Well, low-lying clouds fill my heart when I wake up, when I eat, when I go for walks or watch TV, even when I'm sleeping, and I have had enough of it."

The only failsafe North End grievers' rule had to do with someone thinking of harming herself. So Ruthie looked at Pórdís to see if what Millicent just said qualified, while Jane looked at Frank, to see if he might take the opportunity to confess his bridge jump.

Frank, however, asked out of nowhere, "How about if you're blinking, Mills? Do the clouds go out of your heart when you try to blink?"

Millicent gave him the meanest look she could muster, but Þórdís said, "Believe it or not, that's a real thing. I learned it from my mentor."

They all looked up at Josefine Christophersen-Hemmingsen's unblinking face.

"Well, criminy," Millicent said. "I try to write something after Cornelius's success with it, and we end up talking about blinking. I guess that means if you want anymore from me you're going to have to ask for it, because I'm done volunteering."

"Here's a question then," Ruthie asked right away. "Now that Jonathan's gone, what do you most regret?"

"Not having talked to him properly regarding those affairs," Millicent said.

"Is it a point of pride with you that you had the affairs? Is that why you keep bringing them up?"

That was from Ruthie again, bolder and more forthright than she had even been.

"If you're asking if I was marking territory for myself in a world dominated by Jonathan, then yes, I was. Though I'm not proud of having to admit it to you now."

Jane encouraged Millicent to go on.

"I told you Jonathan was a conspiracy theorist, that he was always deciding the truth of a thing based upon some idiotic notion, and then he rode roughshod over me about it. But I had a 'self,' and a body in which my 'self' resided…so setting down markers and feeling pride in them? Yes, I suppose I was."

"Let me get it straight about them prideful markers," said Frank. "Was it the case that every time Jonathan rode rough-shod over you, you went out and fucked someone else? Is that why you said it twice just now?"

Though he used an obscenity, he also used his gentlest voice. So Millicent said, "If it had been 'every time,' I'd have had more affairs than you could count. But of four, it's fair to say that three were that way. The fourth, however, was for love, and had little to do with Jonathan."

Jane pulled a tissue from the box in the center of the table. Her face was dry but she held it in reserve when she asked, "Now that Jonathan's dead, are you thinking of contacting the man you loved, bring him back into your life?"

"You've been spending too much time on the Hallmark channel, Jane," Millicent said.

"In grieving now, how much of it would you say is for the loss of missed opportunities *not* connected with men, but just as 'you,' just as a person in the world?" asked Ruthie.

"I think you believe there is a right answer to that question and that my answer to it is wrong," Millicent said. She looked from Ruthie to the others. "Ruthie already knows this, but I was studying British monetary policy in London when I met Jonathan. Had I not met him I would have finished my de-gree and gone off to work in the world, but since I did meet him, I didn't. But I never begrudged Jonathan those missed opportunities, that's Ruthie's projection. I knew what I was giving up and did it of my own free will."

"It makes no sense, yet all the sense in the world," said Frank. "Not wanting to cut your losses by leaving Jonathan was like not wanting to sell some bad stock you bought on the chance that it might turn around. I did that with Boeing once."

Þórdís kept no clock in the room but she knew what time it was.

"How about a couple more questions before we let Millicent go?" she asked. "Has anyone got one?"

Since no one did, not long after that they adjourned. And no one felt depressed or even grieved very much during their drives home.

There was too much blinking going on.

19.

How Well Did Grandma Know Mr. Okada?

As soon as he got home from Quickie Too, Cornelius called Emi to talk about Phoebe. To his surprise, Phoebe picked up.

"Mom told me Agatha's back," she said. "That's great news, Grandpa."

"She is, but she's hurt. I took her to the vet. I'm going back tomorrow to pick her up."

"Hurt how?"

"A wounded paw and an abscessed eye. Maybe she fought with a feral cat or even a raccoon. She's also lost a lot of weight."

"I'll go with you. Will you wait till I can get out of the house tomorrow?"

"Sure. Shall I pick you up?"

"Yes, that way they'll know I'm not sneaking, trying to meet Dwayne."

That should have told him it was time for him to seal the deal by getting off the phone, that it was *not* the time to ask if she had anything to tell him. But he couldn't bring himself not to ask, "Is Kenji Okada's workshop a regular hangout for you guys?"

He hoped she would give him a pass. It was the foolish hope of an aging man.

"Listen, Grandpa, you understand that this is about Agatha, right? I want to know right now if I have to build a fence around my privacy with you, too."

"You don't," he said. "I promise I'll worry in silence."

There was a pause before she asked, "How well did Grandma know Mr. Okada?"

"He was just someone she could speak Japanese with, Phoebs. Sometimes she missed her native language."

"Yeah, well, that much is okay, but did you know he was in love with her?"

Now it was his turn to pause, while his heart sped up.

"You went to his studio with her. Did you come to that conclusion during those times, or only last night?" he asked.

"Last night when I saw some drawings he made of her. He has this humongous sketchbook, and the drawings in it were all of Grandma."

"Did he show it to you or did you guys look at it without his permission?"

"He showed it to us. Well, he showed us two drawings, anyway… After that he made us call our parents. And after *that,* while we were waiting for them to come, he left us alone with the sketchbook while he fiddled with some stupid mailboxes across the room. That was when we looked at the rest of them."

"And the sketches told you that he was in love with Grandma?"

"Well, duh," she said, but then she whispered, "You didn't know that?"

"Not exactly," he said.

He wanted to ask if she thought it was a two-way street, the love she was describing.

"Saying that you didn't know it 'exactly' means that it was

in the back of your mind. You didn't want to drag it to the front of your mind, huh?"

"I guess that's right."

"Boy, Grandpa, that's *so* you, But I'll tell you this...*before* yesterday I never knew a bit of it, in the back or the front of my mind. It was only when I looked inside that sketchbook..."

When she stopped, recognizing the territory she was stepping into, Cornelius asked her to describe the sketches with as much detail as she could manage, and then he put his phone on speaker, lay down on his living room floor, closed his eyes and listened to his granddaughter talk.

20.

Three Views of Yuki

1. Yuki in a Yukata

When Phoebe said the drawing that shocked her most showed her grandmother wearing a yukata, severely loosened at the front and falling so far down the back that her shoulders were bared, Cornelius remembered his wife in such a pose fifty years earlier, at a hot springs in Hokkaido. They had gone to Hokkaido from Kyoto for a first examination of a possible life together. They had remained both publicly and privately circumspect until their final night, when, in a tatami room whose doors opened onto the steaming hot springs, Cornelius watched her remove her yukata in slow preparation for their first lovemaking. They had soaked in the spa's steaming water twice that day, once after rising and again after lunch. In the interim they stayed in their room, both wearing yukata, with thoughts of entering the spa again before their dinner was brought to their room by maids. They napped, he remembered, for a hot springs took it out of you, and they spoke in low voices, Yuki saying that living in "far off America" was the only solution if they were to be together, the only medicine that might cure her deep reluctance regarding marrying a foreigner. "Maybe others can do it and stay in Japan, but for me it is *verboten,*" she had said, both of them laughing at the German word. Cornelius must have

said that life in America suited him anyway, for shortly after
that, when the sun abandoned the spa to shadows and steam,
Yuki opened the shoji, and then she opened her yukata.

He saw it all again in the words his granddaughter used
to describe the drawing that shocked her most. She also said
that her grandmother's eyes seemed not to be suggesting sex,
but asking the man who drew her if her pose was correct.
Was the Hokkaido connection gone from Yuki's memory by
the time she posed?

Cornelius could not ask Phoebe that, of course, so he
chased the question away.

2. Yuki and Her Father

"He's my great-grandfather and he's in this funny old military uniform. He's sitting back on his heels with his knees
apart, his hands resting on those knees, and he's not wearing
a hat but a headband, with a red circle right in the center of
it. He looks like he's ready for a picture, Grandpa, so maybe
Grandma brought a photo of him to Mr. Okada to sketch.
But I never saw the photo when she showed me pictures
from when she grew up, so maybe she just described it to
him or maybe Mr. Okada made him up. But anyway, this is
the only drawing in the whole sketchpad with two people in
it, because Grandma's in it, too, at about the same age as she
was in the yukata one. But this time she's wearing a white kimono with birds on it. The birds are getting ready to fly off
of the kimono. They never do, of course, but boy, do they
ever look like it! Grandma's behind her father with one hand
on his shoulder. It seems like he's about to go to war, though

that can't be true because he's old. He's as serious as can be and so is Grandma, and, you know, it occurred to me just now that maybe she's not supposed to be Grandma in the drawing but Grandma's mom. That doesn't make any sense, either, though, cause she's got the same face that Grandma has in the other drawings. So no, it's Grandma and her dad.

"Grandpa, can you shed light on this? In a sketchbook that's all about Grandma, why do you think this drawing is even there? I mean, it's kind of weird, huh?"

Cornelius hadn't spoken during her description of the first drawing, and he didn't want to speak during this one, either, but "weird, yes," came out of his mouth.

During their trip to Hokkaido he and Yuki stopped twice in her hometown. On the way to Hokkaido they stayed only four hours, wandering the streets of Yuki's childhood. On their way back they spent a day and a night at her parents' house. Before they left the hot springs Yuki phoned her parents, telling them to expect her and a man she met in Kyoto, a man who said he wanted to marry her. Cornelius was with her when she called, and though his Japanese was poor, he could tell that she hadn't added the doubly weighty news that he was American. That they would discover after he and Yuki made the walk from the station to their house.

Her parents were welcoming during the early hours of their visit, but after dinner Yuki and her father disappeared for an hour, leaving Cornelius to sit while her mother cleared the table, only speaking to him when declining his help. And when Yuki and her father reappeared, Yuki wore the kimono Phoebe described and her father wore the uniform. He also carried a big box camera and set it up for pictures. Yuki had been crying, her face not remotely the face that Phoebe saw in the drawing, though her father's was as stoic as a judge at a military tribunal. He said, through Yuki, that he would not allow the marriage without a full airing of his war experiences first, and then he proceeded to list the battles he had fought. There were many, dotting the Pacific, but ending on July 21, 1944, when he was severely wounded on Guam. He was gruff in the telling, while Yuki's translation was soft.

3. Yuki Among the Wildflowers

Phoebe's final description almost killed him. Yuki sat on a blanket in the middle of a field of wildflowers, "up in the foothills of Mount Rainier, at that lodge where we saw raccoons..."

Phoebe said her grandmother wore shorts and a tank top and that her feet were bare and depicted in an oversized way, at the forefront of the drawing. She said that her hands were planted behind her, that the blanket she sat on was solid brown, like the dirt beneath the wildflowers, and that her expression - aimed at the person making the drawing - seemed loving. The nearby wildflowers were drawn with precision, while those in the background were slices of green with swarths of pink or yellow on top.

The problem with the drawing, the reason it nearly killed him, was that, time after time, Yuki had refused a springtime visit to Mount Rainier in order to avoid her allergies. When Cornelius asked Phoebe what age her grandmother was in the drawing, she said, "old enough for me to recognize her as Grandma." There was Japanese food on the blanket, too, she hastened to point out, *onigiri* and *yakitori,* plus one of Yuki's sweaters tossed casually down, half on the blanket and half venturing into the wildflowers. Phoebe said Mr. Okada even drew the head of one yellow wildflower peeking out from beneath the sweater's sleeve, like someone calling for help from beneath the raging flow of a stream.

When she said, "That's what makes it art, that he decided to show us that one flower, isn't it, Grandpa?" Cornelius said she had done an excellent job of describing the drawings and that he wanted, someday, to have the chance to look through the sketchbook himself.

He also said, "I don't think Mr. Okada was in love with your grandma, but that he loved whatever he looked at when it became a subject for his art."

"Okay, but it sure doesn't seem like he loved those skinny little men very much, when he broke them and scattered them all over that pink plywood," Phoebe said.

"No, maybe not that time," Cornelius told her.

21.

Kittens

The moment Cornelius got to Emi and Donnie's house on Saturday morning, though he hoped to talk with them, Phoebe ran out to his car, insisting that they leave for the veterinary hospital immediately, with Agatha's basket, a toy she loved, and with the clear rule that no one speak of anything else.

The veterinary hospital reception room was empty, so while Phoebe went into an examination room to wait for Agatha, Cornelius paid the bill. On the walls of the reception room were photos of animals with notes from happy owners praising the services of the hospital - even some drawings, so maybe Kenji Okada had a cat, and came here, too.

In the examination room, however, the posters were treatises on dog and cat health, complete with actuarial tables. "How old is Aggie?" Phoebe asked when Cornelius walked in. "Isn't she the same age as me?"

"You don't remember? You and Grandma found her in a box of kittens in Wright Park, back when you were four years old."

"That story's real? I thought Grandma made it up, since whenever I asked what happened to the other kittens she wouldn't say."

"Because you could only take one home, and you chose Agatha. She hoped other people might take the rest of the kittens, but she didn't know."

"And now I might be having a kitten of my own. Ironic, huh, Grandpa?"

The vet came in with Agatha just then, leaving Cornelius heartsick and with his mouth open. He *had* to speak to Phoebe about this, clear rule against it or not, but Phoebe turned her attention to the vet, who gave them Agatha's meds. When she told them how to administer the meds, Phoebe took notes, and once they were in the car again she sat in the back with Agatha, while Cornelius choked the life out of the steering wheel in front of him.

At his house Phoebe jumped out almost before the car stopped rolling, carried Agatha upstairs to the guest room and closed the door, her grandfather limping along behind her.

"If I'm not here when you give her her meds, don't let her out of this room. You heard the vet, she can't miss any doses," she said. She paused, then added, "Agatha was probably the only kitten in that box who had a life at all, right?"

"Probably," said Cornelius, from the other side of the guest room door.

He thought he could tell that she had sat down on the floor inside the room, so he sat down on his side, leaning against its panel. It felt like an agreed-upon confessional.

"Band sucks now," said Phoebe. "We have to wear these stupid uniforms for the holiday concert, and it looks like Dwayne and I will have our *Midnight Train to Georgia* solos cut now, since some girls complained that the song is sexist. Do you remember that song, Grandpa?"

"Of course I do, honey. Gladys Knight and the Pips, 1973."

He hadn't known that she and Dwayne had a solo. How had he not known that?

"Yeah, well, whoever. But I can see those girls's point. I mean, this guy is at a train station in the song, about to go back to where he thinks life is simpler, and his girlfriend is singing her heart out because she is going with him even though she's got her own good life that she's leaving behind. What a doofus girl, and what a doofus band teacher! She knew the lyrics before she assigned the song, so why is she cutting it after Dwayne and I worked so hard?"

"Did you tell the girls who complained that you saw their point?" he asked.

"Sure, because I did. I told the teacher, too. Would you say it was bigamy, Grandpa?"

She waited for him to say "of course it was big of you," and when he did she laughed. "And get this. It wasn't like we didn't have our own song suggestions. Dwayne wrote a rap about Benjamin Franklin and his sister for history, but the band teacher wouldn't let us use that, either. She said it was more controversial than *Midnight Train to Georgia.*"

"Maybe she'd have let you use it if the concert was on the 4th of July," Cornelius said.

"Ha ha, but my point is, Dwayne's rap is a lot more feminist than *Midnight Train to Georgia,* yet she chose that without even listening to his rap, and now those girls get to boycott it."

"Benjamin Franklin was a feminist?"

"No, he was as sexist as a goat. But he wrote letters to his sister and got letters back from her. *She* was a feminist and Benjamin Franklin listened to her. Maybe a couple of her ideas even got into the Declaration of Independence. In

Dwayne's rap they do, anyhow."

"So you won't have any solo at all now?"

"No, and if we want to challenge the stupid decision we have to write it in a letter, not an email. And that's too big a pain for anyone."

"Benjamin Franklin and his sister didn't think it was too big a pain, and because their letters survived for all these years we know what they thought."

"Like when *you* are dead we'll have your books to remember you by?"

When he let his weight grow heavier against the door she said, "Come on, Grandpa, that was a joke. I know you learned a lot in your long life, but I've learned a few things in my short one, too. Like, do you know what a slut is?"

He sat up straight. "Someone called you that?" he asked.

"Not to my face but online, oh yeah. Online calling me a slut is an intramural sport, almost. I stopped logging on and that helps. So does talking to you since you get angry for me, and when I told Dad the name of just one of the slut-shamers he wanted to send the cops to her house. So he's got my back, too. But oh boy, listen to this! When I told Mom about it she really did do something, cause Mom's a woman and women act. When I told her, she got in her car and drove over to Roselyn Wilkerson's house with a bunch of stuff that Roselyn said all printed out. And now Roselyn's grounded for life."

"Roselyn Wilkerson?"

Cornelius remembered Roselyn from Phoebe's kindergarten class, a sweet little Shirley Temple sort of kid. Had Phoebe told Roselyn that her period was late?

"The one and only. Can you believe that once she was a

devoted finger-painter and now she wants to tear me apart? What makes someone grow up cruel, Grandpa?"

Cornelius agreed with both Emi and Donnie. He wanted to drive over to Roselyn's house that very minute *and* call the cops. But all he could manage was to say, "It's a question for the ages, honey. Even Benjamin Franklin wouldn't be able to answer it."

"Maybe not, but his sister would because here's the awful truth. Every last one of my slut-shamers was a girl. It's what made Mom madder than any other part of it."

Cornelius wanted to cry for her, hold her, cook for her, and read her a bedtime story! Yet all he could do was sit like a sloth on the other side of that door.

"Anyway, the whole thing gave me a goal to concentrate on, and that's good, right?"

"I hope your goal is never to speak to Roselyn Wilkerson again."

"Forget Roselyn and listen. It's not fair that Grandma's ghost never talks to me. I loved her just as much as you did."

"And she loved you more than anyone."

"Maybe, but when I saw Mr. Okada's drawings of her, I saw a woman I didn't know at all. Do you think you knew her, Grandpa?"

The subject change was so jarring that he tried to change it back. "What's the goal that you want to concentrate on? And do you think I'm lying about talking to Grandma?"

"Lying? I don't know. Yes. I mean no. I mean, I guess it's your way of coping."

"And this all has something to do with your new goal?"

She ignored that, but presently said, "It isn't your way of coping, though, is it? You really do talk to her, and I know why."

"I do, too," he said, "grief, longing, loneliness, regret…"

He had never said it so plainly to anyone, let alone to his terribly wounded granddaughter, but she answered blithely. "Nope, it's none of those things. It's because you think you'll die next and you want to know if there are worse things in life than death, so you won't be afraid of it."

"Do *you* think there are worse things in life than death?" he asked. "Because if you do, I hope you'll tell me."

"Oh, Grandpa, you're no better than Mom. Of course I think there are worse things in life than death…like having to go through it being Roselyn Wilkerson, but I'm not about to…Ugh. Grandpa!"

After that she was quiet for so long that Cornelius nearly crept away from the door, thinking she was asleep on its other side. But he chanced asking in the smallest of voices, so that if she was asleep he wouldn't wake her, "Come on, Phoebe, tell me what your new goal is?" and this time he got an answer.

"To keep my kitten, if there is a kitten, and be a good mother to her. Not to, like, abandon her in some park."

22.

Millicent

Having to be 'up' on such short notice didn't bother Millicent at first. She had always considered herself - to use the American vernacular - 'rough and ready.' But when Pórdís called on Saturday, saying that she thought it would be best if Millicent took Monday and Wednesday of the next week, too, leaving Friday for Cornelius and thus placing her and her tawdry affairs in between Cornelius's bewitching ghost story…well, that was too much! And on Sunday morning, when Millicent called Ruthie to complain about the sandwiching, Ruthie said she was just about to launch her boat, with Pórdís, of all people, coming to go fishing with her.

"What? Isn't that a no-no in the therapist rulebook?" Millicent asked.

"Not as far as I know. It's just fishing, Mills, and if we have any luck we'll eat our catch for lunch." She paused before asking, "Do you want to come with us?"

"No!" said Millicent, "It's raining and cold, in case you haven't noticed, and I don't see how you'll be able to just fish. You'll end up talking about our sessions."

She meant, of course, that they'd end up talking about her.

"That goes to show how little you know about fishing," Ruthie said. "It sets you free, not only from the worries you went to bed with the night before, but from all the psychobabble of things like therapy sessions."

"Well, if you tell Pórdís that you think it's psychobabble, I bet it'll be a short trip."

When she got off the phone Millicent thought about calling Cornelius to see if he wanted to come to lunch, maybe do a little fishing at her house, but then she laughed and thought about calling Jane. It was a sorry state of affairs that the only people she could think to call were her fellow grief group members, but aside from Milly over in London, there really wasn't anyone else. Most of her old friends had been Jonathan's, and she didn't really like them all that well. Nor they her, if the truth be told. Maybe if she and Jonathan had had a son he would have stayed near his mom, showing some filial piety, but she was fresh out of luck on that front with Milly. And what was she thinking? She couldn't call Jane. Both physically and temperamentally, Jane was as disheveled and airheaded as Geraldine Page in *The Trip to Bountiful*, complete with Geraldine Page's warmth and likability, she supposed. And if she wanted to lunch with an airhead she could go talk to some stranger in a restaurant. The only people left were LaVeronica and Frank; one a woman who drew her interest, but could she call her out of the blue like this? She was a quarter century younger than Millicent, not to mention a murderess or a 'manslaughteress,' or whatever the term was. *And* she skipped as many therapy meetings as she came to, so she might not even know Millicent's name.

She picked up her phone again, dialed Frank's number, then hung up before it rang. If he called back she would say she had pocket-dialed him. She wouldn't say "butt-called," since Frank would hear that as some kind of entrée. She couldn't help thinking, though, that Frank had not been quite as big a fool during her Friday session, that some of the things he said seemed meant to be helpful. She couldn't remember what those things were, but the feeling remained, so maybe she was being too hard on Frank. But she wouldn't call him again, that really would be grasping at straws. Even if this particular straw showed an eagerness to grasp back.

Ah, loneliness, how difficult it was, and what nonsense she kept spewing at Pórdís's house about how it and solitude were two sides of the same dumb coin! She made that argument with Milly, when battling Milly's insistence that the best thing for her to do would be to move back home. Best thing for who? Milly? So she and Phillip could avoid the trans-Atlantic travel? It was an easy argument to win, too, since solitude's place in the pantheon of treatises on coping was solid. She argued it so well, in fact, that she tried to live it after Jonathan's death, planning her days around solitary activities, weather permitting, that she had enjoyed before. Sometimes gardening, sometimes yoga or rereading the books she had loved… She went to back Middlemarch with George Eliot; to the lighthouse with Virginia Woolf; into mannered England with the Brontës and Jane Austen. She even took Dickens and Trollope for a spin, with their long-winded but oh-so-captivating tales of right and wrong. All of these authors were from her homeland…she couldn't read Americans or Irish writers anymore, with the built-in difficulties of Faulkner or Joyce. Nor could she read those who so stripped down their prose, like Beckett. But anyway, after only a few weeks she stopped all that, until all she had were her walks and that bane of older people all over the world - television. Other than the North End grievers, of course. Millicent put on a raincoat, went out her front door, and turned toward a nearby high school and the fancy houses beyond it. She took three regular walks of varying distances - from two to four miles - any of which she could either cut short or extend, depending on how she felt. She had taken these walks with Jonathan and Fathead nearly every day for the entirety of Fathead's life. And before Fathead, she took them just with Jonathan, who somehow wasn't a conspiracy theorist during their walks. When he put one foot in front of the other and kept his mouth shut, that was when she loved him most. But she couldn't keep him walking twenty-four hours a day, even though she once bought him a treadmill for his birthday with that goal in mind.

Millicent knew that two or her fellow grievers - Cornelius and Jane - lived in houses that she had passed on her walks. Lately, she had avoided those houses, but today she let her feet go where they might and tried to empty her mind, to neither hope nor not hope that Cornelius or Jane would see her from a window as she sped by. If she kept her pace up and her eyes down, after all, what difference did it make who saw her?

At Yakima Avenue and Carr Street, if she turned right she'd be faced with a long downward slope to Old Town, and, as it happened, right past Jane's place. The problem was, if she walked all the way down to Old Town she would have to walk back up. If she turned left, she could go up to I or J or K streets and find her way home from there.

She turned right and when she got to Jane's house saw something that made her double her pace. Giancarlo was pulling up weeds in the front yard, and singing an Italian aria.

23.

Fishing

"Can you tell me the name of a single fish that's anywhere near as pretty as 'rainbow trout?'" asked Ruthie.

"It is a perfect name. When I was a kid I used to look for the rainbow colors on their sides when they were flopping around on the floor of our boat," Pórdís said.

"Roy G. Biv. Mr. Somebody-or-other gave us that mnemonic in junior high school art and I never forgot it. And a rainbow trout's got them all, even indigo and violet."

"It's interesting that you remember the mnemonic but not the name of your art teacher," said Pórdís. "I wonder if that would make him sad or happy?"

They had finished hauling Ruthie's boat from her garage to the slip in front of her house - only a thirty second drive, as promised. Ruthie was far more expert at backing the truck up and lowering the boat off its trailer, than she was at driving the Porsche. Pórdís's job was to take the boat's painter and walk out onto the slip with it, turning the boat lakeward. She waited, after she did that, with rain slicing into her slicker, for Ruthie to come back from parking the truck. And now they were inside the boat's small cabin with the heater on, and motoring out to where the fish were. There were no other boats on American Lake.

"There's really no fishing season?" asked Pórdís. "If so, it's a first for me."

"That's what Ben told me, and I'm taking it to the bank. If we get stopped by a game warden I'll blame it on the deceased."

The boat had four rods, stuck in four rod holders bolted to the gunwale, two starboard and two port. Pórdís's parents' boat in Reykjavik had been twice the size of Ruthie's, but that hadn't kept them safe. Of course, they had been on the Atlantic Ocean, not American Lake.

"I've got a favorite spot. Once we get there we'll drop our lines and see what we come up with," said Ruthie. "We can either sit in here where it's warm and use rod holders, or go out and 'fish like men,' to quote the late great Ben. And once we catch our limit we'll go back and clean and cook them."

"What's the limit?" Pórdís asked.

"Five fish in whatever combination, but my personal limit is three. Otherwise I don't eat them fast enough to come out fishing again the next week. Today we'll shoot for five, though, so you can take some home."

They sat on swivel stools bolted to the deck. The windshield was glass but otherwise the cabin had a canvas top and plastic side windows, harder to see through than the glass. They could remove the sides by unsnapping the canvas, but that would open them up to the rain.

In Iceland, Pórdís's parents had had a favorite spot on Lake Thingvallavatn that took an hour to get to, so she was surprised when Ruthie slowed to a troll, then cut the engine entirely, letting them bob in the relative quiet of the chop.

"We're here already?" she asked.

"We are. I was just thinking that maybe we won't troll at all, since this chop is likely to make our spinners spin…then we can talk without the noise."

"Sounds like a plan," said Þórdís, though talking was something she wanted to avoid. This was her first foray into a social activity with one of her clients, and she didn't want to regret it later on.

"So what's it going to be?" asked Ruthie. "Inside or out?"

"Out," Þórdís said. "I accepted your invitation, not only on the chance of catching a fish, but so I could get the feeling I got when fishing back in Iceland."

It was a bit more of a confession than she intended.

"You mean so you could get shivering cold and wet?"

"That's exactly what I mean," said Þórdís.

Though there were four rods, Ruthie said that they would use only two, otherwise it wouldn't be fair. That was another thing she learned from Ben, not to be greedy, though Ben treated himself to all the toys he could think of during his life, especially toward the end of it.

Þórdís tried not to count how many times Ben's name came up.

It wasn't a small lake but even from the center of it and through all this rain, Þórdís could see dozens of lakeside houses, many with slips like Ruthie's, some with docks, and she couldn't help wishing for their absence; that nature's grim roughness might extend to everything she saw.

The spinner at the end of Þórdís's line was two inches long, shaped like a teardrop, and gold with red and white diagonal stripes. At the bottom of the spinner were three soldered and barbless hooks, their points equidistant, like, she couldn't help thinking, the points of a tiny chandelier. She couldn't help thinking it because such a chandelier was in a dollhouse her mother once gave her, a chandelier that, after coming home from Lake Thingvallavatn, she saw as waiting in the dollhouse for a trout to come smashing through its floor and take in its mouth.

Þórdís stood on the starboard side, Ruthie on the port.

"Let out thirty feet of line. If it flows sternward at forty-five degrees, we're set," Ruthie said.

Þórdís could see her fishing line move to forty-five degrees even before Ruthie finished talking. Now was the time for feeling the action of the rod, for focusing on whatever might be going on below the surface of the lake, the spinner drawing down the last bits of sunlight. Now was the time for quiet, not for more talk.

"So tell me about growing up in Iceland. I read that Iceland's green and Greenland's not, but that's all I ever learned about it," Ruthie said.

She stuck the butt of her rod into a rod holder and stepped back under the canvas cover. It wasn't exactly a violation of the fishing etiquette Þórdís thought they'd agreed to, but it felt like it. If a fish was about to come upon Ruthie's spinner, and thus, quite likely, upon the end of its life, it seemed that paying attention was the least to be expected of predator and prey alike.

"It's like growing up anywhere," she said. "Friends, schools, sports…"

She sensed her lure spinning along merrily, oblivious to the cold and dark, when, to her amazement, Ruthie bolted out from under the canvas, grabbed her rod, and ordered Þórdís to reach down under the boat's stern seat for a net.

Ruthie's rod took on the shape of a serious frown. A fish was heading toward the lake's bottom with her lure in its mouth. No sooner did Þórdís see the rod bend, however, than the fish turned and broke the surface of the lake about fifteen feet behind the boat.

"The net!" Ruthie ordered. "Let's haul it in! 'No more Mr. Nice Guy,' as Ben used to say."

She reeled her line in with no sense of wanting to play the fish, brought it near the boat's port gunwale and Pórdís netted it. It flopped around between them, half in and half out of the net but, no doubt about it, Roy G. Biv in the flesh.

By the end of the morning they'd caught six trout, plus two bass that they released.

Pórdís caught one and Ruthie caught five.

24.

Light Blue Keds

What Phoebe didn't say, regarding their visit to Kenji Okada's workshop - and swore Dwayne to secrecy about - was that she had begged Mr. Okada to let her borrow the sketchbook full of drawings of her grandmother. She spent the time before their parents rushed up the stairs to drag them off to their separate homes, listing the reasons she had a right to the sketchbook, even if Mr. Okada's intention was to make something only for himself. She cajoled, begged, even spoke around the edges of a threat. In the end, Mr. Okada refused to lend it to her, but he did say that she could come "spend time with it" whenever she wished.

And now, on Monday after school, when she was supposed to be in the band teacher's office, fighting for the right to play "Midnight Train to Georgia" in the holiday concert, she sat in that alcove again, staring at the sketchbook. When she came up his stairs he looked at her soberly, not showing any surprise. He motioned her over to the alcove and went to pull the sketchbook from its cubby. She didn't think he would speak until he said, "If you have any questions save them till you're ready to leave. I don't want my work interrupted over this thing."

"This thing," was what he called it.

"Yessir, I mean, no sir," Phoebe said.

The work he did not want interrupted was a painting located about as far from the alcove as it could get, and further blocked from Phoebe's view by a Japanese screen. And as an extra precaution, he had turned his easel so that the painting faced the wall and not the center of his studio. If asked, he might have said that he'd been engaged with the painting for six months, but a closer truth would be that he worked on it for one month and then put it away for five, only bringing it out again after Phoebe's last visit. When he began the painting Yuki sat for him, so it was before the cancer hollowed her cheeks and began the elongation of her previously perfect face. In any case, what he had clipped to his easel now was the final page of his sketchpad, removed before he gave the sketchpad to this inquisitive girl.

"Mr. Okada?" the inquisitive girl said now.

How had she come across his studio without him noticing?

"Are you leaving already?" he asked.

"It isn't exactly 'already,' I've been here for an hour," she said.

Surely not. He'd barely begun to settle back to work.

"Leave the sketchpad. And next time call before you come," he said.

"Okay, but I have questions."

She turned back toward the alcove, making it necessary for him to follow her.

"Look at this one. You've got Grandma wearing light blue Keds in it, and they belong to me. They're the ones I keep at Grandpa's house in case I needed a change of clothes."

"They don't belong to you, your grandma wore them all the time."

"Because I let her, and she was only supposed to wear them around the house. So here's my question… Did you go there to sketch her, or did she sneak over here wearing my Keds?"

It was a question worthy of Sherlock Holmes. He didn't want to lie to her, so he pretended a new interest in the sketch, which showed Yuki standing in territory not of this world but of a past or a future one. He liked to think of it as the world she had flown to after her death. In any case, it held the sense that she had just arrived there, so any recognition, any definition of the world had not yet caught up to her. And the drawing was in charcoal, except for those Keds, which he had nearly put wings on before he thought better of it. That they were pristine was a reflection of the fact that they were that way when she pulled them from her backpack, kicked off her zori and put them on.

"She brought them here," he said.

"Brought them? What do you do mean 'brought them'? She didn't wear them?"

"She brought them in her backpack, with whatever other clothing she thought she might need for our sessions."

"Grandma had a backpack? I didn't know that."

"Perhaps she kept it out of sight at home."

"I'll ask Grandpa. If it's still around maybe I can have it. I don't have anything that's just for me to remember her by. Except for about a million origamis."

Mr. Okada went to a chest with many narrow but long drawers. He pulled one out and removed what at first seemed to Phoebe to be yet another origami. It was only when he brought it over and laid it atop the drawing that she saw it was a woman carved out of something like soap, standing in sweatpants and a sweatshirt and wearing, yes, a pair of light blue Keds. It was stunning. Here was her grandmother looking like she often did at home. Phoebe bent down to look at it closely.

"Can I have this?" she asked, without looking back at Mr. Okada.

"You may. It is why I brought it out," he said. "Think of it as your homunculus."

She didn't know the word, so she tried to commit it to memory. Hummus. It sounded like hummus. She asked if he had a box she could put it in, and then said what she thought at first, that it was made out of soap.

"A soap that never loses its size," he said. "We call it soapstone."

When he brought her a sturdy mailing envelope she slid her grandmother down into it carefully, then hurried out of the studio before he changed his mind. A soap that never loses its size, because it is soapstone.

After she left, Mr. Okada returned to his painting, though he knew before he got there that any attempt to concentrate would fail.

Quite suddenly a question occurred to him: What if he told the girl a more complete truth about her grandmother? What if he told her that, as a young art apprentice in Kyoto, he had taken a part-time job - *arubaito*, they called it there - in a downtown store selling casual shoes, most of them imports and some of them Keds? What if he told her that, on his first day of work, the stockinged foot of an apparition appeared on his fitting stool, an apparition otherwise wearing a sweatshirt and sweatpants? And what if he had told her that, many years later he saw the apparition again, way across the world in Tacoma, Washington, either wearing the shoes he had sold her or another identical pair?

25.

Millicent

Though until about six-thirty that evening Cornelius and La-Veronica both considered skipping their grief group again, at seven they both showed up. Pórdís was relieved to see them sitting there with Ruthie and Frank and Jane. She regretted having fished with Ruthie now, though she had two rainbow trout in her fridge and a third that she ate for dinner last night to honor the occasion.

"Well then, Millicent, when you're ready," she said. "You told me you preferred not to read again. Does that still hold?"

Millicent had brought cannoli, and was just then opening their box.

"Have some," she said. "And yes, it does still hold."

She looked from the cannoli to Jane, who once said Giancarlo made cannoli that was 'to die for,' then apologized because he was dead. But was he? And had Jane seen her trucking by her house yesterday morning, to hear the unmistakable aria?

"Okay, let me ask you, Mills," said Frank. "When you visit Jonathan at the cemetery do you take somethin' like these cannolis along, so you can sit and eat and talk to him? Or are your visits as short as you can make 'em? I'm asking because when I visit Doris I take tuna fish sandwiches, and stay until the cows come home."

When Millicent visited Jonathan she practically set the

timer on her phone.

"I don't take food and I don't stay long," she said. "I think because he's more alive for me at our house, or when I'm out for my walks."

She chanced another look at Jane. She said that Giancarlo made cannoli, but had she also said that he sang opera?

"At home or on your walks, then...when you think of Jonathan what would you say your mood is?" asked Þórdís. "Are you pleased with the memories or..."

"Or do I grumble? At home I do, but I'm happy to think about him on my walks. Sometimes it's even as if we're holding hands, like at the beginning of our marriage. Strange, huh?"

"Nothin' strange about it. It's because on them walks you ain't surrounded by all the household junk you think you oughta get rid of," said Frank. "What's the fancy word for them sorts of things, Þórdís?"

"Household junk works," Þórdís said.

She didn't know what had gotten into Frank lately, but she liked it. She made a note to tell him so during their next private session.

For her part, Millicent felt even more duplicitous than usual, not because she was lying about her walks with Jonathan, but because she only mentioned them to see if she could get a rise out of Jane. Maybe the aria singer had been her gardener...that was possible, wasn't it?

"The household junk doesn't bother me, Frank. It's not about getting rid of Jonathan's things. It's that, when I'm at home, I get angry with him for dying almost as soon as he got his crazy diagnosis. If that makes any sense at all."

"Of course it does. You wanted him to fight harder," Cornelius said. "I was that way with Yuki, too."

Millicent stuffed a half a cannoli into her mouth. She didn't even like the damned things after eating six of them at Milly's wedding, but she had to block her next impulse. Cornelius took a cannoli, too, and so did Jane, but Ruthie only looked at her peakedly, waiting for Millicent to spit it out… not the cannoli, but the truth.

So Millicent said, "No, Cornelius, it's not like that. I am angry with him for robbing me of weeks, or even months, of tending to him well. I am angry with him for robbing me of the chance, at the end of his life, to show my mettle. That is the awful truth, I'm afraid."

While tears ran down Millicent's face, LaVeronica broke a cannoli in half and took the smaller portion. That made Pórdís pick up the other half and toast Millicent with it, in a "Now we're getting somewhere," sort of way. Ruthie, though, probably because she was Millicent's pre-widowhood friend, had more to say.

"Maybe there's a deeper way of looking at it. Not to take away from your confession, Mills, but when Jonathan gave up fighting, I don't think it was your inability to show him your mettle that bothered you, so much as that you really did love him more than you ever loved anyone else, even after years of troubled marriage, and you wanted him to take that knowledge with him. Am I not right about that?"

Millicent's tears, slow before Ruthie's gift to her, flowed like rain.

"I think you are, Ruthie," said Frank. "At that late stage, with Jonathan suffering the ravages of his disease…*finally* Mills weren't pretending. But she was pretendin' with them loads of other guys, and she wanted him to know that they was the fallacy, not the marriage."

More talk came after that, with others trying to say helpful things because...well, because they were fellow members of the North End grievers' group. But though Millicent sometimes parried, sometimes acquiesced, and seemed to be fully engaged, when she got home she would remember only Frank's bon mot, taking it to heart - her marriage wasn't the fallacy, the fallacy was the other guys.

When it was time for them to leave there was only one cannoli left.

Pórdís hoped to eat it later, after she finished her second trout.

26.

Jane

Actually, Jane had seen Millicent on Sunday morning, though only out of the corner of her eye. Still, it troubled her twice; first because she thought that Millicent was probably savvy to her falsity *beforehand,* and had come snooping around to verify it; and second, because if Millicent really was simply out for a walk, then Sam had been far too lax. Singing in their yard! What had he been thinking?

So she kept an eye on Millicent during their Monday session and made sure to leave quickly, not giving her a chance to catch her outside. But would she be forced to quit the grievers if the truth came out?

When Jane got home the lights were on in her living room, where Sam sat reading a book. He was getting thin but shied away from going to the doctor on the ridiculous theory that what he didn't know wouldn't hurt him. Sam was eighty-three, but had a full head of hair. He was 6' 4", too, and he didn't have an old man's stoop.

"How was your session, hon?" he asked.

"Chock full of undercurrents, and it was all your fault," said Jane. "Anyway, what are you reading?"

"Another one of these Lincoln things. Did you know that Lincoln lost the love of his life long before he became famous. She was barely twenty-two, a girl named Ann Rutledge. It says here that her death caused his lifelong depression."

"Come on, Sam, are you comparing me to Abraham Lincoln now?" Jane asked.

"No, since we can't really say that yours is lifelong. But did you satisfy your Sunday worries? Did your fellow griever tell you she saw me cavorting in our yard?"

"Worries not satisfied. I'm sure she saw you, but I think I let her know that I wasn't about to discuss it. She was 'up' tonight, in fact. Talk about your messed-up ladies. It's like her late husband is swinging a wrecking ball all over her insides. She wasn't happy with him when he was alive, yet tonight she complained that he died before she got a chance to show how much she loved him. It made all of us cry. And you weren't cavorting, Sam, you were singing Nessun Dorma at the top of your lungs."

"Yes, I know. I stand accused, and I'm sorry," Sam said.

"You don't stand accused, you stand convicted. But I can hardly blame you now, can I? I think I'm in over my head with this group. Giancarlo must be rolling in his grave. The good news is, I've just about decided to out myself during our next meeting, though I haven't got much hope that they will understand."

"How about if I go with you?" asked Sam. "I can tell them that thing about Lincoln and Ann Rutledge. That might not help them understand you, but maybe it will help them digest it."

You are too good to me, Sam."

"I know I am. I also know that when I'm gone you'll grieve for me with gusto. You and the others, save Frank, don't know what you've got till it's gone, like in that Joni Mitchell song. You said that Frank is the only real griever amongst you. He so missed his wife that he jumped off a bridge!"

"Would you do something like that, Sam, if I surprised you by dying first?"

"Nope, I'd poke along like Lincoln after Ann."

Sam got up, put his book down on his chair, and then walked into their kitchen. Their German shepherd, Rex, looked up from his blanket near the back door. "Come on, Rex," Sam said. "You have some peeing to do and I've got to stretch my legs."

Jane recognized a frustration with her that Sam would never verbalize in any other way. But stretching his legs provided him the solace that long walks provided Millicent. When he came back from doing it, anyway, he usually seemed as relieved as Rex did after emptying his bladder on a tree. It was why not once, in the many years that they had had Rex, had she offered to go with them.

At Sam's command Rex got up and did a thing he hadn't done in months. He went across the room to take his leash in his mouth and turn to look expectantly at Sam.

27.

Dwayne

LaVeronica left the meeting just about as quickly as Jane did. She thought it was, if not exactly a silly meeting, at least one that conformed to something like 1950s America, with all these white people conjuring problems. Or, if that wasn't fair, dealing with problems that were trivial compared to her own. Or, *if that* wasn't fair, then dealing with things that they ought to be able to deal with on their own. The lady who was up tonight was a good example of it. She had an English accent, making it seem as though she could have come out of a Netflix drama.

LaVeronica laughed, partly at Millicent, but mostly to make herself less uptight about what she had to deal with inside her house, now that she was pulling into the garage. She killed her engine, got out of her car and went to stand beneath that apple tree, whose branches, she saw now, formed an easy ladder for any horny girl to climb and bother her son. She would never tell him this, but when she was only a year older than he was now, she lowered an actual rope from her window so Johnny Sylvester could climb up the outside wall of her parents' house. She very well remembered that she would have killed *for* Johnny back then, as opposed to actually killing him. But that didn't make her sympathetic to Phoebe or Dwayne. She didn't want them fucking up *their* lives.

LaVeronica patted the apple tree. The axe she brought out still leaned against it, so she carried it up to her porch before going inside.

"Dwayne! Where are you, baby, come kiss your mama who just got home!"

"You don't have to shout, Mom, I'm in the living room," said Dwayne. "I've been writing raps and reading a Mark Twain story for English."

LaVeronica hung her coat up, got herself a glass of milk and a piece of apple pie, and went in to join him. "You had your pie already?" she asked.

When he said he hadn't she gave him her piece and went to get another one.

"If you tell me you're reading Tom Sawyer or Huckleberry Finn I'm gonna give that English teacher a piece of my mind," she said when she got back.

Dwayne was tucked in neatly on the couch, making her worry that Phoebe might have done the tucking, before running out the front door while she came in the back. "Okay then, what *are* you reading?" she asked.

"*The Celebrated Jumping Frog of Calaveras County.* It's full of stupid ways of saying things, but the moral of the story is okay."

He turned his book around so she could see the story. The book itself, *"19th and Early 20th Century American Literature,"* had a table of contents that surprised her, with "Excerpt from Native Son," by Richard Wright, and "The Negro Speaks of Rivers," by Langston Hughes. She'd been introduced to these writers by Johnny Sylvester. He used to like to quote Langston Hughes after having sex with her.

"What's the story about and what's the moral that you think's okay?" she asked.

Earlier, she'd been 'hands-on' when dealing with Dwayne's homework, but lately she had let it slide.

"It's about this guy, Jim Smiley, who spends three months trying to teach a frog to jump, dumb as that is. He names the frog Dan'l Webster...spelled like this..." He turned the book back around and pointed out the *'Dan'l.'* "I hate that!"

"How come you thought Jim Smiley trying to teach a frog to jump was dumb?"

"Because frogs can already jump, of course. But he worked so hard at it, for three months, and that won me over. Do you remember when I tried to teach Billie how to fetch?"

She said she did remember it. She had given Dwayne Billie for his birthday when he was eight years old.

"Well, I only tried for about an hour and then I gave up. But Jim Smiley would have stuck with trying to teach Dan'l Webster to jump for years if that's how long it took."

"So you liked Jim Smiley's tenacity?"

"Yeah, but what did it get him? Along comes another guy who pours shot down Dan'l Webster's throat so that he can't jump at all."

He paused then asked, "What is shot, Mom? Is it those BB things like in a shotgun?"

"That's exactly what it is. Basically it's lead."

"Then if Jim Smiley had just picked up Dan'l Webster before he bet the guy, he'd have felt that he was way heavier than usual, right? It was only because he didn't pick him up that the guy got away with his forty dollars."

"Maybe the moral of the story is 'check things out before you start.'"

"No, the moral of the story is 'don't get addicted to gambling because people will cheat you if they get the chance.'"

"Not because you shouldn't get addicted to anything? Only gambling?"

"Actually, I'm wrong and you are, too. The moral of the story is that a person's got to believe in something, even if it's a stupid frog. That's why I ended up liking it. Jim Smiley believed that he could make a great jumper out of his frog, but no one believes in anything these days, except for me and Phoebe. I was glad the shot didn't kill Dan'l Webster, though, that when Jim Smiley finally turned him over and shook him, all of it came falling back out of his mouth."

"Yeah," LaVeronica said. "If you pour that much shot into a frog, he's likely to die of lead poisoning. But you can't do that with a pregnancy, Dwayne. You can't turn a girl over and shake her, you get that, right?"

"Geez, Mom, our English teacher would tell you that that was a lousy analogy."

"And I would tell her right back that I don't pussyfoot around when it comes to the welfare of my child… And that means you, Dwayne."

Dwayne closed his English book and put it behind him.

"I still have algebra to do, too," he said.

"Which you can deal with in a minute, but we've got to get down to it sooner or later, son, *without* Phoebe present. And I don't see a better time than now."

She took a bite of her pie. She didn't expect that she would need fortification, but the pie calmed her, especially when Dwayne launched a preemptive strike.

"We won't stop doing it, Mom. We can't and we know we can't because we tried. We think my body belonged to Phoebe and hers belonged to me in another lifetime, so when we fit them back together in this one, it's like we're home again."

LaVeronica bit down on her fork. "So that's what you two think," she said.

"It is! Phoebe says that Roselyn Wilkerson and her crew can put that in their pipes and smoke it. Ha! Phoebe's got a way with words, Mom."

"She's either got a way with words or she spends too much time with her grandpa. But do I have to remind you of the reason Roselyn might be acting out? Wasn't it about a minute before you fell in love with Phoebe that you told me that Roselyn was the love of your life?"

"I made a mistake. Everyone makes mistakes. Do *I* have to remind you of that?"

"I am pretty much reminded of it every day of my life, but let me ask, did you and Roselyn ever 'fit your bodies together' like you and Phoebe do now? You didn't, right?"

Dwayne looked at the floor, but admitted that all they ever did was wrestle around. "Roselyn Wilkinson's what you'd call a big fat tease, Mom," he said.

LaVeronica put her pie plate down in order to reach over and grasp the front of Dwayne's shirt, pulling him closer to her until he stared into her eyes. "Who's in there? Is it my son or am I looking at a kid who just called a girl he's known since kindergarten a horrible thing? I'm beginning to think I might have wandered into the wrong house!"

Dwayne's pie nearly slid off his lap. "I didn't call her anything," he said.

"Yes you did, but listen to me! I went to jail because a man I used to think was the other half of me wouldn't stop believing that he owned me. Yet there was a time when I would have died for him, just like Phoebe thinks she would die for you now. So I won't sit here listening to the one person in the world I really would die for, use a word like 'tease' for a girl who wouldn't have sex with him. You got that?"

"Yes ma'am," said Dwayne.

He waited until she let go of his shirt before adding, "You might not say that, though, if you knew what else Roselyn said about Phoebe online. I understand that she didn't have to have sex with me, but why does she have to be so horrible now?"

"What are you talking about? What else did she say about Phoebe online?"

"That she had sex with half the members of the band, and that she has a special place with a dirty mattress down in the thick of Garfield Park."

"Oh man, does nothing ever change? That little piece of shit!"

"See…I told you you'd change your mind once you heard the whole story."

"No way. There'll be no mind changing as far as you and Phoebe are concerned. But I'll stand up for her, too, when the witches come out. I hope you understand that."

When Dwayne told her he did, she said, "Okay, mister, now go finish your homework."

28

Cornelius Visits Mr. Okada

Cornelius felt it was long past time he - well, the expression "had it out with" didn't fit - but at least had a talk with Kenji Okada. So midmorning on Tuesday, December 17, he got in his car, drove to the man's studio, and walked in the same wrong door that Phoebe and Dwayne had, to see the same strange mailboxes with the same names upon them. Phoebe and Dwayne thought they were authentic mailboxes at first, but one of the advantages of age and education was that Cornelius recognized some of the names as historic or fictional. "Yoko Sugiyama," for example, was the wife of the Japanese novelist, Yukio Mishima, no doubt given a mailbox to honor her forbearance. He also recognized "Deacon Brodie," but for the moment couldn't access how or why. He saw the other mailboxes on the stairway but didn't study the names, and thus get sidetracked from his mission.

At the top of the stairs he knocked, waited, then opened the door and stepped inside the studio to a decades-old recording by João Gilberto. Mr. Okada stood across the room with his back to Cornelius, working on a painting and swaying to the Brazilian tune. Cornelius felt Yuki's presence, felt that she had stood in this exact spot, to look across a vast expanse of time and space from the life she led with him to the one she abandoned when she was, perhaps she thought, hardly finished with childhood. He waited until João Gilberto started into *Quiet Nights of Quiet Stars,* then he cleared his throat.

"Mr. Okada, it's Cornelius MacLeish, come to get to the bottom of things," he said.

Quiet Nights of Quiet Stars seemed inappropriate for the drama that might unfold. Kenji Okada may have thought so, too, for he silenced the tune before he said, "I thought you might be looking for your granddaughter."

"If that were the case I would feel even more aggrieved than I do now."

"Your wife, then," he said. "What do you want to know?"

He put down his paintbrush, took a step toward Cornelius, then thought better of it and gestured with a paint-splotched hand toward his alcove. "There is tea in there and the sketchbook that your granddaughter came to look at," he said. "Let me go wash up."

In the alcove Cornelius poured himself some tea, but found it tepid. He pushed the teacup away and pulled the sketchbook toward him. Did Mr. Okada keep it in this alcove, or had Phoebe recently been back to look at it again?

One of Yuki's breasts was bare in the first sketch he saw, and the sketch itself was bifurcated. Attached to that breast was the mouth of an infant whose body flowed toward the edge of the sketchpad, then disappeared in a puff of charcoal smoke, making Cornelius feel the power and the sadness of departure. He imagined the infant to be Emi, who was gone from both of them now *as if* in a puff of smoke. That side of the drawing so moved him that he might have fallen to his knees were he not already sitting on a *zabuton.* As it was he put a hand down to steady himself before looking at the drawing's other side, where Yuki's other breast slept beneath

an old woman's robe. A frail arm was exposed with an intra-
venous needle taped against it at the elbow. Loose skin hung
from her triceps, and an aged hand with long fingers held the
very pencil from which the lines of the entire drawing came,
making it seem that Yuki had been able to conjure both her
extreme youth and her old age. Though the drawing moved
him, at the same time he thought it unoriginal; something
derivative of Escher.

Kenji Okada came into the alcove to say of the drawing, "It is good that you found that one, for it tells the story
of your wife and me better than I could using words. What
I tried to show in all my sketches was what I believed her
mood to be. At the time I felt a small success, but now I feel
only failure."

When he pointed at the aged part of the sketch, at the
elongated, deeply cancerous face of the woman they'd both
loved, a bird that had been perched within Cornelius's chest
opened its talons and lifted off of him.

"Mr. Okada..." he said, but Mr. Okada stopped him.

"I am glad you saw it, so you may know that you are not
alone."

Not alone? Did that mean this man wanted parity with
him?

When he left the studio another half hour had passed. But
though more words were spoken, he knew only these two
things: that the man believed that they were equal, and Yuki's
ghost would never come again.

29

A Piping Hot Bath

On Wednesday morning, after reading an email from Milly, apologizing for her "bitchy" visit and wishing her mother a Merry Christmas, *and* after realizing that she had let Christmas sneak up on her without a single preparation, Millicent drew herself a piping hot bath, put on one of her old Joan Baez records, then climbed into the tub slowly, so the nearly scalding water wouldn't sting too much. A rubber duck sat in her soap dish - Milly's from a bygone era. The soap itself was on a sponge.

"If the sun never shines in the pines Joan's singing about, don't ask me why she likes it there," Millicent told the duck. "I used to love this song, but now I think it's about suicide. Tell me, rubber ducky, have you given any thought to that?"

The duck looked befuddled, so she brought it down into the water with her, where it bobbed around and nodded, as if saying "yes, these days I have thought of little else."

Millicent was "up" again that night at grief group - it was to be their final meeting before a long holiday break. But she didn't want to be up. In fact, she would *not* be up. She would insist that Cornelius do it.

"That's fair, innit?" she asked the duck. "I mean, I am only up because he bailed."

Millicent still had Jonathan's old record player, plus several hundred of her own, pre-Jonathan, records. She often played "Take Five" or "Kind of Blue," as well as, back to folk music, Odetta, Jesse Fuller, and even the Malvina Reynolds album that she bought on the night that she met Jonathan. The records were in great condition, not only in their original jackets but with those inner cellophane linings still on them. It *proved* she'd had pre-Jonathan values and that they'd stayed steadfastly with her.

She looked at the duck but she didn't ask it any more questions. Rather, she took her soap off the sponge and scrubbed herself from head to toe. She washed her hair *with the soap,* though she would never admit it to anyone. When she felt she was clean she let the water out of the tub, rinsed the soapy residue out, then refilled it, all while sitting in it naked. Her house needed a lot of repairs, but at least it had a good water heater. And a very good view of the bay.

After the new bathwater cooled a bit she submerged all of her but her hair, which spread out like the hair of a corpse in a movie. She had seen movies where something like that happened, not only in bathtubs but in swimming pools and lakes…. She noticed whenever she saw such a movie how unconcerned the hair seemed to be with the death of the poor, fallible, maybe even murdered woman.

Millicent laughed underwater, causing bubbles to come up. Then she came up herself to take a breath. She stayed in the tub, adding hot water until her skin grew more wrinkled than, through horrible aging, it already was. Earlier, she'd placed Jonathan's straight razor on the edge of the tub. He had liked to sharpen the razor on a leather strop that hung on a hook behind the bathroom door. She liked the word 'strop,' which she thought of as onomatopoeic, though she would not have chosen it to signify the sound the razor actually made. Maybe 'swop' or 'sup.'

Millicent held the razor in her right hand and laid its edge against the skin of her left wrist. She had heard that vertical cuts were better than horizontal ones, though that made little sense, for wouldn't a horizontal cut slice through more arteries and veins? She nicked the skin on her left wrist four times, equidistantly. The nicks made the shape of the four of diamonds in a deck of cards. And soon they were the color of those diamonds, also.

She got out of the tub, dried herself, put four pieces of tissue on the spots that bled, dressed and went downstairs to call Þórdís.

When Þórdís didn't pick up she told her voicemail that she wouldn't be up that night. She called Cornelius, too, leaving the same message.

30.

LaVeronica

LaVeronica's new plan was to quit the North End grievers' group that night. They were taking a month off anyway, so the timing was good. She would thank Þórdís - thank everyone if she announced her departure during the meeting - saying that life as a single mother was taking more of her time than she realized. Dwayne had a holiday concert that night, too, but she supposed she could miss it since his *"Midnight Train to Georgia"* solo was cancelled. Dwayne would tell her not to worry, that he was only one dumb musician in a band of seventy. And she didn't want to quit the grievers via text or email, that would make her seem more disengaged than she was. It would make her seem *rude;* something she could not abide. On the other hand, Cornelius would likely miss the meeting for the concert, for he would never bail on Phoebe.

She told Dwayne that morning that she would pick him up as soon as school got out, so they could go Christmas shopping. He had to get something for Phoebe, and for her as well…likely another bottle of bad perfume. She had already bought him a dozen gifts, so would use the time to get a farewell treat for the grievers, like whatshername did with cannolis. Hell, she could she never remember the cannoli woman's name. Not Jane…Not Ruthie.

LaVeronica got into her car but then sat there, without

even opening her garage door. This was not the same car she used when traipsing around town with Johnny Sylvester next to her, dead but with his seatbelt safely fastened. She had kept that car during her trial and incarceration, but the day after her release she took it out to South Tacoma Way and traded it in for the Subaru. And now, all these years later, she had driven the Subaru 200,000 miles and it still didn't seem to be feeling its age.

She opened her garage door and backed out into her alley. When she heard the story of Cornelius opening *his* garage door to find Dwayne and Phoebe - "humping like Romeo and Juliet in Friar Lawrence's cell," was how he put it - she laughed, despite herself. But since then, every time she went to her garage for *anything* she not only pictured her son and Phoebe, but also, God help her, Dwayne as a baby, strapped in his car seat behind Johnny Sylvester's corpse. What mother does that to a child, even if the child is never aware of it?

By the time she got to Dwayne's school, kids were already heading for the parking garage or over to a line of yellow school busses. Her normal place for picking Dwayne up, in front of Rankos Drugstore, wasn't always available since the store had patrons and other parents had the same idea she did. So their backup meeting place was a couple of blocks away, in front of the old Ansonia apartment building, now converted into condos.

If Dwayne didn't see her at the drugstore he knew to go to the Ansonia without calling her cell. Today, however, since even parking by the Ansonia was impossible, she was about to call Dwayne when, heading *away* from their backup meeting place, who did she see but Dwayne and Phoebe, plus, if her aging eyes did not deceive her, the erstwhile love of

Dwayne's life, Roselyn Wilkinson.

"What have we here?" LaVeronica asked her un-dialed phone.

Rather than putting her Subaru back in gear and roaring over to ask that question, however, she slumped in her seat and called Dwayne. She heard his phone ringing in her ear before he heard it ringing in his pocket, so she had time to watch him look at Phoebe before digging it out to see who was calling. She even saw him mouth the words, *"My mom."*

"Yeah, hi," he said. "I can't go shopping, I've got practice for the concert."

She nearly said, "No you don't, you little liar," but saw what she hadn't seen before; that Dwayne and Phoebe both carried musical instruments, she her saxophone, he his trombone. Even Roselyn Wilkinson carried something smaller, like a flute.

"Okay. What time should I pick you up? You still have to get your presents."

"How about tomorrow? There's a chance that "Midnight Train to Georgia" might be back on tonight, and we have to be ready for it."

"I can see you, Dwayne, and you aren't heading in the right direction!" was on the tip of her tongue, but "Okay, call me if you need me. And I'll see you at home *right after* the dress rehearsal," came out of her mouth.

Ah, the traps mothers set for their sons!

"It's not a dress rehearsal, but I'll have to dress up tonight," Dwayne said.

She hung up and watched the three of them walk away from their high school, down toward where Phoebe's grandfather lived, but also toward Garfield Park.

She kept her distance, put her car in gear again, and followed them.

"Tell me what mother wouldn't do that?" she would ask Dwayne if she got caught.

31.

Midnight Train

Cornelius knew very well that the concert was that night. Though he wasn't planning on going anymore, he had had it on his calendar since September. He expected Phoebe, who came for a snack every day, to rail against their band teacher again when she got there. He did *not* expect Dwayne, and when Roselyn Wilkinson traipsed in behind them he opened his mouth and closed it with no words coming out.

"Stop gulping, Grandpa, you look like a guppy," said Phoebe. "Roselyn already apologized about a million times. And I'm accepting her apology as long as she does us a favor."

"Hi Mr. MacLeish," said Roselyn.

She held up an instrument case and waved it at him.

"Hello, Roselyn," Cornelius said. "How goes the finger painting?"

The joke fell flat with Roselyn, but Dwayne and Phoebe both laughed.

"Are you hungry, and what's with the instruments? I thought you were boycotting the concert. That's why I wasn't planning on going."

"Well, Grandpa, things change!" said Phoebe, "I know you've got the Mopesters tonight, but if you don't come you'll be sor-r-r-y."

When she sang out *"Sorrry!"* and Dwayne and Roselyn fell

into each other, Cornelius said, "Okay, I guess you better tell me what's going on."

"It's true that Dwayne and I were boycotting the concert after Ms. Kramer cut our solos, but Roselyn's in the band, too, and when she said she'd do anything if I forgave her, we came up with a plan, which we're here to practice now."

Dwayne put his trombone case on the floor and took out his trombone. When Roselyn and Phoebe bent to get their instruments, too, Cornelius said, "Why don't you guys tell me about it *before* you all start playing."

"The band is doing a bunch of Christmas songs that aren't called Christmas songs anymore, like *'Chestnuts Roasting on an Open Fire,'* and *'Walking in a Winter Wonderland...'*" Phoebe said. "The idea is that Dwayne and I will sit apart in the audience so no one gets suspicious, then in between those two songs we'll march up on stage with our instruments out, Roselyn will join us, and we'll see how far we can get into *Midnight Train to Georgia* before Ms. Kramer stops us."

When Cornelius only stared at her, Dwayne said, "Tell him about our bets, too."

"Each of us has a different idea of how far we'll get. Roselyn thinks they'll haul us off before we get to how LA turned out to be too much for the man; Dwayne thinks we'll get as far as what time the train is leaving; and I think that everyone will be so shocked that we'll get to the part where the girl says she'd rather live with him in his world than alone in her own, which, Roselyn already admitted, is how she felt when Dwayne chose me. We won't be singing, of course, but you know what I mean. Don't you think it will be poetic justice, Grandpa?"

"I do, but I also think you'll be suspended from school,

and I wonder whether you're ready to pay such a heavy price."

"Suspended?" Roselyn said. "But it will only be a joke."

"We figured we might get kicked out of band, but not out of school," said Phoebe. "It wouldn't be like we stole something."

"What about from the kids in the band who want their families to hear them play? Wouldn't you be stealing that from them? You don't think they'd be mad at you?"

"Oh man, Darius Duchamp will hunt me down and kick my ass," Dwayne said.

Like at the end of an eventful round of boxing, just then the doorbell rang. Cornelius kept his eyes on Phoebe, while also managing to let LaVeronica in. He wasn't surprised, but Dwayne furrowed his brow, and stepped behind the two girls.

"Hi Phoebe, hi Roselyn," his mother said.

She didn't speak to Dwayne, but kept her eyes on Cornelius while he told her they'd been discussing an idea for tonight's concert, even while he also told her what it was. She smiled during his telling, but then said more mildly than her words required, "But that's a cowardly plan, my dears, and packed to the top with vanity."

Phoebe heard her words more than her tone, and coiled like a snake about to strike. Roselyn heard her tone as a nearly miraculous way out of this, and failed in trying not to look relieved. Dwayne, who knew his mother's tactic of delivering her sternest verdicts wrapped in velvet - the verdict being: *"You are NOT doing this, Dwayne!"* - let his brow un-furrow like a flag cut loose on its pole.

Until a quick look at Phoebe furrowed it up again.

"Let me get this straight, she said, "You don't think it's an act of bravery?"

LaVeronica turned, ready for battle. Until she saw that Phoebe was looking at Dwayne.

"I didn't say that, Mom did! And your grandpa did, too. He said we'd be stealing from the other kids in the band!"

When Roselyn said an emphatic, "Yeah," Phoebe saw the realignment in the room as clearly as the movements upon a chess board. She stepped closer to her grandfather, in order to survey her enemies from the safe environs of her only friend.

It took a minute for Roselyn to pick up her flute, cast a wan smile at no one in particular, then head out the door. Dwayne knelt to put his trombone back in its case, before he left Cornelius's house, too, his mother not far behind him. It was the sort of vanquishing that rarely took place, whether in the hearts of teenagers or in those of women and men walking along the edges of an ancient geriatric forest. When Cornelius and Phoebe were alone in the living room, and before Phoebe had a chance to head, full throttle, into the meltdown that her grandfather expected, he texted Emi, asking her to come.

She texted back instantly that she was on her way.

"Do you want something to eat?" Cornelius asked, when he saw Phoebe staring at him.

"I wouldn't mind a salmon sandwich."

"The salmon's gone but how about sardines? Or I've got some pretty good ham."

"Put ham on one side of the sandwich, sardines on the other, and coat them both with peanut butter. How does that sound, Grandpa?"

She went into the kitchen to look out his deck window at the same bad weather that had plagued them since they got back from Las Vegas.

"Sounds like a recipe for disaster," Cornelius said.

"Where's Aggie? She didn't take off again, did she? And yeah, it would be about as big a disaster as what just happened in the living room. I think I should go on a hunger strike, Grandpa. Maybe then disaster would leave me alone."

"Agatha's upstairs. I don't think she'll take off again. That was just her way of dealing with losing Grandma. She's attaching herself to me now."

Phoebe turned to look at him.

"There's no better way to deal with anything, is there?" she asked. "I mean, Aggie's way is as good as any. She left, got into fights, lost weight, but now she knows where she belongs."

"I know where *you* belong, Phoebe, and it's with me."

"You, me, and Agatha, huh?"

The door opened again and Emi came in, pretending not to rush. Alone among the members of the family, with even the slightest hint of rain, Emi used an umbrella. She hurried past the two of them to open the deck door and put it back outside, its handle stuck under the leg of the nearest chair.

"How you doing, babyface?" she asked when she closed the door again.

"Fine, but I'm not going back to school until next year."

Before Emi could say that there were only two days left before winter break, a gust of wind lifted the umbrella off the deck and pushed the chair around so that it faced the window. To everyone's relief no ghost sat in it. But it did make Emi relent. "I guess taking a couple extra days off to figure things out won't hurt," she said.

Cornelius remembered when he and Yuki sat in this very kitchen, trying to talk Emi out of going to San Francisco with Eric the druggie, who waited for her at the Trailways bus station. She stole money from her mother's purse and left in the middle of their talk, only to come back after a month. Years later, after hearing that Eric died of an overdose, she cried herself to sleep in her father's arms.

When Cornelius wondered now if she might be thinking of the same time, she surprised him by saying, "I was in your shoes once with the boy I told you about last week, Phoebe. And even your grandmother went through a rough spell when..."

If she hadn't stopped suddenly, Cornelius might not have noticed her rough intake of breath. As it was, however, he did.

"Went through what rough spell when what?" he asked.

"Yeah, Mom, when what?" asked Phoebe.

"It wasn't a exactly rough spell... It's just that she was an artist's model and we didn't know about it."

Phoebe stood shoulder to shoulder with her grandpa again. They both stared at Emi, whose face betrayed her last six words.

"Okay, she mentioned it once," she said. "But she made me promise not tell anyone."

"I'm not anyone," said Cornelius.

"We're both not anyone, Mom," said Phoebe. "Why didn't you tell us *after* she died?"

"I don't know! But I *do* know that I'm no longer keeping anyone's secret."

"Did you ever go with her when she met that man?" Cornelius asked.

"No, I didn't go with her! She didn't ask me, and I wouldn't have gone if she had. But I did go there once on my own, to find out what his intentions were with my mother."

"Really Mom, you did that?"

Phoebe didn't look at her grandpa, lest he see how impressed she was. He didn't look at her, either, lest she see that he didn't want to hear what might come next.

"Eric notwithstanding, I guess I'm old fashioned, so yes, Phoebe, I did do that. And he said his intentions were honorable, that at first they might not have been, but when Grandma got sicker and couldn't visit him anymore, his intentions became so by default."

"And he's been drawing pictures of her ever since. He fell in love with an image no more real than a bar of hummus soap, Grandpa," said Phoebe. "He was just like me when I thought I loved Dwayne."

"When did you go there?" Cornelius asked. "You still haven't said."

"Last Tuesday morning, the day after Donnie and I got Phoebe from his studio."

Emi tried to put her arms around her father and her daughter, but neither of them let her.

"I told him he didn't have a right to draw her," she said.

32.

Þórdís and Lars

For reasons quite unclear to her, on that same day, Þórdís answered a call from her onetime paramour, the guy she met in Iceland and followed back to Tacoma. She saw his name before she answered her phone, of course. He'd called her often after she broke things off with him, first a couple of times a week, then a couple of times a month, but whenever his name appeared she either dismissed the call or waited until the ringing ran its course. This was a guy, after all, who chased his patronymic origins to Reykjavik, instead of going to Sweden where 'Larson' filled page after page of every phonebook. He *had* found one Larson family in Reykjavik, but they came from Sweden in the19th century, had no idea where Tacoma was, nor what this Lars Larson wanted from them.

When her phone rang today and she saw Lars's name, however, Þórdís picked up.

"Lars," she said. "I've been thinking about you."

That was true if 'short term' thinking was at issue.

"I'm surprised," he said. "I was going to leave a message saying I'm leaving town."

"I hope not back to Iceland. The Einholt Street Larsons might not be so welcoming this time." She laughed, to let him know she was teasing him.

"No, not back to Iceland. I'm in contact with someone in

Oslo."

"But 'Larson' with an 'o' isn't Norwegian, Lars."

"I know, but this guy I found online says a lot of Swedes moved to Norway before coming to America. He's research-ing my particulars for me even as we speak."

"I'll bet he is," said Pórdís. "Have you sent him any money yet?"

Lars was quiet on the other end of the line.

"If it's less than a thousand dollars, chalk it up to a lesson learned," she told him. "But why are you so stuck on this 'roots' finding thing, Lars? You've got a good life right here."

"You want to know why, I'll tell you why," Lars said, but then he didn't say anything more. Until he asked, "Why *did* you answer the phone?"

"I don't know…rough week? I guess I thought you were calling to ask me out to lunch."

"Do you want to have lunch? We could meet somewhere, or I could pick you up. I've had a rough week, too," Lars said.

They decided to meet at Doyle's, which had a couple of good lunch specials. Irish stew with bread and a glass of Guinness for thirteen bucks, or corned beef and cabbage for twelve.

"So I give up the bread and the beer to save a dollar?" Lars asked the waitress when he got there first. "That doesn't seem like much of a deal."

Unlike Pórdís, the waitress didn't laugh, so he ordered the more expensive special, though he never drank this early in the day. Pórdís arrived just as the waitress was leaving his table. She ordered the corned beef and cabbage before she sat down.

"Long time no see," she said, but she felt a pleasant jolt.

'You'd think I could get to the bottom of this thing I have for older men,' she often told herself.

"You're looking good," said Lars.

The waitress obviously hadn't liked it, but Lars's conviviality was what first drew Pórdís to him back in Reykjavik. They met at an aquavit bar.

"Thanks," she said. "I think Tacoma suits me. It reminds me of home."

"So you're not sorry you came?"

"No, Lars, I'm not, it's an interesting place. And it's what prompted me to answer your call. I'm middle-aged and living far from where I grew up. I've been here awhile yet don't know anyone personally other than you. Do you think that's sad?"

"A little bit, yes, and it's my fault for taking you away from your home. I always thought Josefine Whatever-Whatever was the star your life revolved around…"

When their lunches came the waitress smiled the smile she hid before Pórdís got there.

"Tough day for you, too, eh?" Lars asked her, then he slid his glass of Guinness across the table to Pórdís.

That put Pórdís in touch with a memory of her first date with Lars back in Reykjavik. Not the night of the aquavit drinking, but a day or two later when she drove him around town, on the lookout for families named Larson. He was anxious, for by then he had yet again realized where his life-long lack of seriousness had led him.

"'Larson,'" he had said in her car. "What kind of fool comes to Iceland in search of 'Larson,' is what I want to know?"

"There are songs about the various kinds of fools people

are," she had told him, "The fool on the hill, the one who never fell in love, the one who rushes in where others fear to tread," and that seemed to cheer him up.

And now, at Doyle's, she cut into her corned beef, then sat her fork back down. When she said, "I've missed you, Lars, but the truth is, I didn't know it until I saw you sitting in here just now," he slid bread across the table to her, too, pushing it up against the Guinness.

She could see, reflected in the glasses Lars wore, the action from various muted televisions, as well as the merest shadows of the backs of the heads of the patrons sitting at the bar. That people in general were "the merest of shadows" to everyone but those who loved them, made her wonder what would happen if she tried to love the person behind the glasses that reflected the shadows now.

When their lunch was over, Lars asked if she would like to drive out to Browns Point with him, where he'd bought a house that once belonged to the parents of his first ex-wife.

"It has tenants now, but their lease is up at the end of the month," he said. "And if you still like fishing, you can fish right off its dock."

"Wait, hold on, really?"

"Yep," said Lars. "And on a clear day you can see the Olympic Mountains."

"The end of the month is the end of 2019," Þórdís said. "Goodbye and good riddance. It wasn't a very good year."

"What do you say, once this current jerk is out of the White House, we try making 2020 a better one?" asked Lars.

33.

The North End Grievers' Year-End Showdown

Pórdís didn't get Millicent's message refusing to be 'up' that night, but Millicent nevertheless stood firmly behind her decision. She was the first to arrive at Pórdís's house, even ahead of Pórdís, who hurried home ten minutes before the session began.

Millicent stood up from her porch swing to ask about the voicemail.

"What voicemail?" said Pórdís.

"I called Cornelius, too, so if he listened to his messages he'll know to come prepared. I was only "up," remember, because he had that family thing."

She smiled, though, during her time on the porch, she *knew* Pórdís hadn't listened to her message, and did not believe that Cornelius had, either. That, however, was their problem. She wasn't talking about herself again. Frank could be up if worst came to worst. Or LaVeronica, who never said a thing about her own grief.

"Well, come in. Let me turn some lights on. The others will likely get here in about a minute and a half," Pórdís said.

She tried not to show her irritation, but she also assumed that Cornelius would arrive not knowing anything about being up. If that happened she wouldn't force the issue. She'd simply let everyone talk for ninety minutes, then send them off to leave her alone until next year. *If* she didn't decide to

move back to Iceland, a thing she'd thought about after leaving Lars and before she got home.

"I didn't realize I turned off the heat. It's freezing in here.
But please, go in and sit down while I wake up my house."

In the dining room, Millicent reached up to touch the
bottom of the Josefine Christophersen-Hemmingsen picture, as if for good luck. She'd never done that before, but it
seemed appropriate now. She even thought she felt a bit of a
shock - would it be of recognition? - coming from the Pórdís
matriarch. To think that only a couple of hours ago she'd
been sunk down in her tub, nicking her wrist with a razor.
She looked to make sure her sleeve was buttoned below the
band-aids she'd applied there.

LaVeronica arrived next with a box of chocolate chip
cookies, three bucks apiece from the Metropolitan Market.
She placed the cookies on the table with as much nonchalance as she could muster. She'd seen Millicent through the
window, touching the matriarchal photo, but feared that if
she did the same thing Millicent might think of it as making
fun. She keenly wanted to, though, and that surprised her.

The others arrived all at once, bursting in as if they had
also been peeking through the window. Ruthie led the way,
rosy-cheeked and beaming; Frank came next, an unlit ciga-
rette in his mouth and with his collar up, like Frank Sinatra
on an album cover; Cornelius carried a bag from which he
pulled a bottle of single malt scotch; and Jane, to everyone's
surprise, seemed to have thought it appropriate to bring a
stranger along.

When Pórdís saw the cookies and the scotch she ducked
back into her kitchen for glasses and plates, thus giving
herself time to think. For a client to arrive insisting she

wouldn't be 'up' was one thing, but for someone to bring an unexpected guest... She returned to the dining room to distribute the glasses and plates.

"It's kind of you to bring treats on our last day, LaVeronica and Cornelius, but Jane, I have to say..."

"No, please, let me say it first," said Jane. "Everyone, this is Sam, my long-suffering husband. Giancarlo died in 1973. My keeping him alive was...well, at best it was a pipe dream. At worst a small insanity."

Frank walked over to stare up into Sam's face.

"She's been comin' here for months, cryin' spilt milk over someone else," he said.

"I know," said Sam. "Most nights I used the time to get some reading done."

Sam's coolness sent Frank over to the scotch.

"Are you gonna open this, Corny, or do I have to do it?" he asked.

Cornelius opened the scotch and poured some for Frank. More than being shocked by Jane's revelation, he wanted to know what Sam read during his time alone.

Frank looked at Millicent and Ruthie. "You two look like cats who ate canaries," he said. "Tell me you ain't been harboring Jane's dark secret right along with her."

"Not me," Ruthie said. "But I can't wait to hear what happened to Giancarlo."

She stared so hard at Jane, that Jane stood up taller in the doorway.

"Giancarlo got hit by a train," she said. "I had a hard time getting over it when it happened, and it's returned to haunt me once again, over this last year or so."

"It returned to haunting her because she started to believe

that I pushed him. But I was at a kiosk buying sandwiches for the ride between Rome and Trieste," said Sam.

Millicent's mouth hung down to the top of a slight double chin. Were they confessing this because she walked past their house?

"Well, *I* certainly didn't push him, and Sam was back from the kiosk before the train pulled in," said Jane. "He asked me to hold the sandwiches, and the next thing I knew Giancarlo was on the tracks and the train rolled over him."

"But you just said you were at the kiosk, Sam," said Ruthie.

"I was at the kiosk when I saw what was about to happen. I ran back and gave Jane the sandwiches so I could grab Giancarlo."

"How were you able to see what was happening from the kiosk?" asked Frank.

"Because I knew his assailants. We both knew them, right Jane?" Sam said.

"They were the lowlifes who drove us to the station in the first place. Not 'drove us' in their car, but drove us to the station because we were afraid of them," said Jane.

"Was you two lowlifes, too?" Frank asked. "I heard it takes one to know one."

He finished the last of the scotch in his glass.

"We were just a couple of American hippies willing to be outraged on behalf of any leftwing cause. So we were easy marks when we met Giancarlo in a bistro one night and he introduced us to Paul and Martine," Jane said. "One thing led to another and for a time - it doesn't shine a very good light on me - but for a time I was the girlfriend of Sam *and* Giancarlo."

"I wouldn't say it shines a *bad* light on you," Millicent said. "But back up a bit. Who are Paul and Martine? And was Giancarlo one of the lowlifes?"

"He was not, but when Paul and Martine let him know that they were thinking of fake-kidnapping Paul, he found some who were willing to help them," said Sam. "I told Jane we were in over our heads and should get out of there, but she only had eyes for Giancarlo by then."

"Wait, I'm lost, too," said Ruthie. "You two went to Italy, met Giancarlo in a bar…"

"A bistro," said Jane.

"Where you fell for Giancarlo and slept with him openly. In the meantime, Giancarlo introduced you to Paul and Martine, who wanted to kidnap a different Paul…"

"It was the same Paul," Sam said. "Paul wanted to fake-kidnap himself."

"Hold on! I remember that! J. Paul Getty's grandson! He was going to scam his grandfather but changed his mind," Cornelius said.

"Yes, but the low-lifes kidnapped him anyway, and cut off his ear when they didn't get their ransom. When the cops started closing in on them they came after us because we knew who they were," said Jane. "We told them we were headed for Trieste, that they would never see us again, but they had second thoughts about Giancarlo, found us at the station, and shoved him."

"I might have pulled him back if not for all those sandwiches," Sam said.

No one pointed out that he'd just said that he gave the sandwiches to Jane.

They'd been standing in Þórdís's doorway, but now Jane

slumped into a chair. "Do you know what we did next, after the cops arrived, and therefore why I started mourning Giancarlo again after all these years?" she asked. "No, you don't, so I will tell you! Since there wasn't another Trieste train until the next day, and since the cops didn't know that we were with Giancarlo, we crossed the tracks and got on the train for Florence. We changed our tickets when the conductor came through, then sat in a second-class compartment and ate those sandwiches! Not just the two Sam bought for him and me, but also the one for Giancarlo!"

Since the start of their story, Frank and Millicent and Ruthie and Pórdís had been drinking steadily, while Sam and Jane and LaVeronica and Cornelius had not. It was a divide that would serve them poorly over the rest of the evening.

"I guess you won't want me back after this," said Jane. "I thought my lies weren't really lies because the emotion behind them was real, but I'm sure you feel hoodwinked."

"Hoodwinked ain't the word. It's got too much harmlessness in it," Frank said.

"I can't believe it, but I agree with Frank," said Millicent. "What you told us is harrowing, Jane, but I feel betrayed."

Jane nodded and stood again, ready to leave. Pórdís, however, said, "Maybe Sam could tell us about himself. That might help us better understand things."

Sam was surprised, but pleased. "Tell you about me? There's not much to tell. I was a radical in the 60s, got freaked out by what happened in Italy, came home and went to graduate school, spent my life teaching, and now I'm retired."

"What did you teach? I bet you were a literature professor," Millicent said.

"Yes, but mostly in literature in translation. It made for a low enrollment in my courses."

"Don't let him fool you. Sam's classes were always full," said Jane.

"They were full because, though Sam didn't know what made people tick in real life, he knew what made them tick in books, right?" asked Frank.

"Actually, quite right, Frank," said Jane. "Sam's students adored him so much more than mine ever did me. And I taught straight-out European history."

Everyone felt that Sam would say that Jane's students had loved her, too, though they hadn't even known she'd been a teacher. But he only said, "In books we expect things to be resolved. In life it doesn't work that way."

When Millicent began to cry, LaVeronica pushed a tissue box across the table to her.

"What's wrong with you Mills?" she asked.

It was the first time she'd spoken to the woman in such a familiar way. Hell, it was the first time she'd ever even remembered her name.

"I was just reverting back to childhood, I guess. I was thinking that that's what God is supposed to be for. To help us find some sort of resolution."

"Come on, Mills, God don't think about us. He sits off tryin' to get his foot up close to his face so he can clip his toenails," said Frank. "You know God ain't hands-on."

"Maybe not 'hands on,' but he's close enough to hear us if we scream loudly enough," said Ruthie.

"You know, Frank, I read the nail-paring thing a long time ago, but it wasn't God's toenails, and he wasn't having trouble getting his foot up near his face," Cornelius said.

"Probly not, Corny. It's likely that God don't have trouble puttin' his foot wherever he wants it. I musta misspoke. Seems like every time I open my mouth what comes out of it is corrected by someone, even if I'm home alone."

When LaVeronica laughed, Frank bowed. And picked up one of her cookies.

"This might be the whiskey talking, but the idea that books give more direction than real life does, makes me fonder of my profession than I have been lately," said Þórdís. "Perhaps it means that we can learn more by reading and thinking and talking about it, than we can by simply letting the days drift by."

"You been down on therapy lately, Þórdís?" asked Frank. "Well, if it's the whiskey talkin,' don't worry, cause whiskey may have a way with words, but that don't mean it's right. If it's you talkin,' though, let me say that I think you direct things well here, so thank you for that."

Though she still worried about getting kicked out, Jane was impressed by Frank.

Millicent was, too. She said, "And if you happened to have any more booze sitting around, Þórdís, I'll thank you, too. Look at how empty Corny's bottle is."

Þórdís went into her kitchen to get two cold bottles of aquavit. When she brought fresh glasses, Cornelius helped her pass them out.

"Do you know what I want from this? Do you know why I came here with Jane tonight?" Sam asked, once they were settled again. "I came to get a good definition of grief. I mean, I felt grief for Giancarlo, too, back in 1973. But what made Jane return to it so fully last year, that she felt she had to join your group? What does she get out of coming here three nights a week?"

He looked from one to another of them. He didn't look at Jane.

"That's easy. Grief is a hole in the bottom of your soul and when you're around other holey souls they know what you're goin' through," said Frank. "So what Janie gets out of coming here is support."

Sam hawked out an irritated laugh. "I support her at home. And almost fifty years have passed since Giancarlo's death!"

Still, he raised his untouched glass to Frank.

"I wish you had done that, too, Jane," said Ruthie. "I mean supported Sam at home instead of bringing him here tonight to suffer all this ridicule."

"I didn't exactly bring him, it was his idea. And what ridicule?" Jane asked. "All of you are being nice to him."

She looked to Sam for agreement but Sam only swayed in his seat.

"The ridicule is telling us, right in front of him, that you preferred Giancarlo," Frank said. "If that ain't ridicule, then I don't know my own name."

This time, when Frank toasted Sam, Sam took a drink.

"Well, I don't think bringing Sam here ridicules him," said LaVeronica. "In fact, I think that, after tonight, maybe they'll both get free of Giancarlo. Though I will be the first to tell you that the ghosts of those we kill do have a habit of sticking around."

Þórdís looked like she would like to hear her talk about that right now.

"I'm sure that's true, Veronica, but not long ago we all sat here listening to Jane go on about the man, when a living, breathing, Sam waited for her at home," said Frank. "If I'd done that when Doris was alive, she'd have killed me every time I walked back through the door."

"I must be drunk because everything Frank says makes sense," said Millicent. "I felt I knew Giancarlo as well as I did Doris or Ben or Yuki. Even Johnny Sylvester. Yet I didn't know Sam from Kellogg's Corn Flakes."

She stopped short of saying, "Until I walked past their house the other day."

Changing from scotch to aquavit made Pórdís lose her sense of time, so she looked through the door to her kitchen, where a clock told her that they had not only passed their ninety-minute mark, but nearly doubled it. And she still hadn't made her announcement.

"Okay," she said. "What can we say to help Jane understand why her grief for Giancarlo came back? Is it because he was dearer to her than Sam was, or even is right now?"

"He's not dearer to me," Jane said. "That's not right."

"It's because he's dead, so she can't get him off his god-damned pedestal," said Ruthie. "That's number one."

"If that's number one, what's number two?" Pórdís asked.

"Jane weren't shy about lettin' us know how Giancarlo was in bed," said Frank. "She got off with him in them olden days, and fifty years later the memory of it came back to haunt her."

Jane looked hard at Frank. If she said "That's not right," again, it would be a lie.

"Okay, good," said Pórdís. "If number one is Jane's pedestalization of Giancarlo, and the memory of sexual satisfaction is in the mix - let's call it number three for now - then what do we think is the second reason for Jane's late devotion to him? And then we'll stop. It's getting late."

"I can hazard a guess. Sam is a thinker and Giancarlo was the opposite, a doer, which she preferred," LaVeronica said. "So maybe - sorry, Sam - maybe she simply loved Giancarlo more, and that truth came back to her after decades of denial. Does that not seem likely to you all?"

Frank let his mouth fall open, while Cornelius clamped his shut. Ruthie nodded and Millicent finished off her aquavit.

"No more lying, Jane. Is what this lady just said the truth of it?" Sam asked.

"Of course not, Sam! I love my life with you. Mourning Giancarlo anew and coming here to talk about him was just…"

When she paused too long, Frank spoke up.

"It was your hobby, Janie. Like havin' affairs was Mills's, makin' up ghost stories is Corny's, and, well, like lyin' about things too much is mine. A person's got to have an outlet."

"This from a guy who jumped off the Narrow's Bridge," Cornelius said.

Frank swung around to stare at him, both eyes glazed and small. But after the briefest instant, he said, "And I lived to come give Sam this good advice - go home with Janie and take up where you left off, Sam, before this awful night."

Frank stood and walked out of Pórdís house.

Cornelius stood, too, to go after him, but Sam beat him to it. That seemed to mean that Jane had to be next, so he waited while she waved back over her head at them and left.

"There are still cookies. If you want them, eat them," LaVeronica said. "Otherwise I'm taking them home to my son."

Those weren't what she envisioned *her* final words would

be, but to her surprise everyone took a cookie, leaving only two for her to wrap up.

"Thanks, Pórdís, thank you, everyone," she said. "And Cornelius, we still have some things to straighten out, so I guess I'll be seeing you around."

"Wait!" Millicent said, but LaVeronica didn't wait, so a few seconds later their number was down to four. Such is the nature of attrition, whether through death or by people simply standing up and leaving a room.

"I can't drive," said Ruthie. "Pórdís, do you mind if I call a friend? It means I'll have to stay a little longer, but I'll help you clean up."

"I can't drive, either," Millicent said. "Cornelius, will you give me a lift?

"Sure, but first tell me why you asked LaVeronica to wait just now," Cornelius said.

"I know the answer to that and it isn't what you think," said Ruthie.

"Here's a question for you, Ruthie. Why is it that every time anyone asked me something, you feel compelled to say that you know the answer?" Millicent asked.

This was the moment, just before everyone departed, that Pórdís had reserved to make her announcement, but too much drinking made her say, instead, "You still haven't made your call, Ruthie, and I don't need help cleaning up. So Cornelius, how about giving them both rides home, so I can go to bed?"

Though Cornelius was aghast at that idea, he tried not to show it.

"Can we stop for dinner on the way?" Millicent asked. "Those cookies were a piss poor substitute for food. Cornelius, if we can do that, dinner is on me."

Cornelius could have said he ate before the meeting, which was true. He could have said that issues with Phoebe were such that he couldn't afford the time, which was also true. Or he could have said that he didn't care if he ever saw any of them again, which was true at the moment but might not be true tomorrow. So what he did say was, "You've got yourself a deal."

Thus it was that at eleven p.m. on Wednesday, December 18, 2019, a month before the onset of the coronavirus pandemic and only two weeks after the start of this narrative, Þórdís was left to climb onto a dining room chair, take down Josefine Christophersen-Hemmingsen's photo, then sit with her laptop in front of her and look up flights to Reykjavik. She would text the grievers that she was going home for the holidays… Later she'd decide what to tell Lars.

Cornelius, meanwhile, caught a break when Millicent suggested that Ruthie stay with her that night, and that they stop at the Forum downtown, a short drive away.

So that was what they did.

No one ever asked, again, why Millicent wanted LaVeronica to wait.

34.

A Bit Like That of the Cheshire Cat

The eaves of Cornelius's house extended far enough out from the roof to protect the seven drawings. Also, there was no wind so the rain fell down straight.

When he pulled up in front of his house and saw them lined up, the drawings - three to the left and four to the right of his front door - at first he thought that his inside shades had been pulled down to the flower beds that ran below the windows on the *outside* of his house, though he didn't have nearly that many windows. He also thought that there were figures on them, but who would draw figures on his shades?

He turned off his engine, got out of his car, and stood in a slowly dawning knowledge of what he was looking at, half expecting the artist himself to step from behind his rhododendrons.

That the drawings were meant to be viewed from left to right seemed clear, for there was a comprehensive movement, a story to be read in them as clearly as if there were in a book. It was the story told in art, of how his wife lost herself with Cornelius then found herself again in the embrace, whether literal of figurative, of a man from her homeland.

He found a spot equidistant from the front of his car and the edge of the flowerbed, shoved his hands into his pockets, and moved along from one drawing to the next. He imagined the outer edge of his flowerbed to be a velvet cordon, stretching along the ground instead of waist high, but nevertheless preventing him from getting too close. Because of a row of lights embedded in the eaves when the house was remodeled, he could see the drawings as clearly as he might in a museum. In the one at the far left, Yuki sat at their kitchen table, dressed in her white yukata, sipping green tea from a Japanese cup. Only the right side of her face was visible, and that only in part, her sadness evident in the way she held her cup and blew across the steaming surface of it. The artist had caught the steam flowing to the right, locking it there with the same white paint that he used for the yukata. A saucer sat on the table, a soapstone version of Yuki leaning over it, as if the saucer were a pool in which she could see her reflection, though Narcissus, she wasn't. Even as he grew colder and wetter, a closer scrutiny allowed him to notice the beginning of a shadow coming across the table that could only be his, as if he were arriving in the kitchen to find Yuki sitting this way.

Oh, how many mornings were like that one? Who let the artist see it so well?

It hadn't registered with him at first, but each drawing was framed, as if meant as a gift that could be carried inside to hang on his walls.

In the second drawing Yuki was in yellow, sitting beneath their willow tree, while Agatha, also in yellow, tried to escape her grasp. Despite knowing that this one, like the first, must have been drawn at his house, Cornelius loved it, for Yuki's eyes weren't focused on the artist, but on the windows of their upstairs bedroom, where Cornelius so often looked out. He felt that if he could turn to see what she saw, he would discover himself smiling and waving to her.

So much better than finding her abject in the kitchen.

The next two drawings, the last on the left side of his door, plus the first one on the right, were those that Phoebe described to him on the phone.... Yuki with her shoulders bared, as she had been at that Hokkaido hot springs; Yuki with her father in his military uniform; and the one most painful to him, Yuki among the Mount Rainier wildflowers.

There were two more drawings, but the wind had changed and the rain increased, until it worked its way under his collar to soak his shirt and back, making him decide that he couldn't stand there shivering and miserable any longer, no matter what the message from this artist. So he walked up onto his porch, unlocked the door, and went in to flip the switches of various lights. He supposed he knew that he had to bring the drawings in, preserving them so they could play havoc on his emotions when he was dry and warm, but he fought against it. Knowledge might be king for a man like Sam, but did he need to know that he hadn't been enough for Yuki seven different times? Weren't five enough? Or three? Or one?

He found clean towels, even dried off his face and hair, before he saw her sitting at the kitchen table, staring out the window at the rainy backyard, precisely as she did in that first drawing, though without the teacup or the homunculus, and despite the fact that he had known that she would never come again.

He kicked off his shoes and bent to pull off his socks, all while watching for a reaction from her, for an *explanation*. But she was unaware of him; as alone as alone could be.

When he sensed another presence in the room he turned to find Agatha, having come downstairs to greet him. He hurried to pick her up, lest she get it into her head to run out the still-open front door, and when he looked back to the table, half expecting Yuki to be gone, she began singing a Japanese song: *"Until we meet again I do not want to talk about whose fault it is. For some reason I was lonely. For some reason I was empty. Little by little I lost everything…"*

She faded after that, from bottom to top, until all that was left was her ineffable face, a bit like that of the Cheshire cat.

35.

Humpty Dumpty

By the time he walked outside again, to rescue the drawings, the rain had slanted further toward his house, soaking the ground under the eaves and climbing up the bottom few inches of the frames, which were thin and unprotected by glass. He picked up the two drawings nearest him, rushing them into his living room to lean them against the furniture. By the time he went back for the next three, and then the final two - those he hadn't yet looked at - he was not only doubly drenched but his hallway's hardwood floor was as slippery as the ice in a skating rink, waiting for his feet to hit it at just the right angle, which they did on his final return to the house.

When his legs flew out from under him he arched his back like a high jumper, somehow thinking that might help him land correctly. The final two drawings flew even higher than he did, and turned the same way he did, so he was able to see them briefly, yet as clearly as he had those outside. In the first, Yuki stood in the artist's studio in a spring kimono, one hand raised as if about to touch the cherry blossoms on a tree she stood beneath, while her other hand grasped an open parasol that rested on her shoulder. There were yellow cranes in flight, both on her kimono and inside the parasol.

In the last drawing, done entirely in charcoal, there was no Yuki. Only a man flailing and falling through space, before slamming into whatever unforgiving surface awaited him.

He was sure that the man was himself. And then he was sure it was the artist.

And then he was sure that it was an amalgam of them both.

36.

Death Comes for the High Jumper

Some hours later he drifted up off his hallway floor.

He found Natalie's card, picked up his phone, and called her.

She said, I am just getting out of the shower.

It's Cornelius MacLeish, he said, do you remember me?

I do, are you back in Las Vegas?

I am, will you have dinner with me tonight? At eight-thirty? At Red Square?

Order me a Kettle One martini if you get there first.

His kitchen swirled around him and his house lifted up, like Dorothy's when heading for Oz, but it landed without killing anyone outside Mandalay Bay.

He put a grim expression on his face, but the hotel's air conditioning soon wiped it off.

He wanted to freshen up, so he asked to be directed to a men's room, ducked in to stare at himself in the mirror for what seemed like an eternity, then left again and stepped into Red Square, which happened to be next door.

There were two empty tables. He sat at one while the other, which had three chairs, was taken by a group of four, who asked if they could use one of his. When he nodded they curtsied, like they were about to start dancing a minuet.

He ordered a Kettle One martini and asked the waiter to bring another as soon as someone joined him. His martini was cold and clear. The bar was crowded with drinkers tossing down drinks that were, like his, impossible to see in their glasses.

The waiter sat a second martini down when Natalie walked in.

She flew across the bar to glide into the chair across from him, cast a shawl across the back of her chair, picked up her martini and drank it. I'll have another, she told the lurking waiter, then she offered Cornelius her olive toothpick, as if it were an olive branch.

Mea culpa for acting strangely the last time we met, she said.

You weren't acting strangely but do you mind if I ask how you knew what I was thinking at the blackjack table?

I didn't know what you were thinking. I was only there, as I am now, to meet someone at Red Square.

She pointed down at the floor of the place.

But you didn't meet someone. They had you on camera passing Red Square by.

You so disconcerted me that I had to get away.

When the waiter brought her second martini, she ordered white wine.

Disconcerted you because I was winning every hand?

Disconcerted me because I had a feeling that I was your muse. I went to Bellagio to ask if you felt it, too. I was relieved when you didn't come to my house.

I almost went to your house, but I thought better of it.

Two glasses of wine showed up, plus a plate of calamari.

Natalie ate a piece of calamari and sipped her wine.

May I call your cellphone? he asked. Not to be coy, but do you mind?

She had a small bag on the back of her chair, from which she pulled her phone. He found his and called her. Hers did not play Beethoven, but Sophisticated Lady, an entirely different rendering of life's melancholy. She let it ring until its message started and then hung up.

He said, I was expecting a different song.

My mother gave me this phone. It comes with a rotating ringtone service. At first I thought I'd change it, but discovered that it was easier to take bad news when introduced by music selected by someone else.

Do you often get bad news? Do you have cancer, too?

As a matter of fact, I've got a chronic lymphocytic leukemia. They told me I had a seventy percent chance of making it past five years. That was four years ago.

When my wife got sick I pretended she wasn't, even when time grew short. Until one day she died, without a single word about her illness from me.

I think words are overrated, Natalie said.

When the waiter brought their check she collected her shawl and left Red Square on higher heels, it seemed to him, than those she had walked in on.

He paid with cash and when he left Red Square, who should he find with a leg up on a balustrade, but his grandmother in a nylon tracksuit. She said she had come to take him home.

I think I'll stop at the blackjack tables first, he told her. Do you want to come?

He hesitated to call her Grandma, lest she turn into someone else.

She followed him to the blackjack table where he met Natalie. The dealer was a woman whose nameplate said Lilith.

He sat down and reached into his pockets, but he didn't have any more money.

When he looked at his grandmother she turned her tracksuit pockets out, so Lilith said, as if he'd asked, Okay, just this once, and slid a twenty dollar chip across the table.

She dealt him two kings, herself a ten and a seven, so he won.

He let his winnings ride and got two queens to her jack and eight, and won again.

His grandmother walked over to a shop selling Vegas memorabilia. When she picked up a pair of fluffy dice, he pushed a twenty dollar chip back across the table to Lilith, stood and went to the gift shop. But his grandmother was gone and the dice were gone and the shopkeeper was in the doorway. When he asked how much the dice were, the shop-keeper took a chip out of his hands, but Lilith, who had followed him, snatched it back.

She paid the man with a twenty dollar bill from the folds of her skirt.

Let's go find your grandmother, my break won't last forever, she said. You can cash those chips in at the cage or use them to play again.

There were other blackjack players now, but the last thing he wanted was join them, so he said he would cash in.

His grandmother waited inside the casino cage, the fluffy dice around her neck.

He wants to cash his chips in, said Lilith.

He can tell me what he wants, said his grandmother.

She came out of the cage, took the dice from around her neck, and placed them around Lilith's, who nodded and left.

He put his chips in his grandmother's hands. He said, I don't want to gamble anymore.

Part Two

The Song Is Ended, But the Melody Lingers On
-- Irving Berlin

1.

Waiting Outside the ICU

"Christ on an old wooden crutch, I just finish losing Doris and now I gotta lose my best friend?" moaned Frank.

Neither Millicent nor Ruthie looked at him.

"Does Pórdís know about this?" Ruthie asked.

"Pórdís won't be back until next year. I told her what happened in an email but she hasn't replied yet," said Millicent.

"Why not? Corny's sick!" Frank said. "And what about Veronica?"

All of them, even LaVeronica, had long since ceased correcting Frank.

"She's at church. It's Christmas Eve. But she told me she'd be here after the hosannas," Millicent said.

"Can you stop with the snideness, Mills?" asked Frank. "The last thing we need is to piss off Jesus while we're prayin' for Corny's life."

Since no visitors were allowed in the ICU, they were sitting in a waiting room, below a couple of televisions that were on, but mute. Throngs of people crowded around the Church of the Nativity in Bethlehem on both TVs.

"How long are you staying here tonight?"

Millicent was asking Ruthie, but Frank said, "Until the cows come home. I already told Beatrice to start dinner without me."

I'll stay until his family gets back," said Ruthie. "Maybe

they'll have an update."

"Yeah, them doctors won't tell the rest of us Jack. When I asked one of 'em he looked at me like the cat just dragged me in."

Millicent and Ruthie looked at him that way, too. It had only been a week, but Frank's hair was wild, he hadn't shaved, his eyes were as red as the devil's, and he was wearing the clothes he wore at their last meeting.

When they heard someone coming they stood, and when LaVeronica walked in with her son, Frank ran to them, scaring the bejesus out of Dwayne.

Millicent and Ruthie hurried over to pull Frank back.

"Tell me quickly what you heard," LaVeronica said. "He's not dead, right?"

She believed that hearing bad news quickly dulled its pain.

"He's alive, but that's all we know. We're waiting for his family now," said Ruthie.

She and Millicent held onto Frank like wardens might at a mental hospital.

"Can I go back to the car, Mom?" asked Dwayne. "Or go eat if there's a restaurant?"

LaVeronica walked to the doors of the ICU without responding to him, hit a button until the door opened, and stepped inside.

"They're gonna toss her out of there faster than they did me," said Frank, while
Millicent told Dwayne, "We know your mom from grief group, and you know Cornelius, right?"

"He's Phoebe's grandpa. Phoebe's my friend from school," Dwayne said.

"Yes," said Millicent. "I think we heard about that."

The thing about their grievers' group was that everyone heard everything if they simply tuned in, and Millicent's greatest asset was her tuned-in-edness. The exception being that she hadn't known about Sam before her walk.

She looked at Frank and Ruthie. "Did either of you remember to call Jane?"

Neither of them had so, though she was still mad at Jane, Ruthie stepped over by Dwayne to make the call.

"Your mom's been in there a while. Maybe she'll find something out," she said.

"Ha! You don't know my mom. She'll find it all out," Dwayne said, and when Ruthie laughed he smiled.

When Jane didn't pick up, Ruthie left a message. She wasn't sure why she was so mad at Jane, but even after a week her anger was palpable.

A few minutes later the ICU doors opened again and LaVeronica came back out. Frank and Millicent and Ruthie hurried over to her, but Dwayne stayed where he was. "One of his nurses is Regina Johnson's daughter. You remember Regina, don't you, honey?" LaVeronica called over to him. "Big fat lady from church?"

Dwayne shrugged, while the others waited to hear what Regina Johnson's daughter said about Cornelius.

"He's got a fractured skull, a fluid build-up that's pushing against his brain, and a rib came loose and got stuck where it shouldn't. Regina's daughter said it's more like he tumbled off a roof than fell down in his hallway. We can't quote her, though. She went out on a limb telling me that much."

"Jesus wept!" said Frank.

"Mom, can I go wait in the car?" asked Dwayne.

LaVeronica was about to say that she would take him

home, when Emi and Phoebe came into view, arm-in-arm and walking slowly. Phoebe saw Dwayne and stopped, while Frank sat down again and Millicent and Ruthie hurried over to tell Emi what LaVeronica found out.

"We know all that. Let me go see what's new on my own," Emi said.

Phoebe wasn't about to talk to Dwayne while her mother was gone, so she took out her phone to text her, saying she would wait in the cafeteria. But Dwayne used her texting time to get up close to her.

"Sorry about your grandpa, he was a really good guy," he said, making her nearly drop her phone.

"What do you mean 'was!'"

"I didn't mean 'was.'"

"Yeah, well don't mention his name. What are you doing here anyway?"

"My mom made me come after church. She wouldn't take me home first."

He meant that, against all odds, his mother hadn't thought that he might meet Phoebe here, a thing she was as set against as Phoebe was herself.

"Go home anyway," said Phoebe. "I need to worry about my grandpa."

If Dwayne said anything more she would shove him down on the stinking hospital floor. Maybe he'd fracture his skull, too, or get a rib stuck somewhere.

Dwayne, however, took a terrible chance. "I heard Mr. Okada brought some pictures over. He was in love with your grandma, huh?"

"Well, she wasn't in love with him! She loved Grandpa like the moon loves the stars."

"Love's a one-way street," Dwayne said. "Like, I still love you but you don't love me."

Phoebe was saved from having to shove him down on the stinking floor when her mother came back out of the ICU and hurried over.

"His vital signs aren't good, honey, a little worse than yesterday," she said. "Dr. Russo's going to drill a hole in his skull, to take the pressure off his brain."

"What Dr. Russo? If it's Rudy Russo, you're in good hands," said Ruthie. 'He's my neighbor out at the lake."

"And it's a well-known fact that there's no better day for havin' a hole drilled in your head than Christmas Eve," Frank said.

"Was Dr. Russo in there?" asked Phoebe. "Did he tell you that himself?"

"He was and he did," said her mother. "He might come out here before the surgery, though, so you can ask him things yourself. They're prepping Grandpa now."

Dwayne came to Phoebe's side again, and when she noticed him there she took his hand. Then she let it go and ran down a hallway to lean against the wall, Dwayne only a couple of steps behind her.

"I don't want to get ahead of things here, but this happened to Jonathan once and it wasn't any more difficult than letting the pressure out of a tire," Millicent said. "No real invasion, and not a very long procedure, either."

LaVeronica stood where she could keep an eye on Phoebe and Dwayne. She had seen Dr. Russo walking in and out of Cornelius's room, and heard him talking about this hole-drilling business on the nurse's station phone. Though she'd intended to drive Dwayne home, she couldn't do that now, so she stepped up to the others and said, "How about we give the family some privacy? If you'll follow me to the cafeteria I'm buying coffee and doughnuts."

"Cookies last week and doughnuts today," said Frank.

"It's Christmas Eve," said Ruthie. "Maybe the cafeteria's closed."

"It's not. It don't matter what day it is, the relatives of sick people got to eat," said Frank.

2.

Jane and Sam on the Old Town Dock

Jane didn't answer Ruthie's call because she and Sam had left their house to walk down to Old Town Dock a few hours before dark on Christmas Eve. They walked to the end of the dock where there were benches to sit on under a cover that kept them dry. They hoped they might come to some rapprochement, some tie-up of the loose ends, some calming of the emotion that both of them had felt since that grievers' meeting.

"Fishing's not allowed here anymore," said Sam.

"Yes, that's right, it's not," Jane said.

To their right, a ramp led down from the dock to a float where people could tie up boats. The angle of the ramp was slight because the tide was high. When the tide was low the ramp had a much more radical angle, sometimes greater than 45 degrees. A few years back the dock had had a makeover, but both Sam and Jane liked it better the old way.

"Come on, Sam, why not go ahead and say it, get it over with?" said Jane.

She meant that Sam should say whatever he hadn't been able to say at their house, like "I want a divorce," or "Let's do what we always do, and smooth things over."

"Are you waiting for me to thank you again first, for putting up with me?" she asked.

"I don't want thanks and I don't want to say anything,"

Sam said. "I want to sit here."

No one else was on the dock, and no boats were tied to the float. It was a day for whitecaps, for seagulls putting their shoulders into the wind; a prelude to the birth of Christ.

"I didn't think it was possible to make too much of it, but I did make too much of it, Sam. I can see that now," Jane said.

The thing that she didn't think it was possible to make too much of, was having stood next to Giancarlo on that train platform when a pack of Italian hyenas pushed him in front of the train. She told Sam as much when they arrived in Florence - that she'd never get over it - and to prove herself right, she hadn't. The face of one of the hyenas still stood in her memory. It was a sharp, crescent moon of a face, if crescent moons were evil and hadn't shaved. Giancarlo's face, too, often looked up at her from the tracks.

"I felt grief and I thought a grief group might help," she said. "Was that such a crime?"

Sam sat on his hands, his shoulders hunched like those of the gulls.

"Not if it was recent or you were alone," he said. "But almost fifty years have passed, and I have been with you the whole time."

"Yes," said Jane, "I know that."

She stood and walked to the ramp that led to the boat float. The ramp rose and fell when the float did. Slats were laid at intervals across the ramp so people could secure their footing when walking down. She looked back at Sam then stepped onto the ramp and walked to the float herself. Now, when she looked back at him, she could see only his head, then his head and shoulders, then only his head again, as the float rose and fell with the swells. She had let him bear the weight of her depression for fifty years, and presenting herself as a widow to the other grievers was an *unforgivable* erasure of him. Yet Sam never complained. And that made her hate him. And hate herself for doing so.

Large metal cleats were spaced eight feet apart along the edge of the float, there for tying up boats. Jane went to the nearest one, scraped the sole of a shoe across the top of it, then moved to the next cleat, working her way around the float. To do such a thing, to take up some activity, was how Jane accessed deeper thought. She'd never been able to do it while sitting around her house or talking to someone. Only by driving and counting stoplights, or going out into their garden to shovel dirt, could Jane dig down deep. Sam knew this, and watched her as she walked around the float.

There were eight cleats, but Jane didn't think there was enough room for eight boats. Still, she walked around it twice, performing her ritual, when what should she see looking up at her from just beyond the cleat closest to the ramp, but a harbor seal, treading water like Jane had been doing for all these fifty years.

"Hello there," she said, in an unsurprised voice.

It was a small seal, not a baby, but not fully grown. It had long whiskers and its eyes were so deep and welcoming that Jane, alone on the float yet only thirty feet from Sam, feared it might jump up out of the water and come to her. As it was, its head and shoulders were out of the water, its flippers working hard below the surface to keep it that way. She had read about the dead inhabiting animals at the beginning of their journey to the afterlife, but Giancarlo had been dead for decades. This seal *was* Giancarlo, though, she knew it.

How did she know it? Because of those eyes! She also knew he had a message for her, so she gathered her courage and took a step forward, so if he delivered the message in words, he wouldn't have to use a loud voice.

After only one step, the seal moved that much closer, too, its nose just on the other side of the cleat. If she took a second step she felt sure that the seal really would jump onto the float and she didn't want that, on the very slim chance that it *wasn't* Giancarlo but a rabid, and therefore overly aggressive, seal. Aggression disguised as friendliness, aggression disguised as the transmigration of souls.

"Hello," she said again, "Do you have something to tell me?"

The seal blinked a couple of times but it didn't come closer.

"Are you Giancarlo, or do you have a message from him?"

This time the seal's eyes narrowed, as if saying, "You know the answer as well as I do."

Maybe Sam got tired of waiting for her, for just as Jane was about to speak again, he appeared at the top of the ramp, startling the seal so much that it sank back under the water. She could see it there, a foot beneath the surface, before it disappeared.

"It's getting cold," said Sam. "How about we head home?"

"You go. I'll stay here a little longer. When I do get home, there is something I would like to ask you, though, so be prepared."

Sam nodded, sure that she would not so much ask him, as tell him to divorce her.

"Okay, but don't be long," he said. "Once I get up that hill I don't want to have to come back down it again, looking for you."

When Sam walked back past the bench he'd been sitting on and then off the dock entirely, Jane moved around the float in order to steadily watch him. And then, though she didn't think there was much chance that the seal would reappear, she made her way around the float a few more times.

After another thirty minutes, she climbed up off the float and walked home alone, soon to be angry at Sam again, for guessing, and dismissing out of hand, what she had to ask him.

3.

Thick Skull

Though they expected him previous to the surgery, several hours passed after the surgery was over, before Dr. Russo came into the waiting room with a grim expression on his face.

"Did anyone ever tell you that he has a thick skull?" he said.

It was a line he sometimes used to help ease the tension when facing a worried family, but it rarely succeeded in creating much levity.

"What are you saying? Did something go wrong? Was his skull too hard to drill through?" asked Emi.

Dr. Russo decided to drop the stupid line from his repertoire. He learned it during medical school, in a "Bedside Manner" chapbook written by one of his professors.

"It went well," he said. "We drilled two burr holes in his skull, cut through his dura, drained the fluid - partially clotted blood - that was putting pressure on his brain, then we closed the dura in one spot and left the second spot open to drain any fluid that might build up again. We'll close it, too, when we're sure there'll be no more swelling."

"What's a dura?" asked Phoebe. "And how come you didn't talk to us sooner? We've been waiting out here for hours!"

One look made him decide that dumbing down for her

would be a mistake.

"The dura is the outermost layer of the meninges. It lies directly under the bones of the skull and vertebral column," he said. "It's thick, tough and inextensible, which means it can't be stretched. I cut through it with scissors and sewed it back up with thread."

He stopped to gauge her understanding, then added, "The meninges is the sac that surrounds and protects our brains from the daily bumps and bounces that our skulls endure. There were no surprises. I know it must have seemed like it took forever, but the whole procedure took less than three hours."

"And you'll sew up his other dura when the draining stops?" asked Emi.

"Well, it's the same dura, but yes, that's the plan."

"Does draining the fluid mean Grandpa will wake up soon?"

"Let's not think too far ahead. A fractured skull and its concomitant concussion, *and* a rib poking his heart, is a lot for a man of his age. Let's watch what happens over the next few hours, maybe over the next couple of days."

"Can we see him?" Phoebe asked. "Where is he? Is he still behind those doors?"

"He's in a recovery room. I'll send someone to get you when he's ready for a visit. But one at a time. After that, I think you should go home, eat your dinner and get a good night's sleep. There'll be nothing more you can do today."

"Ha! Only if you don't count sitting with him and telling him jokes," said Phoebe.

"Yes," said Dr. Russo. "Only if I don't count that."

"What about his lungs? You haven't said a word about

them yet," Emi said.

"He's got several pulmonary contusions, with a fluid buildup of just under twenty percent in one lung. But with mechanical help he's breathing well. When he's conscious and can tell us the level of pain he's in, and we see how he breathes *without* help, maybe we'll fix it then… With luck, his ribs will heal on their own."

Dr. Russo noticed that each time Emi tried to take Phoebe's hand or put an arm around her, or simply stand close to her, Phoebe pulled away.

"She wanted to stand alone, let the weight of things settle on her without mitigation," was how he would put it when he finally sat down to his own dinner that night.

When he said he would chance going home himself, but would come back if anything changed, Phoebe said, "I think you should *not* chance going home. I'm not going anywhere and I don't think you should, either."

"How about this, then," he said. "I'll go get his post-op room assignment, find out what time he's likely to get there, and we'll wait together until he's settled in?"

It was the first time in years that he had offered such a thing, but it made him happy to do so. He would call his daughter, tell her to expect him later, that they should start dinner without him. She would say that they would not, that she would feed her kids if she had to, but she would wait for him.

Oh, how he loved his daughter. Oh, how she reminded him of his late wife.

4.

Lee Marvin

Where was his check, had he put it in the bank?

Where was his deposit slip?

What was his bank account number, wasn't it Phoebe's birthday?

No, that was his password. When he deposited the check - ah, he had deposited it! - the teller asked if he wanted to see a financial advisor so that he might make more money with his money, but he declined. The teller was a woman with a laconic manner and a fuzzy blonde mustache. He had seen her at the supermarket, next to the unshucked corn.

When a bright light came into his eyes he remembered such intrusive lights during ontological exams. Wait, not ontological, ophthalmological. He didn't know what ontological meant. Wait again, yes he did. It dealt with questions regarding the existence of God.

"Ah!" he said. "Too bright!"

Someone said, "Did you hear that?"

"I did, and he squinted, too."

"Turn off that light," he said.

"I think he said that he's too hot."

Someone pulled the blankets off of him, letting a cold wind blow in from the north. He saw snowcapped peaks and felt the chill of an Arctic winter.

"Can you hear me, Grandpa? It's New Year's Day, 2020, and I can tell you right now. it'll be a great year as soon as you wake up. You've been blabbering on like one of those malaria guys in the World War Two movies you and Grandma used to make me watch. Remember the one with a delirious guy in a hammock when Japanese soldiers are nearby? The guy won't shut up so his pal, Lee Marvin, has to kill him with a pillow so they won't get caught. I'll never forget how Grandma laughed at what the Japanese soldiers actually said. She told us they were talking about shopping for cars once the movie was done. She couldn't get over it. She thought Lee Marvin was great, though. Anyway, stop blabbering if you don't want to be like the guy in that hammock."

Phoebe fluffed his pillow. She found herself talking more the longer this went on. When her mom was here, or one of the Mopesters…even with Dr. Russo, she could not shut up. And this was only day eight. What would she sound like if more days went by?

When the light disappeared, he was cast into a serene and merciful darkness.

"I need to tell you something. I mean, I want to talk this whole thing out in front of you since you're probably not listening anyway, before Mom gets here and takes over the telling. When you weren't listening before your accident I always knew it, by the way. I only pretended not to notice, but you, Grandma, Mom…you were all bad listeners. Only Dad listened well, but he never knew what to say after the listening part was done. So it was hard for me to decide whether to talk to people who didn't listen, but had opinions, or a man who listened but was stumped by it all."

She sat down on the edge of his bed to run a finger around the tape that held his IV in place, on the back of his liver-spotted hand.

"Okay, about Dwayne," she said. "First, do you remember who he is or what we did? In a way, it would be great if you didn't, because then you could wake up and meet your virgin granddaughter. That would be something, huh? Except it wouldn't be true. It would be an illusion that I would have to clear up for you sooner or later."

She could see through the tape how the needle went into a vein. She could see the angle it went in at. How would that be for a geometry problem? Figure out the angle of the needle going into an old man?

His bed was narrow, but she managed to stay on it by draping her left arm around him, with her head beside his on his pillow and her mouth next to his ear. It was the *only* way she could say what came next, though she could have said it to her grandma just by sitting with her in the kitchen over at their house. And she had said it to Dwayne over the phone.

She said, "Ok, the thing is…" but then she lost her balance and was barely able to keep from falling onto the floor. Meanwhile, he turned his head.

"The thing is what?" he asked, in a voice of a whispering frog.

He closed his eyes again, while tears flew from Phoebe's like they'd been shot out by squirt guns. "Grandpa you're awake!" she cried. "Grandpa, say something else!"

"I had a bright light in my eyes."

"Is that why your eyes are still closed? Because of the light?"

She jumped up and ran over to lower the blinds, darkening the room so severely that she banged her shin when she tried to make her way back to him. When she said, "Ouch!" he asked, "How long have I been gone?"

"You knocked yourself out on December 20th or 21st, we think, and didn't get found until Mom went over there on December 23rd. You had surgery on Christmas Eve and now, well…Happy New Year, Grandpa!"

She wanted to say it was her fault for staying away from his house for so long.

He opened two small eyes, like two chocolate chips stuck in dough. But he could see out of them, and what he saw told him everything.

"Light is your enemy when it shines in your eyes, but when you shine it on your troubles it helps you understand them," he said.

His regular voice tried to chase the frog's away.

"Stop talking! Let me get the nurses, call the doctor, call Mom. And the Mopesters have been coming around non-stop…even Dwayne's mom."

"Yes, I *do* remember Dwayne," he said.

Phoebe found his remote and poked the call button.

"Nurses are coming and I'm texting Mom. She'll be sorry she wasn't here to see you wake up. She's been here as much as me, only just not right now."

"Is there a chance she'll be a grandmother? Is that what you were about to say?"

Phoebe looked up from her phone. "Yes, but there's no more 'chance' about it," she said. "I peed on a stick and got a blue line! Mom made me do it four times!"

Before he could react to that, a nurse rushed in to do what needed to be done when a comatose patient woke up. Like shouting into his bedside phone.

Phoebe's phone rang then, making her think that the nurse was calling her.

"Yes, awake! Yes, now!" she told her mom, while the nurse said Dr. Russo was in the hospital, and would be right down.

When he arrived a few minutes later, Dr. Russo had Ruthie with him, and when Emi got there ten minutes after that, they all danced around, relieved and joyful that their father and grandfather and patient hadn't died.

For his part, Cornelius lost the sense that Phoebe was pregnant, was captured, instead, by a dawning memory of carrying framed drawings into his house; by a certain knowledge that it had been raining; and by a deeper knowledge that the final drawing had sent him all a-tumble.

Which came first then, the tumble or the awareness of it?

5.

Mrs. Dr. Russo

For the rest of that day Cornelius was isolated so his doctors could observe him without interruption. On the second day after his awakening, and on the third and fourth, he was allowed visitors unless he said he was too tired, but on the fifth day, when his urine turned tea-colored, indicating the presence of rhabdomyolysis, they returned him to the ICU. He had been on an IV drip to infuse his body with the fluids and electrolytes necessary to flush built-up toxins, but the rhabdomyolysis had "fought hard to gain a footing in him," as Dr. Russo put it, and could lead to kidney disease. Or, if they weren't careful, to renal failure and dialysis.

"What are you saying!" cried Phoebe. "I was there when he woke up and he was fine."

"Let's just say he's not out of the woods, but we'll get him there in a few more days."

Dr. Russo was her grandfather's surgeon, not his doctor, but he kept coming around. He was true to his word, though, for on January 10th Cornelius was back in the general hospital population, and he was ready for discharge on the 15th.

"He's got partial pneumothorax, which was caused by the lung contusion, but his ribs seem to be on the mend without our help, so that, too, should take care of itself. If it doesn't…well, we'll cross that bridge when we come to it. He'll need physical therapy, regular visits to his G.P., and a watchful watchfulness on the part of his loved ones."

It was the longest speech that Dr. Russo ever gave them, but while Emi took notes Phoebe *knew* that the "watchful watchfulness" thing was aimed at her. It meant she hadn't been a good granddaughter, that it was her fault he stayed unconscious in his hallway all those days. She tried to think if she had *ever* not seen her grandpa for that long before, and could not. Nevertheless, she didn't accuse Dr. Russo of blaming her. She simply helped take Cornelius to a hospital bed set up in his living room, since climbing stairs was still too much for him. School had started again, so she stayed with him after dismissal each day, Emi the rest of the time. When one or another of the Mopester came with food, and during his physical therapy sessions, she took breaks, walking around his neighborhood to think about herself.

Things went on like that for a month and a half, with Cornelius's progress adequate according to his physical therapist, but slow according to Phoebe, who, when the pandemic closed her school in March, took over his guest room nearly full time. She was fourteen weeks pregnant and beginning to show by then, but she made it clear to her parents in numerous talks and one screaming fight, that there would be no abortion. She said it to others, too. To her grandfather, to Dwayne, and, surprise of surprises, to Roselyn Wilkinson, who called almost every day to see how she was. Who knew what evil lurked in the hearts of teenage girls, how it got there or how it departed? The only person who didn't need persuading, regarding her decision, was LaVeronica, who had already taken one life and would not be party to taking another. Whether or not she transferred the firmness of her position to Phoebe, was the subject of conversations at everyone's house.

One day, at her mother's insistence, Phoebe, who had never even seen a doctor other than her pediatrician, made an appointment with Dr. Russo's daughter, an OB/GYN, whom Emi heard about from Ruthie, her father's Mopester friend. Emi drove her, went in with her, and asked the questions that Phoebe either couldn't think of or was too shy to ask.

They discovered through an ultrasound that Phoebe was carrying a girl. Mrs. Dr. Russo, as they called her, said that the health of the fetus was good, and that they would call her due date September 1, with a margin of error of plus or minus a week. Before they left the doctor's office they scheduled appointments through the spring and summer, though Mrs. Dr. Russo said that if the pandemic got worse they might do some of them online.

On their way home, Phoebe told her mother that she wanted to put the baby up for adoption, but when they got there she told her father, who waited for them in the driveway, that she was thinking of naming her Cornelia, after her grandfather. Or maybe Cassie, after her grandfather's grandmother.

"My mom's name is Mary and my grandmother's was Alice," her father said. "How about letting my side of the family in on it? How about calling her Mary Alice?"

"I like 'Mary Alice.' Not 'Mary' and then 'Alice' as a middle name, but 'Mary Alice' all together," Phoebe said. "Her last name might be Williams, though, like Dwayne's."

"Mary Alice Williams," said Donnie, and with that, for awhile, at least, it was decided.

6.

Phoebe's Choice

It may have been decided 'for a while, at least,' when Emi and Phoebe got home from the doctor, but it wasn't decided a couple of nights earlier, when mother and daughter spoke in their kitchen, sometimes calmly, sometimes throwing words at each other like plates pulled down from the shelves.

It started when Emi said for the umpteenth time, "You're still in your first trimester, honey, there's nothing viable about what you're carrying. And ending a pregnancy is safe and accepted now, if not routine."

She was drying one of the nearly thrown plates, and pointed it at her Phoebe's abdomen.

"Don't say 'ending pregnancies,' say 'abortion,' Mom. I hate the word, but we have to use it if we are going to talk about this…there'll be no more deflecting."

'Deflecting' was her grandfather's word, but Emi didn't point it out.

"Abortion then, and I don't like the word, either. But it has freed a lot of women and girls who were nowhere near ready for motherhood."

Emi put the plate on the counter, then turned and asked her daughter to sit down. Phoebe recognized the tone and did as she was told, while Donnie came to the door of the kitchen, to lean against its jamb.

"You remember I told you about Eric, right?" said Emi.

"I remember you *finally* told me about him when you came to get me at Mr. Okada's place. Are you about to say you made him up? Cause if you are, I'm saying first that I thought that was what you were doing when you told me."

"No, I didn't make him up. Why would I do a thing like that?"

"To try and teach me a stupid lesson."

"I promise you Eric was real, and more important to me than anyone at the time."

"Even more than Grandpa or Grandma?"

"Yes, hands down."

"Well, it's not that way for me with Dwayne, cause I hate him now. Are you about to tell me that you never hated Eric, so I'll feel even worse about things?"

"I am trying to tell you something serious. So please stop guessing and listen to me."

Though it was after dinner and dark outside, those words, said with great portent, brought a dawning into Phoebe's mind like it was morning.

"Wait! What?" she said. "Are you saying Eric got you pregnant?"

"I discovered I was pregnant in San Francisco after Eric and I broke up. When I came home I didn't tell anyone, until one day I told my mom."

"Grandma? You told Grandma?"

Donnie moved all the way into the kitchen to put an arm around his wife.

"Grandma and only Grandma. It was the biggest secret of my life, and she saved me, Phoebe, first by talking to me for a couple of days, next by taking me to get an abortion and staying with me every step of the way, and finally by keeping my secret, all the way to her grave. No one else ever knew about it except your dad, whom I felt I had to tell before we got married."

"Oh god, I could have had a…! What year was this? I could have had a brother or sister who was twenty years older than me?"

"More like thirteen, but yes, you could have, if I hadn't ended the pregnancy. But by doing so I was able to turn my life around, fall in love again, and give birth to you when I was ready."

The color drained from Phoebe's face and her lips and mouth grew straight. Both hands held onto the seat of her chair beside her thighs. "Do you know what sex it would have been? Do you ever even think about her or him?"

"No, about the sex. But yes, I think about her or him sometimes. Do I regret it, though? Do I feel remorse or guilt? No, honey. The fact of the matter is, I almost never do."

"Why not? That's why I'm not doing it! Because this baby would come back and haunt me worse than Grandma haunts Grandpa! And it would turn me into a terrible person!"

"It would not turn you into a terrible person, nothing could do that," said Donnie, but neither his daughter nor his wife seemed to hear him.

"You want to know why those feelings rarely come to me, and why I don't think I'm a terrible person now? Because I had a mother who taught me well, a lot better than I've taught you. She was strong and made me strong, at least when it came to a woman's right to choose the path that her life will take, each and every time a turn in that path comes along."

"Are you talking about the Grandma I knew?"

"The one and only. She was clear-eyed and a whole lot tougher than she looked."

"Did Eric know about it? Did you name the boy or girl? Did you think of aborting me when I came along?"

"Eric didn't know. I didn't look for him to tell him, and then, it seemed in almost no time, he ODed and died. And no, of course I didn't think about aborting you. If fact, your dad and I tried hard to have you. It took me a year to get pregnant. We wanted you desperately."

"Like you desperately didn't want that other baby! You did name it, though, didn't you? That's why you skipped over that part of my question!"

"Eric Junior. I called that bit of drugged-out tissue 'Eric Junior,' for a while. Until your grandma put a stop to it, took me to the clinic, and saved my life."

"And you or she never told Grandpa? How unfair was that? Don't you think he had a right to know?"

"A right? I guess he did, if loving me gave him such a right. But Mom and I were trying to save him from a lot of heartache. Over the years, though, I have thought that might have been a mistake. Mom made a mistake with him again, too. He always loved us both so openly, but we didn't show our love for him by coming clean."

"You sure didn't! And now you expect me to keep your secret for you!"

"I only told you because I wanted you to know that I have been where you are, and that you have a choice, Phoebe, not to give you an extra burden. But I did give you one, I can see that now."

"Well, I made my choice, and it's to have this baby!" Phoebe said. "But you called it a 'bit of drugged-out tissue.' Does that mean if Eric Junior had been born he would have had fetal alcohol syndrome, but with drugs?"

"Very likely, yes. Eric was heavily into everything, honey, and I didn't exactly abstain."

"So he might have gone to juvie or maybe even jail, but then cleaned himself up and visited us? And he might have always been nice to me, because I was his little sister, even up to, like, right now?"

There stood Emi and Donnie. In their lonely kitchen. Having to listen to that.

Donnie told Emi later, that it would have been better to leave Phoebe in the dark. A few days after that, though, Mary Alice invaded the imaginations of them all, quite like Eric Junior did that night, complete with years of dealing with a drug infested DNA.

But what would Phoebe do now, tell her grandpa or keep her mother's secret?

Her mother hadn't asked her not to tell her grandpa. If she had she would almost certainly have told him. But since her mother left it up to her, she almost certainly would not.

7.

Millicent on Pórdís

At the end of March, when Millicent came over to Cornelius's house in a mask and with two pieces of rhubarb pie, individually wrapped on paper plates and with plastic forks in cellophane, he told her that he'd once loved rhubarb pie, but hadn't since people started adding too much sugar and mixing in strawberries. He also told her that when he was a child he had an aunt who made it properly.

"I can't believe you said that! I learned to make it from an aunt of my own in London, and it's bitter to the point of making you pucker."

She was right about the pie, and when he told her so, she said, "Okay, pour me a glass of that wine, because I need fortification to tell you what I came to say."

Cornelius had put some white wine in an ice bucket and carried it down to the table under his willow tree when she called to say she was coming. It would be his first alcohol since getting home from the hospital. He still saw his physical therapist once a week, and he sometimes used a walker to get around his house, but he'd carried things down to the willow tree without it. He'd lost twenty pounds since his accident and skin hung loose from various parts of his body.

He filled Millicent's glass while pouring himself a taste. The wine went well with the pie.

"I've been talking to Pórdís, who wishes you a swift recovery," Millicent said.

Cornelius got a card from Þórdís saying exactly that, but he nodded and asked her to thank Þórdís for him.

"She says the pandemic is keeping her away, but no one knew about the pandemic in February and she didn't come back then, so I'm a little miffed at her."

"Maybe she's had enough of us. Does she say she'll return once it's over?"

"You know, when I asked her that question, she told me she'd already left Iceland, moving to Denmark, where she's living in the house of her mentor - the battle-ax who stared at us like Moses in drag from her dining room wall. Remember her?"

"Josefine Christophersen-Hemmingsen," Cornelius said. "What's she doing in Denmark?"

"She's back in school, isn't satisfied with her Choke Hold degree, she says."

"Chokkold," said Cornelius, pronouncing it correctly.

"I know, but would you care to guess the name of her new school? It will make you laugh."

"The only thing I know of Denmark is their open-faced sandwiches," he said.

"Ha ha, Mr. Funnybones, then listen up. She enrolled in 'The Hans Christian Andersen Fabulist Therapy Institute!' How much better is that than 'Chokkold?' And don't say 'What's so fabulous about it?' because, when I said it, Þórdís wasn't amused."

"What do they teach there? How therapy can turn ugly ducklings into swans?"

He didn't mean to be facetious, but if he was Mr. Funnybones he thought he better act the part, since he looked like the grim reaper wearing jeans two sizes too big for him.

Millicent dutifully laughed. "It wasn't on the phone, but on one of those video call things that she told me, so I could see her as well as hear her, and by the end of it I was a believer. You will be, too, if you stop being snide."

"I'm a believer now. How could I dislike a school named that?"

In fact, he didn't know much more about Hans Christian Andersen than he did about Denmark. Only that he wrote "The Ugly Duckling," and "The Little Mermaid," stories he read to Phoebe when she was seven years old. When he admitted as much, Millicent said, "Do you remember what 'The Little Mermaid' is about?"

"A mermaid gives up her longevity so she can gain a human soul. When I read it to Phoebe, she said the mermaid had a soul already because she desperately loved the prince."

"Smart girl. If she decides to study therapy, you should send her to the Andersen school. That's what they teach there."

"That we all have souls because we can love?"

"That no one is born ugly or with angst or anger or inferiority complexes, or with the desire to fuck everyone in sight - I think Þórdís threw that last one in for me. They teach that happiness comes from accepting ourselves and getting on with it. I'm sure it sounds simplistic when I say it, but I was thrilled by Þórdís's rendition of it."

"It doesn't sound simplistic, but it does sound old-fashioned. Things like fetal alcohol syndrome or the ravages of our sociopathologies aren't taken into account. We're a lot more ruinous than we were back in Andersen's day."

"'Sociopathologies,' eh? I like that. Þórdís called them something else, but says that they are medical problems and should be treated by psychiatrists, with drugs… In other words, in those cases, according to the Andersen Institute, therapy punts. For grief and loss, though, they teach that it all boils down to the stories we tell ourselves, and that the key to survival is better storytelling."

"But Hans Christian Andersen told his stories un-ironically. They were just about whatever they were about."

Millicent sighed. "It isn't 'The Hans Christian Andersen Fairy Tale Institute.' It's got 'fabulist' in it. And you know what fables have at their ends."

"Morals. They're supposed to be instructive. I remember the one about The Fox and the Grapes from Aesop. A fox can't jump high enough to get the grapes he wants, so he talks himself into believing that he doesn't want them. Is that the kind of moral they mean? I hope not, because sooner or later that fox's grape desire will come roaring back in, and he'll be facing the same old problem."

"Please, I'm imparting Þórdís's beliefs secondhand, while you keep calling them nonsense. I remember the Fox and the Grapes story, too, but I thought it had to do with a crow."

"A crow is in a different fable, and I don't think they're nonsense. I agree that pretty much all we do is tell ourselves stories. I guess I'm just wary of the attributed morals more than of the fables themselves."

"You think too much, that's the moral of your story. And mine is that I haven't thought enough over the years, that I've too often acted on impulse on the one hand, and denied my true desires on the other. Just like your fox. Is it too late for me to stop doing that, Cornelius?"

Her glass was empty, but Cornelius didn't refill it. His physical therapist was due soon, and he wanted a nap before he came. Millicent sensed it, looked around for the bag she brought the pie in, and swept the paper plates and plastic forks back into it. She swept the crumbs in, too, then tied the bag shut, untied it again, and stuffed in the napkins. She poured the last of the wine into Cornelius's glass.

"I'd drink it but I'm driving. Will you rejoin Þórdís's group if she comes back?"

"Wouldn't miss it for the world," Cornelius said. "And it's never too late, Millicent."

When she said she'd see herself out, rather than argue about it he told her there was a path around the side of the house that would take her to her car. She called something back over her shoulder that he didn't catch. It was then that he saw Phoebe in her bedroom with the window slightly open. When he waved she waved back, though she didn't think it was good for him to have visitors, and remembered the doctor saying he ought to cut back on alcohol. That was why she was sitting in the window, not to eavesdrop.

She *had* eavesdropped though, and heard not only the old lady's parting words, but most of their conversation. She remembered "The Little Mermaid," and liked it when he said she said that thing about the mermaid having a soul. She wouldn't put it past him to make that part up, but she hoped it was real since it was such a cool thing to say. It also made her decide to read "The Little Mermaid" to Mary Alice when she was old enough. Only, she wouldn't be able to read it to her if she put her up for adoption, where her name might not even be Mary Alice. She had asked her mother if you could put a baby up for adoption with a name already attached, but her mother'd said she didn't know.

When Cornelius pushed himself out of his chair, she ran down to help him back into the house. She wouldn't ask him the naming-a-baby-before-adoption thing, any more than she would tell him about Eric Junior, but she might ask if she really talked about souls when she was seven years old. And she would tell him what Millicent said before she left, which was, "Call if you feel like dropping by some night."

She might also say, "The lady's hot for you, Grandpa," if he looked up for a little teasing.

8.

Ruthie on Jane

Four more weeks passed before anyone else came to visit, not only because of Cornelius's slow recovery, but because of the pandemic. The nation was in tumult, and in Washington State - with those nursing home deaths up in Kirkland - schools were closed or closing, as were restaurants and bars.

One day in April, however, who should show up without calling first, but Ruthie, wearing a mask and carrying a pizza from the Cloverleaf Tavern. It was one of Cornelius's brief times alone since Emi and Phoebe had gone to interview prospective parents for Mary Alice.

He went to the door without his walker. "Ruthie, what's this?" he said.

He cocked his left hand and shot its index finger at the pizza box.

"I remembered this was your favorite, and I wanted to bring a peace offering," she said. "You're not still mad at me, I hope."

"Mad at you? When was I ever mad at you?"

He led her through the kitchen and out onto the deck. If Emi and Phoebe came back to find her *inside* the house, he'd get another scolding from them. Ruthie said she didn't intend to eat with him, but sat down when he asked her to, admitting that she hadn't yet had lunch.

"Beer? Wine? I think I've got some fruit juice in the

fridge…"

"Just water," Ruthie said. "A Cloverleaf Tavern pizza! I haven't had one in years."

It was the reaction she hoped to get from him, but he was beyond effusiveness now, except in response to the pain inflicted on him by his physical therapist. When he heard her knock he'd been upstairs googling the aftereffects of head injuries. His had been severe. He still had headaches and wore a neck brace at night. Everything he read suggested that three months after his fall he should be more substantially recovered. He asked his various doctors what the problem was, but heard only that recovery often came at a snail's pace.

He brought water, plus napkins and plates for them both.

"You've lost *so much* weight," said Ruthie. "I hope you put it back on. Rudy says that at our age a few extra pounds is just the buffer we need."

"Rudy?"

"Dr. Russo. I knew him before your accident."

Cornelius nodded, but instead of asking more about Rudy, he asked why she thought he was mad at her. "I've been mad at most people in our group at one time or another, but I can't remember ever being mad at you."

He moved a piece of pizza from the box to Ruthie's plate as if to prove the point. He moved another to his own, just for show.

"There's no need to be coy. I've called you a dozen times and you never pick up. You're just like the rest of them. You think I'm scandalous."

"Trust me, Ruthie, I don't think anyone's scandalous. It's just that most of the time I keep my phone turned off. And returning calls is still beyond me."

"Really? If that is true I'm so relieved!"

She ate her piece of pizza in six quick bites. Cornelius took one bite of his.

"Now that I think about it, I guess it's Jane's fault that I thought you were mad at me. When I saw her at the hospital she came right out and said so, or just about."

"Jane's in the hospital? I didn't know that. What's wrong with Jane?"

"Jane's not in the hospital, Sam is. You didn't hear? He's got COVID, and is in dire straits. He's on an incubator and everything."

"'Ventilator,'" Cornelius said. "'Intubation' is how they put you on one."

"That's what I said. Why do you have to clarify everything?"

"Old habits, I guess."

"Well, I can understand that some people think Jane should get a pass with Sam in such bad shape, but I'm here to tell you, she's an outright weirdo. Where does she get off, saying you are mad at me after all the wool she pulled over everyone's eyes?"

Cornelius said he didn't know where Jane got off, and once again insisted that he wasn't mad at Ruthie. He even served her a second slice of pizza. He hoped he might be able to save the rest for Phoebe and Emi when they got back.

"Poor Sam, sitting at home and reading while Jane was up at Pórdís's house, Giancarlo this-ing and Giancarlo that-ing. And now he's at death's door with Jane gearing up to mourn *him!* Can you fathom that?"

"Sam really might die?" Cornelius asked.

"Not 'might,' will! And Jane can't even go to his bedside. She has to look at him through a window. It's enough to make you think that instead of watching your life fall apart you are watching a television drama."

"Poor Jane," said Cornelius. "Poor Sam, too."

Ruthie took a *third* slice of pizza.

"So tell me why Jane said I was mad at you," he said.

"Because you lost Yuki and I lost Ben at about the same time."

"I remember," said Cornelius. "No crime in that."

"Well, she sure thinks there is! She says those of us who lost our spouses last need to get in line when it comes to meeting someone new. She actually said that Frank should be first, Millicent second, and that you, because we are tied regarding grieving time, will be furious with me for jumping ahead in her stupid queue."

Ah, the Rudy thing...

"I couldn't be happier for you, Ruthie. And I don't doubt that Ben would be happy for you, too."

"Ben? Oh, man, when you're wrong you go all in. Ben is spinning in his grave. Not only did I find Rudy, but I'm selling his boat, his motorcycle, even that Porsche I drive around."

"What about Rachel and Yehudi?"

He meant, 'wouldn't Rachel or Yehudi want Ben's toys?' but she misunderstood.

"Believe it or not they *are* happy for me. Rachel's met Rudy, and it turns out Yehudi studied for his Bar Mitzvah with Ezra, Rudy's son."

"Rudy Russo's Jewish?" Cornelius asked.

"Sure he is. Why not? 'Russo' is one of those names that's

derived from a town, Rudy says. People are forever thinking he's Catholic, though."

Cornelius tipped the pizza box closed, then said again that he couldn't be happier for her, prompting her to nod, but then turn the conversation sideways.

"Are you in love with anyone?" she asked. "I mean any one of us?"

Cornelius's mouth fell open. If he wanted to close it again he would have to use a hand. "I love you all," he said.

"You know what I mean. And I think you know *who* I mean, too."

He did, and he didn't. Was she asking about Millicent? Certainly she didn't mean Jane, who was up to her ears in dead and dying loved ones. And LaVeronica or Þórdís were each about a million years too young for him. Was she asking about herself? Had she come to test whether or not her Rudy revelations made him jealous?

Now he did reach up and push his mouth shut. "To give your question the answer it deserves, no, I am not," he said, though the answer it truly deserved was silence.

He laughed. She had asked why he was mad at her, and then proceeded to make him mad at her in about a half an hour.

"Well, I don't believe you. And let me just say that if you don't act quickly you are going to let her get away."

She stood, leaning down and kissed the bridge of his nose, though she was aiming for his mouth. It was the sort of near-miss that she had experienced all her life.

When she walked back through his kitchen he hobbled after her, his anger gone as suddenly as it came, replaced by something like sorrow. But he wasn't able to speak again before she opened his front door and fled down to her car like his house was on fire.

He was slower than she was… slower in more ways than one.

9.

Phoebe and Emi on the Browns

"Mary Alice Brown is no kind of name! Not when you compare it to Mary Alice Williams or Mary Alice MacLeish."

"'MacLeish' in the running now?"

Cornelius had worked his way downstairs again when he heard them come in.

"It is for me," Phoebe said. "Mom likes it, too, but the Browns, OMG! When we said we would only consider letting them adopt her if they called her 'Mary Alice,' their eyes rolled back in their heads. Or Mrs. Brown's did, at least."

A line about Mrs. Brown having a lovely daughter came into Cornelius's head. He didn't try to sing it to them.

"Maybe Mrs. Brown's did, but Mr. Brown was okay," said Emi.

"Only if a doormat is okay. Mrs. Brown rules that house!"

"So the Brown's are out? Did they outright say they want to adopt Mary Alice?"

"Oh, they want her desperately," said Emi. "They even have a room set up for her with dancing bears and such."

Cornelius led them into the kitchen, where the pizza still sat on the counter. He offered to heat it up for them.

"Who brought that?" asked Phoebe, but without waiting for an answer she found a plate, put two slices of pizza on it, and popped it into the microwave.

"It won't be crispy that way," said Emi.

She put a piece in the toaster oven for herself.

"My fellow Mopester, Ruthie, brought it over. She lost her husband around the same time we lost Grandma," Cornelius said. "She was kind enough to check on me."

"I bet she'd be kind enough to do a lot more than that," said Emi.

"Shush, Mom. None of those old women want sex anymore."

` Phoebe pulled her pizza out, saw how limp it was, but started eating it anyway.

"Oh, I don't know. Old people aren't dead yet, right, Dad?" said Emi.

Because of Phoebe's pregnancy, her own marital problems, and his recent health issues, Emi rarely teased. So Cornelius laughed, though he hated ageist jokes.

"Come on, Dad, don't patronize me. It wasn't even funny," she said.

"I was laughing about the Browns," he told her.

"See Mom, even Grandpa knows if we gave them Mary Alice, she'd end up on drugs."

Emi took her pizza out of the toaster oven and carried it over to the table. Agatha was on the chair she wanted, so she shoved her off of it. Cornelius thought that would earn her Phoebe's wrath, but she only took his arm and led him to the table, too, so they could all sit down.

Down at the end of the yard, his willow tree had new shoots of green all over it.

"Spring is the season of rebirth unless you happened to have COVID," he said, then he told them what he heard about Sam, who'd been Jane's husband for half a century, yet wasn't the one she mourned. When he also told them the Giancarlo story he thought they'd be shocked, but they moved right past it.

"Was it Jane who brought the pizza? I thought I heard another name," said Emi.

"You did, you heard 'Ruthie,' Mom," Phoebe said. "Ruthie came over and told him about Jane. That's what these old ladies do. They say they want to visit Grandpa, but really they want to rag on someone else. The first one who came here did that, too."

She smiled at her grandfather, but all of this was putting him out of sorts.

"No one ragged on anyone. We talk about the others because that's our frame of reference, it's how we even know each other. It's not like you two don't go on about...say, Dwayne and his mom, or Roselyn Wilkinson."

"What are you talking about? All we ever try to do is come to a good decision about Mary Alice!" Phoebe nearly screamed.

She burst into tears and ran from the room.

"Smooth move, Ex-lax," said Emi.

Cornelius went after Phoebe, who was slumped in the corner of his hospital bed.

When she looked at him her tears were gone, but their tracks were still visible. Like in the Smokey Robinson song.

10.

Jane on Frank

First off, never mind what Ruthie said, Sam wasn't dead. According to the others he was in about the same condition as he had been a month earlier. Still, Cornelius was surprised to find Jane at his door one Monday in May, unannounced and with something to say to him. He'd been walking around with those final two drawings he slipped and fell with, looking for a place to put them. The living room was too prominent, his bedroom too intimate, the guest room Phoebe's territory, the upstairs hallway too transitory, and his bathrooms out of the question. He was still considering his office, but feared that if he put them in there, he'd do nothing but stare at himself falling through space.

When the doorbell rang he leaned the drawings against a wall. His condition, quite in opposition to Sam's, had improved until he no longer needed his walker or his physical therapist, except on rare occasions. He stretched every morning, and went outside for stints of weeding his various flowerbeds most afternoons. He'd enjoyed gardening with Yuki, and was discovering that doing it alone was okay, also. He still slept in his living room, but expected to get permission to go back upstairs at his next doctor's appointment.

"Jane," he said, when he saw her. "To what do I owe the…"

He stopped before "pleasure," fearing she had come with

news of Sam's death.

"I needed a break, and, well, I feel guilty that I didn't go to the hospital when everyone thought you were dying. But here I am now, apologizing. I wanted a chance to explain that Hob Nob thing you witnessed back in December, as well."

She extended a sack of takeout Thai food from down on Pacific Avenue. It wasn't until she said she hoped he hadn't eaten dinner that he realized how late it was. Not only hadn't he eaten dinner, he hadn't eaten lunch. A continuing and difficult problem, concerning his recovery, was that he hadn't gained any weight back.

He led Jane through his kitchen to the deck, paused a minute, then continued down the outside stairs and across the lawn to the table and chairs beneath the willow. Just yesterday he had trimmed around the tree and washed the chairs and table with his garden hose. Jane wore a mask, which she kept on inside the house, but took off when they both sat down outside.

"Pad thai, lemon grass soup, and some waddaya call 'ems," she said.

"You've thought of everything," said Cornelius.

She pulled out napkins, too, then said, "If I have thought of everything it's a first, for I'm a person who has thought of almost nothing throughout her life."

She gave them each a 'waddaya call 'em' - they turned out to be spring rolls - then opened the pad thai and the individual soups.

"I hear Sam's hanging in," Cornelius said.

"He is, and do you know who is up there staring though the window at him most days? Our dear friend, Frank!"

She said it like it was about the worst thing Frank could

do.

"I didn't know visitors were allowed. I bet Frank said he was Sam's brother."

"You know him well. He even brought a dog once, telling the attending nurse the dog was Sam's 'emotional support animal.' She let them stay until a doctor came by, threw them both out, and yelled at the nurse."

For the first time since his fall, Cornelius let out a genuine laugh. It hurt his still-mending ribs. "I've never known anyone quite like Frank," he said.

"No one has! And I am here to tell you that you still don't know the half of it."

She ate a spring roll, lingered over a spoonful of soup, and said, "Okay, here's the half you still don't know, and why I acted so strangely up at the Hob Nob that day. Once, about three years ago, Sam and I saw Frank at the opera in Seattle. We have been opera lovers since those years we spent in Italy - In Milan we saw La Bohème with Luciano Pavarotti, no less - and the Seattle Opera had La Bohème on for the night I'm talking about now. This is way pre-grievers, at least a year before I fell into the snake pit of Giancarlo delusions, and Frank still hadn't lost Doris. So we didn't know each other, but here's the thing, Frank and Doris were sitting one row in front of us at the opera, talking to another couple who apparently went with them. They were dressed to the nines, the men in tuxes, the women in evening gowns...that happens at the opera sometimes, especially in the orchestra seats. Sam and I, though, always dressed down, as if in counterbalance to the hoity-toities. We were also early, since we wanted to read the libretto notes and also have a full night out."

Cornelius closed his eyes in order to see the picture Jane

was painting.

"Anyway, while Sam read the program, I listened in on the conversation of these four strangers, and who do you think was holding court?"

"Frank, of course," Cornelius said.

"Yes, indeed, but in a distinctly un-Frank way. They weren't talking about the opera but about…get this…'cold fusion,' and what it would mean in terms of stopping global warming if an earlier success in it could be replicated."

She waited for Cornelius to open his eyes again.

"Do you know what cold fusion is?" she asked.

"Nuclear fusion without the heat. Nuclear energy achieved at something like room temperature. I remember someone claimed to have done it couple of decades ago… *That* was what Frank and his friends were talking about?"

"You know, Cornelius, you and Sam could have been great friends. You both know a little about a lot of things. But they weren't talking about a couple of decades earlier. Frank was holding court on recent breakthroughs at *his own lab!*"

If Cornelius's lemon grass soup had been whiskey he'd have spit it out.

"Frank doesn't have a lab," he said.

"Maybe not now, but he did. And he was speaking very knowledgeably."

"The answer is simple. It wasn't Frank. It was someone who looked like him. You just said it was years before you met him properly."

"You don't think I thought of that? At the opera I wasn't only eavesdropping, but studying the four of them. At intermission I saw them again, drinking champagne out in the lobby, but still, when I met Frank at Pórdís's, though I recognized him instantly, I began to doubt myself. I kept my own counsel about it during his 'up' week and my own, but it began to nag me so much that I asked him to meet me at the Hob Nob that morning, drank two Bloody Marys, and asked him straight out, 'Are you a physicist, Frank?' And right after I asked it, you came along."

Cornelius laughed. "Forgive me, Jane, but that's impossible. Come clean now. Did you and Frank concoct this story as a way of cheering me up?"

"It would have been a good concoction, but no. It turns out he's a chemist, not a physicist. If you don't believe me, look him up. That's what I did, and it's quite a story."

"I don't believe you and I will look him up," Cornelius said. "What would make the man you're describing turn himself into the guy who jumped off the Narrows Bridge? We both saw him at the hospital after it. That was no chemist, but a lost and broken man."

"It's the same question Sam asked me, and you just answered it. Frank was, and *is*, a lost and broken man. And I think grief is what not only made him jump off the bridge, but fake being an ignoramus."

"Grief can do a lot of things, but not that."

"Grief can do a lot of things *including* that. I should know. At the Hob Nob, let me tell you, even after you left I questioned him like Perry Mason, but he didn't break character. He only admitted that there was another Franklin Blessing who was his doppelganger, making his life miserable by outperforming him at every turn. Still, I kept at him until he said he was going to get his gun, drive to Seattle, and shoot the other Frank Blessing. I backed off after that, since I took it as a suicide threat from a guy who'd already tried it once."

"And that was it? Nothing more since then?"

"No more confronting Frank, but Sam and I spent a lot of time trying to learn what we could about him and Doris. I said no one spoke much except Frank at the opera, but during intermission, when they were discussing La Bohème, Doris said that the character, Mimi, reminded her of herself a few years back, sick and knocking on Frank's door in search of …but she couldn't come up with the word, so the other woman provided 'succor,' pissing Doris off. She said, 'What are you accusin' me of?!' It took the other woman a minute to understand that Doris didn't know what 'succor' meant, but then she made things worse by saying, 'sustenance, aid, help, relief, support,' with her nose up in the air like one of those prissy ladies from a New Yorker cover. That sent Frank into a rage. He swore at the other woman, turned to Doris, and said in the voice of the Frank we know now, "Come on, darlin', we're gettin' out of here…' Do you see what I'm getting at, Cornelius?"

"Actually, Jane, not quite."

"Frank sounded like Doris then, and he has continued to sound like her since she died. I think it's his way of honoring her, a body and soul homage."

"Come on, Jane, that's impossible, too. We know this guy. And you only heard him say a line or two at the opera."

"A line or two at the opera, but Sam and I discovered that Doris went to Lincoln High School right here in Tacoma, dropped out in the 11th grade, took a course in cosmetology, worked in the University District in Seattle, and met Frank one night when she wandered into a party… I guess, like Mimi in La Bohème, in search of succor."

She waited for Cornelius to scoff, but he only sat there

with his soup spoon in his hand.

"It's amazing what you can find out about a person these days, but ready or not, Cornelius, Frank is either suffering from a deep psychological transference, or he's Lawrence fucking Olivier. I know you'll look them both up after I'm gone, so let me prepare you. Doris Blessing didn't die of cancer, but in the cold waters of Puget Sound, after leaping off the Narrows Bridge. It happened a year or so after we saw them together at La Bohème.

11.

Phoebe and Emi on the Ruckelshauses

As soon as they got to his house, before they could even open their mouths, Cornelius told them everything about Jane's visit. He even had them read the printouts he made of The News Tribune's article on Francis Blessing, the chemist, and on Doris Blessing's bridge jump.

"It never came up during a Mopester meeting?" asked Emi. "That seems odd."

"It certainly didn't. And it still may be that it's a different Frank, but there's no question it was Doris."

"So Frank assumed her personality and told everyone lies about the way she died?"

That was Emi again, intrigued while pretending to be mystified.

"Wow, Grandpa," said Phoebe. "How did Frank say she died?"

They didn't seem nearly as interested in the chemistry part, as they were in the suicide.

"He said she died of cancer, maybe because cancer killed Grandma and Millicent's husband and Ruthie's, so we could relate. Jane's fake husband got hit by a train and, well, you know about Johnny Sylvester."

"Ha ha," said Phoebe, surprising them both.

"I was just thinking of what Dwayne did once back in third grade. He brought newspaper clippings of his mother's trial for 'show and tell.' He was proud of it, and we were all *so* impressed. But what are you going to do, Grandpa? Confront Frank?"

"No, I'm not going to confront him. Chances are the Mopesters will never meet again. But if what Jane said is true, I hope somebody offers him some help."

"How about calling his kids? Or will that take too much out of you, when you're just getting back your strength?" asked Emi.

Cornelius hadn't thought of Frank's kids, but their names popped into his head as soon as Emi spoke - Beatrice and Bucky. Maybe they were Frank's inventions, too.

"Or your therapist. Does she know the story yet?" asked Phoebe.

Though he'd been thinking about Frank since Jane left, he hadn't thought of his kids *or* whether Pórdís knew Jane's story. He was no better at solving the mysteries surrounding him now, than he had been when trying to solve them in the books he wrote. Maybe that was why he stopped writing... maybe he hadn't been good at it.

"Anyway, you didn't come for the latest on Frank," he said. "Tell me about the Ruckelshauses."

"They said we should call them Ricky and Audra," said Emi. "Audra was okay, but Ricky lived up to his stupid name. Ricky Ruckelshaus, jeez!"

"What about you, Phoebs? What did you think?"

"They were fine. They said that they'd be happy to keep "Mary Alice' as a name."

"Mary Alice Ruckelshaus...yikes," said Emi.

'Jeez' and 'yikes' in close proximity. Emi wasn't a Ruckelshaus fan.

"Audra is a nurse and is so tired from taking care of COVID patients all day long that she nearly fell asleep during our meeting," Phoebe said. "And Ricky's the owner of a German tavern called 'Ruckelshaus Haus.' Have you ever heard of it, Grandpa?"

Cornelius said that he had not.

"Do they have a chance?" he asked. "Did they say why they wanted to adopt her?"

"Audra was kicked in the stomach by a mule when she was my age, so she can't have children," Phoebe said. "It made me feel sorry for her. It might be sort of cool if Mary Alice could help heal a wound like that."

"But Ricky!" said Emi. "After we told them that naming her 'Mary Alice' was a part of the deal, he said, 'Good, cause Audra was leaning toward 'Rapunzel.'"

"He was joking, Mom, trying to break the ice. Maybe he wanted to show that he could be a funny dad to Mary Alice. That's what I thought."

"Maybe so, but you know what *I* thought?"

"That divorce is right around the corner. You already told me that a dozen times."

"I did not. I told you once."

"You said that Rapunzel thing was racist, since Rapunzel's hair was blonde and Mary Alice's is going to be black or brown. You went on a rant about it, Mom."

"Ah," said Cornelius.

"Ah what?" Emi demanded. "Are you going to pile on, too, Dad?"

His "ah" meant that not only hadn't he considered whether Frank's kids or Þórdís knew about the two Franks, but he hadn't given a thought to Mary Alice's hair color or skin color or anything else of that nature. It made him proud that he hadn't, but also a little worried. Who didn't think of a thing like that?

"Not piling on, just realizing what Mary Alice will have to face during her life."

"Now you sound like Mrs. Williams. Has she been over here, too, Grandpa? Don't any of you know that there's a pandemic going on?"

"No, she hasn't been here. You must have talked to her though, to be able to tell me that I sound like her."

"Believe me, Phoebe's done her best *not* to talk to her, but Mrs. Williams is a force," said Emi. "Surely you noticed that at your club."

"The Mopesters isn't a club, Mom! Why do you have to put everything down? First you make fun of Mr. Ruck-elshaus, and now the Mopesters, while I thought your only care these days was to not have Mary Alice 'crying up' your house?"

Suddenly - though not for the first time - Cornelius felt ashamed for letting Emi, his only child, slip from under the tender arm of his affection in favor of Phoebe, his only grandchild. He was sure she *had* said "crying up," but he couldn't let that define her.

"Come on, Phoebs, give your mom a break. How many times have you said something you don't mean? I know I've done it just since Grandma died."

His words brought Emi's head up from its gradual sag.

"How do you know I didn't mean it, Dad?" she asked.

"I just do," he said. "We both do, don't we, Phoebs?"

"I guess so," Phoebe said, and that unearthed a ton of emotion in them both. When Emi moved to hold her hand,

Phoebe fell into her arms. Buckets of tears waited just off-stage.

"So what about the Ruckelshauses?" Cornelius asked. "You still haven't said whether you think they have a shot?"

"I don't think I want Mary Alice growing up in a tavern, so probably not," said Phoebe. "Can you imagine all the drinks she'll sneak when she's hanging around behind the bar?"

Her mother said she could imagine it, while her grandfather said that he hadn't given it a thought until now.

12.

Frank on Millicent

By the time Frank came knocking on his door yet another month had passed, during which time communication between anyone other than family members took place by phone or online. Of Cornelius's various illnesses, he was more or less fine now, except for continuing issues with poor balance and with difficulty putting weight back on. Nevertheless, Phoebe kept up her "watchful watchfulness." When she noticed that his balance was poor she told her parents about it, but she kept it to herself when talking to him. He had enough to worry about with her, and she didn't want him worrying about himself.

When Cornelius heard Frank's knock Phoebe wasn't home, so he supposed it was her, key misplaced again and back with news of another failed adoption interview. There had been seven thus far, two since the Ruckelshauses.

Seeing Frank at his door took him back to what seemed like the beginning of all the craziness; the day of Frank's bridge jump. Frank wore a mask with a picture of a guy wearing a mask embossed upon it.

"Hi there, Frank, come in," he said.

"How come you ain't surprised? It's been a month a' Saturdays since we seen each other, Corny," said Frank.

"I am surprised, but please…" He swung the door open wide.

Frank started talking before he was over the threshold. "Where'd you hang 'em, them pictures by the man who cuckolded you? I want you to know, when I heard about that, I told the person who told me that I was never prouder to have such a solid friend. Hanging them pictures, man! If that ain't the pot callin' the kettle black!"

"I wasn't cuckolded," Cornelius said. "But who'd you hear it from?"

"My lips are as sealed as Millicent's weren't when she told me."

He walked into the living room, looking for the drawings.

"As a matter of fact, I haven't hung them," Cornelius said. "They're leaning against the door to my basement."

When he pointed to the kitchen Frank headed in there. "Well, that one's got love written all over it, and the other one looks like you went for a ride in your clothes dryer," he said. "But I'm sure you know as well as I do where they're headed."

Cornelius didn't, and said so. He also said that they should go out to his deck, and offered to put some coffee on. Frank said, "fine" and "fine" regarding the deck and the coffee, then, "They're headed down to your basement, maybe up over the dryer I just mentioned, or next to where you keep your firewood. They're right there waitin' for you to let 'em in."

He walked out onto the deck and sat down. Cornelius looked from the drawings to the back of Frank's head. "Chemist, my ass," he said.

When the coffee was ready he took two cups out, plus milk and sugar and a couple of the same big cookies that LaVeronica brought to the grievers' group that time.

Frank broke a cookie in half, and dunked it in his coffee.

"Are you okay now?" he asked. "I mean you bumped your noggin like you meant business. Tell me you ain't thinkin' of doing it again."

"I bumped my noggin by accident, Frank."

He wanted to dunk a cookie, too - it was something his grandfather did when he was a child. But Frank might think he was making fun. So he left the cookies alone.

"When did you see Millicent? Or was it only a phone call?"

"Oh, I saw her alright, but for a long time she didn't see me."

Frank's smile was salacious and smug, making Cornelius change the subject.

"I wonder if Þórdís will come back, or if we'll have another session if she does."

"I think she will, but Millicent thinks she's gone for good," Frank said.

"What makes you think she will? Did you talk to her, too?"

"No, but Þórdís is invested in us. We are an experiment she's runnin' and she wants to see the result. Like whether or not we mend or bond."

'Bond like in cold fusion?' Cornelius thought to ask.

"We'll mend," he said.

"That makes you a bigger optimist than me, cause I ain't sure about the mendin,' and I ain't bonded with anyone since Doris died 'cept you. Millicent now... She's a better bonder than gorilla glue."

He laughed, but Cornelius had had enough.

"Come on Frank, spit out whatever you have to say about Millicent. That's why you came over here, isn't it?"

"No, I came to be neighborly. I came to see you!"

"Thanks, but I'm fine. I got the 'all clear' from my doctors a couple of weeks ago. Now I'm paying attention to the COVID protocols. How about you, Frank?"

He picked up the other half of Frank's cookie and ate it dry.

"I ain't good at bein' alone, so no, I ain't fine. I stalk my kids, Corny. I bought a car they won't recognize and started following 'em hither and yon in it… Except that there ain't much hither and yon'n goin' on these days."

"Beatrice and Bucky," Cornelius said.

"That's what they asked us to call 'em, but their birth names were Marty and Stanley. Beatrice thought 'Marty' was a boy's name and picked Beatrice for herself, while Stan's teeth came in crooked so he got tagged with Bucky and it stuck."

Cornelius knew a wild ride was coming and he didn't have the energy for it. But it came, ready or not.

"And that car I bought took me spyin' on others, too. I tell you, man, a different car and a new set of clothes, maybe a hat or a pair of glasses, and a person can reinvent himself. Did you ever try somethin' like that? Except in them books you wrote?"

"Not that I can remember. Who else did you follow, Frank?"

"Ruthie and Jane and Pórdís, before she left. Not you, though. And not LaVeronica, neither. That woman scares me. After the virus ruined things, I mainly followed Millicent, since she's the only one who still went out. The final time I did it, she went to The Spar. It was March 16, the day before COVID closed the place, and since it was my last good followin' chance, I went right in after her, wearin' a disguise. I wanted to sit close enough to eavesdrop but not close enough to get caught, so when she took a seat at the bar, I did, too, only a few seats down, so she couldn't get a good look at me."

"Forgive me, but you're not someone people don't notice, Frank."

"Thanks, but that night I was pretendin' to be Doris. She had a bunch of pantsuits that you'd never in your life think I'd put on."

"Wait! You went into The Spar in drag?"

"No, I just told you, I went as Doris. During the last few months of her cancer she had hats that covered most of her head, too, so I wore one of them and I shaved real close. I looked like one of them androgynous types. I ordered a beer, but otherwise kept my verbalizations to a minimum, while down the bar Millicent was one Chatty Cathy. She told the bartender that Jonathan had been friends with this tough old guy who worked at The Spar named Don, and when the bartender told her Don was dead she ordered a burger and three beers, one for Don, one for Jonathan, and one for herself. Can you believe it? If I wanted three beers I'd just order 'em one at a time, but not our Mills."

"And she really didn't see you, peering out from under your 'Doris' costume?"

"No one saw me! One thing I learned that night is that people look straight through an old woman outta fear that they might have to talk to her. Anyway, when the guy sitting beside her asked, 'Why not three burgers, too?' she said, 'because I don't want three burgers worth of guilt around my waist.'

"I thought that was a good one, but when the guy added, 'It's Millicent, isn't it? You don't remember me?' it nearly knocked me off my stool. Are you listening to me, Cornelius?"

"Like a dog listens to his master. What happened next, Frank?"

"Well, the guy was right. She not only didn't remember him, but said she'd never laid eyes on him in her life. I thought, 'Good for you, Mills, you ain't as easy as I thought you was.'

"I asked for another beer myself, but before my beer came the guy started tellin' Mills that he was a friend of Jonathan's from back in the day, that he was a retired judge, if you can believe it, and a three-time loser in marriage. Or a two-time loser if divorce only counts, since his second wife died."

"Holy shit," Cornelius said. "So it wasn't just a pickup line?"

"You say you listen, but you don't, Corny. It weren't no pickup line right from the start because he knew her name."

Frank had finished his coffee, so when he broke another cookie in half there was nothing for him to dunk it in.

"I already said more'n I should, but while Mills ate her burger in that hoity way of hers, the judge drank one of her beers when she offered it, then he told her in his most judicial voice that a common element of property law was that a third beer should be split between the litigants, and, dumb as it was, that won Millicent over. She turned on her stool and coquetted the man, Corny, sayin' he made it seem like they had come to The Spar together to divide up their stuff like some failed, but still speaking, married couple. Well, before they even finished splittin' the third beer, that commenced 'em to arguing over who'd get this or that piece of furniture, who'd get a vase they loved and spent too much money on, even who would get which car. Each of 'em was reasonable or unreasonable in turn, complete with flashes of anger over some long-ago slight, and both of 'em remembered how they loved Streisand and Redford in *The Way We Were*, and how, looking back on it, that story was also theirs. It was the weirdest thing I ever heard in my life, and, as you may know by now, weirdness and I ain't strangers.

"By the time The Spar closed both of 'em were too drunk for anything save goin' home to bed, but when the judge said if they was gonna continue parceling out their stuff they should do it where the stuff resided, Millicent climbed down off her barstool and left with him anyway."

"Good Christ," Cornelius said. "Did you leave the bar then, too?"

"Of course I did. I paid my bill and went outside in time to see them getting in his car and leavin' hers right there on the street. So I followed 'em. The judge lives on Prospect Hill. You ever been there? It's got these windin' roads that don't lend themselves to follow'n, but I did it so I could find out where he lived. When he parked in his garage I went down the street, then made my way back on foot though I was bedeviled by a couple of neighborhood dogs.

"Now, if you can guess what happened next I'll buy you dinner," said Frank.

"Please don't tell me you got caught or watched Millicent and this judge…"

"You don't have to say 'please' for me not to tell you that! I weren't no peepin' Tom! I was a private eye of the kind who don't get caught."

"Well, damn it. What did happen next, then, Frank?"

"The judge didn't close his garage door when they went into his house, that's what happened next. So I went in there and poked around."

"That's trespassing. Breaking and entering. You're getting into criminal territory."

"There weren't no 'breakin' 'cause the garage door was open, Corny, and man, was it ever some garage. This judge - I might as well tell you that his name is Andy Follett - had its walls lined with photos of himself gettin' awards, of him handin' down opinions and sentencing folks to prison, even photos of him up on Mt. Rainier hikin' around in them Swiss yodelin' pants. I mean, he still used his garage as a garage, I knew because his car was in it, but this is some kind of narcissist, this Andy Follett."

"Believe it or not, I've met him," Cornelius said. "And you are talking about a house I've been in. Yuki and I went there once for a Tacoma Arts fundraiser. The guy who drew Yuki was there as well."

He nodded back toward the drawings in the kitchen.

"You mean you was a cuckold and partyin' with the cuckolder at the home of a narcissistic judge?"

"I told you, I wasn't a cuckold, and no, it was long before that. It might have been the night that Yuki and the artist met, the night she realized..."

"Realized what? Come on, man, you been wrapped up tighter'n a drum majorette and right now you started to unwrap. Don't stop, Corny, what did Yuki realize?"

"That she missed her homeland, and maybe he could give it back to her."

"Christ on a step stool! Are you sayin' somethin' fused

between 'em because they were both Japanese?"

When 'fused' popped out of Frank's mouth Cornelius looked him in the eye and said what he thought to say before. "I only hope it was a cold fusion, Frank. I don't know whether you are wrapped up as tight as a drum majorette, too, or so unraveled that you can't get back to where you once belonged. But if there was ever a time to come clean about things, now would be it."

Frank was quiet for a long few seconds, but then said, "I assume you're talkin' about the amazing thing I saw in that garage, Corny. Cause I'm not talkin' about anything else."

After a pause of his own, Cornelius said, "Tell me what you saw in the garage."

13.

Phoebe and Emi on the Moodys

Fourth of July fireworks shot up from boats out on the bay, and from across it at Browns Point. Every year Emi and Phoebe came to watch the fireworks from Cornelius's deck, with or without Donnie. This year they came without him. Also, this year, for the first time in anyone's memory, no clusters of people were allowed in Old Town, and large gatherings were discouraged at people's houses. The pandemic had taken its toll.

Cornelius grilled salmon and corn on the cob, and he made a large Caesar salad, his most energetic efforts in months. Emi brought wine, and Phoebe brought word that her due date hadn't changed. She said, "Dr. Russo told me if I was one week late I'd be giving birth on Labor Day, and I told her that half the reason we even have a Labor Day should be because women go through hell, and what's a better reason for a holiday than that?"

"Nothing, but strangely, you forget the 'going through hell' part the moment you fall in love with your child," said her mom.

Phoebe fell into a waiting deck chair, knocked there by her mother's comment. The fireworks wouldn't begin until dark, and dark didn't come until after nine o'clock during the abomination of nature called daylight saving time.

"Tell me about the Moodys," Cornelius said.

He opened the wine and brought it out with a glass of seltzer water for Phoebe.

"They're a biracial couple. Mr. Moody is black, Mrs. Moody is white, and they've got this nine-year-old Down Syndrome kid named George," said Phoebe. "He told us how much he wanted a baby sister."

"Wow," Cornelius said. "They're using George for sympathy, huh?"

"Mr. Moody's name is James, and Mrs. Moody's name is Janet. She's a ballet teacher and he is the owner of 'Moody's Mood for Love,' a lingerie store," said Emi. "And no, they weren't using George, except to show us how much they loved him."

"Is he a sax player, and maybe a singer, too, this Mr. James Moody?"

Emi and Phoebe both broke out laughing.

"We had a bet! I guess Mom knows you better than me, Grandpa," Phoebe said.

"I told her you'd say something like that, within a minute of hearing the name of his store," Emi said.

"And I thought you'd be too interested in whether or not the Moodys were contenders to show off your secret knowledge of jazz."

"What are you talking about, secret knowledge? Everyone knows James Moody. And of course I want to know if they're contenders."

To his surprise, he was miffed.

"How did Mrs. Moody strike you both?" he asked.

"Mrs. Moody said she'd have Mary Alice in tights and a tutu before she could even walk. She was a beautiful and a nice lady," said Emi.

"But?"

"There are no 'buts.' I think the Moodys fit the bill. Don't you, Phoebs?"

Phoebe gave her a ponderous look. "Mary Alice Moody, though," she said. "Kids will make fun of her name as soon as she starts school. They'll call her moody even when she's happy, and they'll rag at her online."

"Well, I think it's a melodic name," said Emi.

"I do, too," Cornelius said.

"I'll tell you one thing. She's not getting a computer till she's old enough to vote! I'm putting that in the contract."

"Come on, Phoebe. How did they act when you told them the 'Mary Alice' thing? Can you tell me that, at least?" Cornelius asked.

"You tell him, Mom, since you seem to like them so much."

"They said it was a lovely name. And I don't like anyone but you, honey bunch."

Phoebe usually couldn't be cajoled. Attempts at doing so often sent her into an even deeper funk. But this time it worked.

"George said he would stay by Mary Alice's crib every night, singing to her until she fell asleep," she said.

Moody's Mood for Love, no doubt, Cornelius thought.

"So how did you leave it with them?" he asked. "Time is getting short."

"Looks like we'll have a second meeting with Dad there, too, this time at their house so they can show us the room they have for her. Dad might be less fair to them than me, Grandpa, but he agreed to go."

"Why do you think he'll be less fair? He hasn't met a single family yet."

"That's right, he hasn't. How unfair is that?" Emi asked.

"Plus, you know what I found on a paper in his waste-basket when I was taking out the trash the other day?" said Phoebe. "'Mary Alice Cassavetes' written over and over again. Dad wants us to keep her, Grandpa. He just isn't say-ing so out loud."

"Maybe that's right, so here's where we are now," said Emi. "She'll be Mary Alice Moody, Mary Alice Williams, or Mary Alice Cassavetes, with people loving her no matter what."

Cornelius went inside to get the salad. When he came back out the fireworks were starting in three different spots. He couldn't help thinking that each set of fireworks was cel-ebrating one of Mary Alice's possible names.

He also couldn't help wondering what *he* truly wanted her name to be when she was old enough to vote.

14.

LaVeronica and Dwayne on Ruthie and Mary Alice

Two days later Cornelius was upstairs answering an email from Pórdís when his phone rang beside him on his desk. If it hadn't been LaVeronica calling he would not have answered, but he was typing her name into his email just as the phone rang, and that made it seem portentous. Before Yuki's death he'd have considered it coincidental, but he was different now.

"Hi, I was just now thinking of you," he said.

"Good," she said. "Come open your front door and you can see me, too."

He'd been telling Pórdís that each of her North End grievers had visited him *except* LaVeronica. He saved his email, went downstairs, and opened his door to find LaVeronica's right hand firmly grasping Dwayne's left forearm.

"Let's go through to the backyard where the breeze will keep us safe," he said.

"Sure," said LaVeronica, while Dwayne hunkered down.

While he led them through his kitchen he hoped they wouldn't notice the drawings. "Go on down beneath my willow tree," he said, "I'll bring drinks."

"We don't want drinks," LaVeronica told him, so they all went down to the willow, pulled out chairs and sat in them.

Cornelius saw right away that he'd left his deck door open and went back to close it lest his cat get out. He told them

Agatha was still grieving over Yuki. It wasn't true, but he wanted a moment to gather himself in case they'd come to talk about Mary Alice. When he got to his deck he went inside and closed the door. What if he didn't go back? Was there a chance they would leave by his side gate? He opened the door again, yelled that he was getting himself a coffee, and made his offer of drinks again.

"No thanks," said LaVeronica.

"I'll take a coke," said Dwayne.

Since he didn't have a coke, he grabbed a bottle of sparking water, poured himself a coffee and went back outside.

"It's effervescent, at least," he said about the water, while LaVeronica said, "You'll never guess who called me this morning."

Cornelius shrugged.

"A woman named Ruth Stern, whom I had never heard of. It wasn't until she mentioned you that it dawned on me..."

"That she was our Ruthie?"

"We're not supposed to call her that, since it was the name Ben saddled her with. Now she wants us to call her Ruth Stern... And she called Ben her 'ex,' too, not her 'late' husband."

There was no one else to share his surprise with, so Cornelius looked at Dwayne, who had slid down in his chair until his butt was halfway off it.

"Posture, Dwayne," his mother said.

"She told me she was 'with' a guy named Rudy now, and that she considered herself 'well and properly suited' for the first time. Who talks like that?"

"She was here a while ago, and Rudy is Dr. Russo, who drilled the holes in my head."

"Lord save us!" LaVeronica said, "And Dwayne, sit back up!"

"How come Ruthie called you? I don't remember you being close during meetings."

"Since she's busy killing her past, I figured she thought I might understand it because of Johnny. But when she told me why she was calling, I just about hung up on her."

Cornelius knew she was waiting for him to ask why Ruthie called her, and when he wouldn't do it, LaVeronica said, "You tell him, Dwayne. Tell him how far we've all fallen, and how we'd better get back up before the roof caves in!"

The feeling Cornelius had when he opened his door - that Dwayne was in trouble - came back.

"Why do I have to tell him?" Dwayne asked. "She's you guys's friend."

"Because she talked to you first, baby, now don't make me ask you again."

"Well, one of you better tell me," Cornelius said.

His irritation surprised him. For the first time since December he wished that Pórdís were there so she could straighten things out.

"She asked us to consider something," LaVeronica said. "What did she ask us to consider, Dwayne?"

"Letting her adopt Mary Alice. I thought she was Mrs. Moody so I said okay, since Phoebe already said that the Moodys were okay with her," said Dwayne.

"She told him she was Ruth Stern, but he decided she was Mrs. Moody!"

"I said a hundred times, Mom! I heard about the Moodys! I only forgot their name."

"Well, that's part one," LaVeronica said. "Now here comes

part two. When I got on the phone and found out who she really was, I just about tore her a new one. What did she think, that I would let a seventy-five year old white woman raise my only grandchild? Where did she get off, and who did she think she was? Stuff like that. All good questions, too. You would have done the same thing, right?"

"The same thing and more," Cornelius said.

"Good! But then, when I was in the middle of it, she started saying she had grown kids and that one of them, her son, married a black girl who can't have children, and wouldn't it be perfect if we let that son..."

"Yehudi," said Cornelius.

"Yeah, wouldn't it be perfect if we let Yehudi and his barren black wife adopt Mary Alice! She said they would give her the best education, a Bat Mitzvah... She even said they wouldn't change her name to Sarah if that was, as she heard, a dealbreaker. By then I'd have wrung her skinny chicken neck if I could of gotten my hands around it."

Dwayne started laughing, so Cornelius did, too, first out of sympathy for the kid, but then for real. LaVeronica had worked up a strong head of steam, so was the last to come around. But soon all three of them were laughing beneath the willow tree.

"Tell him what the thing of it was, Mom," Dwayne said.

"The thing of it was, I didn't believe she called us on behalf of her son and his wife. I still thought she was calling for herself and her dumb-assed beau, and used Yehudi as a fallback when I yelled."

"And so?" said Dwayne.

"And so, to make her admit it I doubled down, saying that Phoebe and Emi and Dwayne and me would be happy to meet Yehudi and his wife on the chance that it might work out."

"Tell me you didn't say that!" Cornelius said.

"She did, and now she's in over her head because Yehudi and his wife are for real and she hasn't told Phoebe or her mom about them yet."

"So you came over here because you want me to tell them?"

"No! You know me well enough to know I clean up my own messes. We came over to ask if we could meet them here, if we have to, in your backyard."

"Mom and Mrs. Moody both agreed on that," Dwayne said. "They think you are fair and that your house is neutral territory."

"Not Mrs. Moody, Dwayne! Mrs. Stern!"

Cornelius didn't know what to say so he did what he always did and started talking.

"I'm not fair, I'm biased. And my house is not neutral territory. I don't want Mary Alice having a Bat Mitzvah, and I can't stand the idea that Ruthie would be her grandmother. So if you must have a meeting, have it somewhere else."

He stopped and glanced up into his willow tree, as if looking for support.

But the tree was as quiet as a mouse.

15.

Pórdís to Everyone

The email Cornelius was answering when Dwayne and his mother showed up, turned out to be the same email, with variations, that Pórdís sent to each of her North End grievers. So though it appeared to be personal, it later came to light that everyone received a rather generic farewell. That irked Cornelius, but it also bonded him with the others in ways that would not have happened without such a note.

The note read as follows:

Dear Cornelius (or Millicent, Frank, Jane, Ruthie, LaVeronica)

I am writing from a room in Copenhagen that once belonged to my mentor, Josefine Christophersen-Hemmingsen, whose photo hung on the wall of our therapy room (aka my dining room) in Tacoma.

When I was her student she urged me to come here (not to this room, but to Denmark) to properly study the therapeutic tools she used so expertly when helping people answer the question, 'What becomes of the broken hearted?" Do you remember that old song?

So when the pandemic hit, and when I couldn't deal with a man whose affections I both spurned and encouraged - on again, off again, like a water spigot - I decided she was right and hightailed it over here, with a brief stop in Reykjavik to catch my breath. And now I am sleeping in her old bed, surrounded by her old books, in a house that belonged to her parents and now belongs to her younger brother, Einar, and his wife, Annegrete, who plays ABBA tunes all day long - an

ABBA freak at this late date, if you can believe it! But both of them are kind, and urge me to tell them all I can of Josefine's life in Iceland, which, it turned out, she told them almost nothing about in letters that she almost never wrote. So I talk about her, go to virtual classes at the Hans Christian Andersen Fabulist Therapy Institute, and listen to ABBA tell me that Chiquitita was enchanted by her own sorrow, a condition that I believe afflicts you, too, my dear Cornelius. You are the Chiquitita of the grievers, did you know that? Some therapists use the word 'drowning' when describing how grieving people feel about their losses, and some do drown, but my advice to you is to consider the word 'enchanted' when dealing with yours, for it seems to me that you embrace, desire, and are seduced by your sorrows, Cornelius… Put that all together and what do you get? Not bibbidi-bobbidi-boo, like in Disney's 'Cinderella,' but 'enchanted,' like in ABBA's near accusation of Chiquitita. But from me, concerning you, it's not a 'near' accusation, it's a direct one, for I think you think that if you look upon it as enchantment you will disarm its mystique, bring it out from behind its heavy curtain, like Dorothy did with her own enchantments in Oz.

Okay, enough with the Hollywood references and the ABBA ones. Josefine's young sister-in-law, Annegrete, likes me. And when I say likes me I mean 'likes me, likes me,' for she whispers through my door at night, sometimes asking 'Are you sleeping?' or 'Do you hear this old house creaking so forlornly?' I can't tell her that I'm asleep if I am asleep, of course, so I tell her that I'm not when I am not, and also that I like old-house sounds. I tell her this through the door, for if I open it I fear that I will also be opening a can of worms that I have thought of opening previously, but have never actually opened. Too many variations on the word 'open' in that sentence, but you get my meaning… This is my confession to you, after sounding off about you for too long. What if I fell in love with Annegrete? Would that not be one helluva turnaround? Would I then feel compelled to console Einar over the loss of his wife, like I consoled you concerning yours? I bet Josefine would disown me if I did that, and I also bet that Einar would throw me out of the house. So I will listen to Annegrete's entreaties but leave my door closed. Is that a cowardly way out, or a wise one?

When my course is finished I will stay in Denmark or return to Iceland, for in both countries Fabulist therapy is finding a foothold, while Americans are too skeptical for stories to work their wonder anymore. I nearly wrote 'cynical,' but though you have all been skeptical of the things I tried to tell you, only one or two of you have been cynical…one for sure, who isn't you, and you if there are two. So now I've given you a little guesswork as my final assignment.

I wish I had known what I know now when we had our sessions. If I had I would have used more parables, stories, fables, rhymes, even songs, to bring my therapeutic points home, not because I think your grief isn't worthy of the deepest probing, but because the deepest probing doesn't come when one faces others in a group - I have come to believe - but when one is alone. And parables, stories, fables and such, are medicines that one can more readily take home. None of us are unique in this world, Cornelius, however much we like to think so. Each of us is a variation on a theme, each a reconstruction, imagined and reimagined, like the billions of stars and planets in our nighttime sky. That is what the H. C. Andersen Institute teaches us.

I'll close now, for I am going with Einar and Annegrete to see Swan Lake. The ballerina playing Odette, the princess-swan, is a friend of theirs whom I have met. Her name is Ingeborg Ingeborgsen. Einar and Annegrete both have what you would call "crushes" on her, though both would be offended were I to accuse them of it. So I will leave you with the promise that I won't write again until one or another of them has won Ingeborg's heart. That will be something to look forward to, will it not, a new love story from me?

With warm affection,

Þórdís Jakobsdóttir
Fabulist-in-training
H. C. Andersen Institute
Copenhagen, Denmark

16.

Donnie on Mary Alice

Donnie called to ask if Cornelius would like to take a walk with him down along the waterfront. To his surprise - since he had never much warmed to his son-in-law - Cornelius was glad to hear from Donnie, maybe because he hadn't been out of his house, except for medical appointments, or maybe because something in his makeup, since his accident, had softened toward people who saw the world in starkly different ways than he did. In either case, he said they should meet at the fish market by Old Town Dock, walk down Ruston Way, and walk back.

Donnie had got there first and was standing outside his car.

"Thanks for this, thanks for meeting me," he said.

Donnie's ever-ready earnestness was part of what put Cornelius off. Emi often said that she, too, wanted to kill her husband when he tried to say he understood her during an argument.

"I'm glad you called. I miss walking, and I need someone to help me get back on track," Cornelius said. "Getting old's no fun, Donnie. There's not enough to look forward to, and too much looking back."

Donnie, however, was as incapable of pessimism as a duck was of staying dry.

"Well, there's no law against looking back, but you've got

a lot to look forward to, Cornelius. Mary Alice is coming!"

They headed toward Point Ruston, a new development that sat atop the grounds of the old Asarco smelter. The Town of Ruston had been the victim of arsenic-laced smoke from that smelter for a century, and now it was the beneficiary of high-end condos and apartments that few of its residents could afford. A deadly pollution replaced by a aesthetic one, Cornelius thought.

"If we walk to the ferryboat it's two miles," Donnie said. "Four miles round trip."

He pointed toward a permanently docked old ferry that they couldn't see yet.

Such a distance had once seemed easy for Cornelius and Yuki, the whole thing doable in a little over an hour. Now, however, he felt like he couldn't go half that far. Just as he was about to admit as much, Donnie said, "My daughter is about to have a daughter of her own, and I don't know what to do about it, Cornelius."

Cornelius looked at the low-hanging clouds. "You seem to think the baby's name is secure," he said. "I'm guessing that means you want Phoebe to keep her."

Donnie stopped, though their walk had only just begun.

"It didn't mean that, at first. I only suggested that they call her Mary Alice because I knew Emi would hate the names, and the felonious mother of the baby's father would hate them even more. Dumb as it seems, I figured it would spur them all toward adoption. But now everyone calls her Mary Alice, like she's someone we know."

"Yeah," Cornelius said. "It makes her closer to you. I feel that."

"It makes me close to her, makes me worry about her, and

start looking forward to taking her to the park. Yet Emi and Phoebe keep finding people who want to adopt her. They roped me into meeting one couple…you know about that, I suspect."

"The Moodys. You went to their house. How did it go?" Cornelius asked.

They had started walking again.

"You want to know how it went? It broke everyone's heart, that's how it went. They had a crib and a mobile set up with ducks and bunnies and such. They had a music box with four different nursery rhymes, all coordinated to four different colors. On top of that, they're good people, waiting for our decision like their lives depend on it. And it isn't even 'our' decision. Somehow that belongs to Phoebe alone. How did such a thing happen? She's fourteen years old! When did I lose my ability to help her grow up, or give her advice on anything at all?"

When they got to the Les Davis fishing pier they turned and walked out onto it, to look over its railing at the water. A small harbor seal poked its head up out of a swell. Nobody knew, not even the rain, that it was same seal that had popped up next to Jane.

"I don't know when we lose our ability to help others, and I don't know how," Cornelius admitted, and then, to his mild surprise, he told Donnie about Ruthie's call to LaVeronica, and that she and Dwayne had visited him.

Donnie had his elbows on the railing. He didn't ask questions, nor frown at the mention of LaVeronica, nor laugh at the mixup over Ruthie's name. He simply listened like Solomon listened to the women who claimed to be the mother of the same child.

"Why did you tell them they couldn't meet at your house?" Donnie asked. "Don't you see how that will cause more difficulties for everyone?"

In truth, Cornelius didn't know why he'd been so against it. And now, before Donnie's version of Solomon, he felt ashamed of himself.

"I don't know. I'm sick and with sickness comes exhaustion that not only overwhelms me but feels like a permanent condition. I feel it today. I'm surprised I could walk as far as this pier."

"Every stage of life feels like a permanent condition when you're in it. You haven't figured that out yet?" Donnie asked.

"I don't know if Emi and Phoebe even know about it yet, but I'll call them when I get home and offer my house for anything they want," Cornelius said.

"And I'm meeting them in the next couple of hours. I'll tell them that when it comes to the Moodys, they really do have to shit or get off the pot."

That didn't sound very Solomonesque, but Cornelius nodded.

17.

Millicent on Frank and Judge Follett

"Of course I know Yehudi. When Jonathan and I went to dinner at Ben and Ruthie's he sometimes ate with us. And I've met his wife. We went to their wedding. Her name is Bess."

Cornelius and Millicent were on WhatsApp or Facetime, he wasn't sure which because she called him. He'd been sitting in his office again, this time trying to write the beginning of a memoir. Never mind that memoirs were generally abhorrent to him, he wanted to capture Kyoto in 1972, his first encounters with Yuki, their love and eventual marriage. He hoped he might write his way into knowing who his wife was, into understanding this un-understandable thing that plagued him now.

But Millicent hadn't called to talk about Ruthie. She'd called to talk about Frank. Still, she answered Cornelius's question and asked, in turn, "Why? Did something happen to Yehudi?"

"It's more like something didn't happen," he said, then he told her everything he knew about Bess's inability to conceive.

"Poor Bess," said Millicent. "And poor Yehudi, too."

That was as enthusiastic as Millicent was likely to get. She'd already used her daily quota of it, talking about Judge Follett at the beginning of their conversation. Cornelius pretended surprise when she did that, until she said she knew about Frank's foray into the judge's garage and his eventual visit to Cornelius. How did she know about it? Because Frank told her.

"Frank's a busy guy," Cornelius said.

"Andy wanted to have him arrested. I mean, who invades a judge's garage whether the door is left open or not?"

"That would be Frank. He's got a deeper well of disturbances than the rest of us," Cornelius said. "But I guess congratulations are in order. I met Judge Follett once, you probably heard, when Yuki and I went to his house for a fundraiser."

"So you know whence I'm calling. That's what I like about you, Cornelius. A person doesn't have to explain too much."

"One thing I don't know, is what Frank got so worked up about in that garage."

"Really? He didn't tell you? That's why I'm calling."

"He wanted to tell me but he was being coy, so I feigned disinterest."

"God, that is *so* you! Yuki must have been a saint."

Irked again, Cornelius said, "Just tell me what was in the garage."

"As you know, Andy was the presiding judge at LaVeronica's trial and, well…maybe he got a little more into it than he should have, but he saved everything that was ever written about it, and I mean every snippet, from newspapers and magazines far and wide."

"And he hung them in his garage? That sounds more like relegating than anything else."

"Ha! I told him that, too! And he *was* relegating them, only maybe not fast enough. First he hung them in their den and even in their bedroom - he was married to his second wife at the time. It was part of the reason she divorced him. When she moved out he transferred the clippings to the garage, I guess as proof that his ex was wrong. He says now, after Frank got in there, that he should have thrown them out."

"I'm sorry, Mills, but what are we talking about here? It sounds like the story of a judge who was proud of his most famous case."

Since they were on camera he could see her pained expression.

"I am trying to be sensitive. Do I have to spell it out? Frank got it right away."

Cornelius nearly said that she did have to spell it out, when the smoke blew away from his addled brain. "Wait! Did something happen between them? Did the judge have a thing for LaVeronica?"

"Don't sit there telling me she didn't tell you. Everyone knows how close you are."

"Close, not close... All we ever talk about is Phoebe's coming baby."

"Then define 'thing.' He didn't walk in on her when she was taking a bath.... He wasn't some new Johnny Sylvester in her life, if that's how you define it."

"No matter how anyone defines it, it's scandalous! I believe what LaVeronica did was justifiable. She was defending her ground, or 'standing' it, or whatever. But your Judge Follett sent her to prison and then...? Come on, Millicent, what did he do, follow her around in his car?"

"Now you sound like Frank! Damn it, we are talking about a dignified man, an elected official, an officer of the court. All his 'thing' amounted to, past the collection of those clippings, was visiting her in prison *once,* to see how he might help with her - and I'm quoting him now - with her 'post incarceration life.'"

She waited for him to say what Frank did - "You mean he went to see if he could fuck her when she got out!" but Cornelius said only, "You told me that was a quote for a reason, and the reason is you think your judge is lying about that visit."

"Jesus Christ, I quoted him because that was what he said. I don't think he's lying! Why do you have to be such a peculiar man?"

"Do you love this judge?"

"Well, I'm here at his house, looking out at the morning sun."

"And are you feeling uninspired?"

She paused before admitting that she was.

"How can I deal with the fact that all the roads I choose turn out to be dead ends, Cornelius? How can I face a thing like that at seventy years old?"

Her confession made him realize that of all his fellow grievers, Millicent was the one who kept him most off balance. Probably because she was the most like him. Never mind seventy, was he facing something like that now, at seventy-five? Was that why he was trying to write a memoir? So that he might rewrite his life?

"I can't answer that for you, Mills, but I will tell you that I think Judge Follett visited her for one reason only; because he thought his sentence was wrong. I don't think it was a 'thing.' I think he went to ask if he could help her as an apology. And I think he kept those clippings to teach himself not to make the same mistake again."

Millicent put her head in her hands, her elbows on the arms of her chair...probably Judge Follett's chair, in Judge Follett's home office.

"So, you think he hung them in self-flagellation, a mortification of the flesh without the flesh, so to speak."

"How you come up with the things you say is beyond me, Mills, but yes, I do. Are you going back home now? I can't help hoping so."

"Where else do I have to go?" said Millicent, after a pause.

If he said his door was always open would she misunderstand? Was the treadmill she was on more like a Mobius strip, not only going round and round but also upside down?

"My door is always open to you, I hope you know that," he said, "but right now I've got a piece of writing that I'd like to get back to."

When she asked him what he was writing, he found himself doing what he *never* did, and describing it to her in detail.

18.

Cornelius on Love

He spent so much time thinking about his talk with Millicent that he didn't get back to his memoir until the next day. But when he did, he was surprised to find its opening paragraphs better, in a way, than he thought they'd be:

I was nine years old and in bed with my grandmother in the rundown old house where my parents often parked me, when I first got the feeling that I had been there before, also at nine years old, but something like a decade earlier.

Grandma's dentures were in a glass on the edge of her sink in the bathroom. I could see them through a partially open door. We were together in her twin bed. The other bed was empty because Grandpa was in the hospital. When he was home I slept in the living room, but I'd begged Grandma to let me sleep with her that night, not only because I was afraid in the living room, but because I loved her as much as it was possible for a person to love another person, and she, though she had other grandchildren, loved me in that same way...that is to say, she loved me best. My mother's theory on it was that Grandma lost her youngest son, Cornelius, four months before my birth, and therefore transferred her love for him to me. Uncle Cornelius was killed during World War II. I heard a ton of stories about him, he was my mother's baby brother, after all, but I didn't begin to get the idea that I might actually be my dead uncle, until that night. It wasn't the greatest feeling in the world for a kid to have, but I let it stick around.

Indeed, he must have let it stick around, for though he

meant the memoir to chronicle his life with Yuki, he started with his grandmother, and by admitting he was named after his dead uncle. It wasn't that the origin of his name was a secret, only that he'd thought he was past it.

Cornelius's desire to get back to Yuki, made him resolve to quit the nine-year-old portion of the memoir in four pages, thus aging himself from nine to twenty-five in a couple thousand words. Still, he couldn't help thinking that the visits from Yuki's ghost were planted back when he was nine and spent so many nights at his grandmother's house. Hadn't she come to him when he was unconscious in his hallway, after all, to lead him back to wherever he was now, to keep him, as it were, from cashing in his chips?

He had only just asked himself that question when Phoebe blew through his front door like a pregnant bomb about to go off.

"Grandpa!" she bellowed. "Grandpa, come here right now!"

He walked out of his office behind Agatha, who ran downstairs to Phoebe's urgent cries.

"What happened? Why are you screaming? Are you okay?" he asked.

"Okay? What okay? Are you kidding me?! I'm having a baby in six weeks and I hear I have to meet *more* people who want to adopt her, *more* baby-stealers arranged by you, Grandpa! Oh, oh, oh! Aggie, let's get out of here, leave this backstabber alone!"

"What are you talking about? I didn't arrange anything. All I did was listen when Dwayne and his mom came over."

"So you *do* know! Dwayne isn't having this baby, Grandpa, I am! I get to decide things! I should never be the last to know!"

"Of course you shouldn't, but listen, honey, the time for deciding things is over. If you're having a baby soon, then whoever adopts her should know about it with time to spare. Time to get ready, I mean."

"Stop saying 'a baby!' Her name is Mary Alice!"

"Okay, listen. I took a walk with your dad the other day, and this 'Mary Alice' business stood over and under and around everything he said. It made me think that we've been seduced by the name, letting it give her a place in our family. But if the Moodys, or these new ones...if they adopt her, then making them call her Mary Alice is a bad idea, sweetheart. It's cheating them out of a right they would normally have as her parents."

Phoebe would have crumpled if she hadn't been as big as a dirigible. As it was, she leaned against the wall and slowly slid down it, her legs splayed out across the floor and her hair hanging over her face.

"What if they name her Myrtle or Helga? Oh god! What if they named her Francine!"

Cornelius struggled to navigate the stairs and sit down on the floor beside her. "You'd be better off saying Myrtle or Helga are out, than by making them name her Mary Alice," he said. "And I don't think 'Francine' will be in the cards."

"I knew you and Dad went for a walk. Dad likes you better than you like him, Grandpa."

"I like him fine. What'd he say about the Moodys? And what did you all think of the room they set up for her, whatever her name turns out to be?"

"Mom said the room was 'generic,' like a baby's room in a furniture store. Dad said it was worse. He said it reminded him of those 'staged' rooms that real estate agents think look nice but really look horrible, with slinky curtains everywhere. He also said he didn't like that Mr. Moody was so much older than Mrs. Moody because he might die and leave Mrs. Moody to raise Mary Alice by herself. Mom said that he wasn't allowed to say that because it was ageist, so they fought on the ride home. Both of them think we ought to cut the Moodys loose, though."

"What about you? What did you think after the visit?"

"I didn't care how old Mr. Moody was. I mean, you're a lot older than him and you could raise Mary Alice if you had to. And I liked them both. But I double-down hated the room, for the reasons Mom and Dad said, but also because I've seen a room exactly like it before, and do you know where? At Roselyn Wilkinson's house! You put a baby in that room and she'll grow up to be like Roselyn, so the Moodys are out with me, too, even if it's unfair."

"Then why did you burst in here in such a state? Was it only because you heard about Ruthie's son and daughter-in-law?"

"*Only because!!* Isn't that enough? Here I thought I was in the clear after the Moodys, when along comes Dwayne's mom and YOU, with a whole new set of wannabe parents. How do you think it made me feel to be blindsided like that?"

"I can see how it made you feel. I wasn't thinking and I'm sorry. I promise I'll be more on top of things from now on."

Past experience made him believe that Phoebe would show her forgiveness by falling into his arms. But she didn't. Rather, she pushed the hair out of her eyes, grabbed his forearm, and said, "How about we help each other stand up?"

"Okay, but you've gained 50 pounds and I've got bad knees, so it won't be easy."

"Forty pounds," she said, but it took a minute for him to stand, and another for Phoebe to get her legs far enough under her to help him when he pulled her up.

"Okay, here's what we're gonna do," she said. "We're going into the kitchen for some food, then you are calling Ruthie or Dwayne's mom, or whoever you have to call, to set up one meeting with these new people. One! With them and me and Mom and Dad and you. No one else except Dwayne's mom, but not Dwayne, unless he insists, which he won't. We'll pick a nice day and stay outside. We'll see what these people are like and then we'll decide. Period and finito, as you used to say. How come you don't say it anymore, Grandpa?"

"Dunno," he said, though, for the life of him, couldn't remember saying it at all.

"And if they have a room set up for her then, to be fair, we'll go see the room, but after that we say yes or no, and if it's no we'll take it as a sign that Mary Alice is supposed to be raised by me. Is that a deal?"

"It's a lot of people to have over here in the middle of a pandemic. I already know one person who died of COVID, Phoebs. But okay, it's a deal if we don't mingle and if we set the meeting for an hour."

"You mean, like, give them a start time and a stop time? That's a great idea, especially if Dwayne shows up, cause then I won't have to see his dumb face for any longer than I have to. So one o'clock to two o'clock."

"Dwayne doesn't have a dumb face, sweetie. Dwayne is handsome."

Phoebe thought about arguing, but then it occurred to

her that Mary Alice might have that very same face, so she conceded the point.

19.

Prison Visit Fallout

When Millicent called her the following Saturday, LaVeronica thought she was doing so in order to lobby for Ruthie's son, and was curt.

"Of course, I remember you, do you think I'm demented?" she asked, after Millicent identified herself.

"Actually, I think you're the least demented of us all," Millicent said. "But that might only be because you're younger."

"What do you want?"

LaVeronica intended the curtness. She didn't want the thrust and parry of talks like this one. What she wanted was to get on with her life.

"I realize that it's early. Perhaps I picked a bad time, but there's something I want to ask you," Millicent said. "Should I call back?"

"Unless it has to do with Ruthie, you better ask now," LaVeronica said.

Of all the North End grievers she liked Millicent least, with her prissy name and her self-satisfied manner. She tried to think why she even joined, but came up empty-handed.

"Okay, do you remember Andy Follett?" Millicent asked.

LaVeronica nearly said, 'Of course I remember him, do you think I'm demented' again, but the question so shocked her that she eased up. "I do if he's 'Judge' Andy Follett," she said.

"He's emeritus now. These days he mostly sits around his house, mulling over his old cases," she said.

She paused, before adding, "I won't say he's obsessed with you. That would be unfair, though it might not be untrue. But he is obsessed with your case. He thinks he judged it wrong."

"I have nothing to say about Judge Follett."

"I know how intrusive I am being, to bring it all back up. And on the phone, no less. I am sorry for the call."

If that was a tactic it was a good one, since LaVeronica, like most of us, was more susceptible to cards laid on the table than those played close to the chest.

"I will say that he didn't actually judge me, the jury did that," she said. "And my sentence was prescribed, so in that, too, there wasn't much he could do about it."

"So you liked him? I mean, you think he did a good job?"

"He did his job: good, bad, or indifferent. The bone I had to pick was with Donnie Cassavetes. You know who he is, I suspect."

"Cornelius's son-in-law and the prosecutor who made a name for himself with your case. But Andy Follett's house is full of everything that was ever written about you, and when I try to talk to him about it, he clams up." She paused again before making a fatal mistake. "Do they have conjugal visits at the prison you were in? They do, I bet."

"As a matter of fact they do," LaVeronica said. "Washington is one of only four states that allow them. If you can name the other three, I'll send you a crate of lemons to suck on."

She then hung up uniquely, by putting her phone on mute, shoving it into the pocket of her jacket and hanging it in a closet between two belonging to Dwayne. After that, she went upstairs to where Dwayne was watching TV, sat down beside him and took both his hands in hers.

"This is a long time coming, but I want to tell you something about your father," she said.

Dwayne turned off the TV. Even as his body raged with hormones, his eyes were like they had been when he was a little boy.

"Well, you know he was a musician. And you remember that your trombone belonged to his father, who played with a lot of famous musicians."

"Don't tell me what I already know, Mom," he said.

"He adored you. But after what happened with Johnny Sylvester, he didn't adore me."

"No he didn't adore me! I don't know if he's alive or dead."

"He's alive but incarcerated, baby, for trying to do to me, what I really did do to Johnny."

Dwayne jerked his hands away like the shock he had been waiting for throughout his life came flashing into his body from the base of his chair.

"Maybe you're not ready for this, with everything that's going on with Phoebe, but I don't want you hearing it anywhere else."

She felt a moment of cold hatred for Millicent, whose dithering around the edges of what had happened scared her into this confession. That Dwayne *wasn't* ready was as plain as the fact that Phoebe was pregnant. But he wouldn't let her stop now.

"Back when I was in prison he took care of you like the best dad in the world, but he was also planning his...revenge,

I guess you'd call it…on me. Whenever he visited me he brought you along, until one day he didn't. Wait, let me back up. The reason he could bring you, was that Washington has these things called 'Extended Family Visits,' and he applied for them. So we were all together every week. Again, until we weren't."

"I don't remember that. I don't remember that he took care of me, either. I don't remember anything about him except that he took me to the store once."

"Of course you don't, honey, all of this happened before you were old enough. But at the time you loved him more than you did me. And I didn't know you remembered him taking you to the store. What did you buy?"

"He bought cigarettes, but what happened next? The time he didn't bring me."

"On that day we planned what's called a 'conjugal visit.' It means when a husband visits his wife, or a wife her husband, or I don't know, any couple maybe…they can spend a few hours in bed together, making love."

Dwayne spit out, "Love's what Phoebe and I had, Mom, not you and my dad!"

"Okay, sex then, but please let me finish. There'd been no sex between us, except for a bumbling time or two, since you were born. But we talked about it during the visits when you came with him, telling each other that a conjugal visit might set things right again. So one day they gave us four hours alone in a room with a bed and four walls."

"One hour for each wall," said Dwayne.

"Yes, and a different couple might have had sex four times, but not us. I got to the room first, had fifteen minutes to settle in, which, in my case, meant calm down. I brought a nightgown that I changed into so I'd be ready. Only I wasn't ready. I feared this visit, Dwayne! I wasn't lying when I said I hoped the visit would set us on the right track. It's just that down deep, in that place where you keep the things that you can't admit even to yourself, I knew that wouldn't happen."

It wasn't until she looked into her son's eyes again that she saw the tears streaming out of them, for he had been silent.

"Do you know that place, honey?" she asked. "It's like a basement in your soul."

Oh, how could she tell this boy what came next? And also, how could she not?

"I hate myself when I'm down in that basement," said Dwayne.

Now she wanted to ask him what was in his basement, instead of telling him what she'd kept locked away in hers for such a very long time.

"Everyone does, but the truth will set you free, Dwayne. You heard that before, right?"

"Jesus said it in the bible. The preacher at our church talks about it sometimes."

Now, no matter how much she wanted to get the words out, she couldn't help quoting, *"So Jesus said to the Jews who had believed him, 'If you abide in my word, you are truly my disciples, and you will know the truth, and the truth will set you free.'* It's from chapter 8 of the Book of John, baby. It's my favorite verse in the bible."

"Jesus was talking to Jews? What'd he do, run into them on the road? Cause that seems to be where he did a lot of his talking. Do you think Jesus was real, Mom?"

"He didn't run into them on the road, baby, everyone he knew was a Jew, even Jesus himself. And yes, I think he was as real as the child that you and Phoebe are bringing into this world. And that basement you hate yourself in? Jesus will help get you out of it if you let him."

Dwayne's tears dried as his interest grew, but he was also incredulous. "So we can let Mrs. Stern's son adopt Mary Alice? Since he is Jewish, too, it would be like letting Jesus do it?"

"That depends on what Phoebe and you think of Mrs. Stern's son and his wife. But Jesus would want your baby to have a good and loving family, I know that. I don't call her 'Mary Alice,' by the way."

"You don't? I thought everyone did. What do you call her?"

"That doesn't matter, not when I am trying to tell you the inside truth about your dad."

Dwayne wanted to say, "Why'd you bring it up then?" but said, "Oh yeah, the visit where you didn't want to have sex with him."

"It wasn't the sex, exactly, I have always been free about that. But sex is sometimes a tool, Dwayne, a weapon, even, more than it is an act of love."

She waited for him to yell at her about 'love' again, but he only said, "That doesn't sound like much fun."

"It's not, and thank you for that."

When she reached out to take Dwayne's hand again, this time he didn't pull back.

"When your dad got to the room he was wearing good clothes and he had a haircut, but he was as nervous as a cat. Still, I held him against me and soon we commenced to getting ready for the sex part, with me determined to have it mean what we said it would...but he... he had snuck a horrible weapon into the room with him, one that no prison guard would find no matter how hard he looked."

"Was it a knife made out of ice?" Dwayne asked. "A guy got stabbed with one of those in a rap I wrote once. Do you know *Mack the Knife?* It was a parody of that."

Something calmed in LaVeronica's un-calm heart.

"Calling it a knife made out of ice is a better description of it than I could ever come up with, for it was just as cold and just about as deadly. Do you remember when I frightened you and Phoebe with talk about the sexually transmitted diseases Johnny Sylvester gave me? Well, what your father brought was worst than those; a sickness he carried in all his bodily fluids, which he gave me during the sex that we did eventually have. The name of the sickness is acquired immunodeficiency syndrome. Your father not only got himself infected on purpose, but went untreated until he came for our conjugal visit, so he could be sure that he would give it to me. And he was successful in that."

She watched Dwayne for signs of how quickly this was sinking in *without* her uttering the horrible acronym "AIDS."

"You don't look sick, Mom," he said.

"I know I don't, but this all happened more than a decade ago, and it took about half that time for my doctors to get me squared away. You know that pill I take, the dull pink one that comes in that envelope? Well, that pill makes it *as though* I'm not sick. And I'm really not, just as long as I keep taking it."

"For the rest of your life?"

"Maybe. We'll see what happens with the research that's going on."

She had never seen Dwayne's face more *disengaged* than it

was now.

"What your father also did - which, ironically, helped me - was go to the police once he left the prison, and turn himself in. He knew there was a law against doing what he did, and for reasons I will never understand, he wanted to be convicted of breaking it. So he's over there in Walla Walla, and you and I are here, living our lives."

"Is there a way that I could get it, too? Like, from using your toothbrush or something?"

"Not a chance. I asked my doctor questions like that a lot of times."

"Is Dad sick now? Or is he taking the pink pill, too?"

"I don't know. You might be able to guess that we don't talk much."

"Is he ever going to get out?"

"Yes...and maybe fairly soon. The law regarding what he did was recently changed from a felony to a misdemeanor, and that could have an effect on him. But we will deal with that when we have to."

Dwayne's face began filling in. She could see him deciding what he ought to think, instead of simply thinking it.

"How come you didn't tell me this before? Why did you wait until now?"

"Because you were too young before. But you've been forced to do a lot of growing up these past few months."

She wouldn't tell him that Millicent forced her hand. She also wouldn't tell him that Judge Follett visited her in prison after hearing about Vernon's confession, with the news that he was doing what he could to expedite her parole.

"A person's not supposed to hate his father, but I hate mine," Dwayne said.

"A person's not supposed to hate anyone. It's not only my hope that this truth will set you free, but that you will find it in you to turn the other cheek, since there's a baby coming soon who is going to want to know who you are."

"That cheek thing was Jesus's, too, right?"

"You bet. It's from the Sermon on the Mount. And let me tell you, when your father does get out, I am going to let things be. Will you join me in that?"

"Do you think Mary Alice will really want to know me? Even if we give her away?"

"I think she'll come knocking on your door someday, and I want her to find the man I know you can be."

"What do you call her instead of Mary Alice? I never heard another name."

"I'll keep that to myself. If I don't I won't have any secrets left, and that might not be good for my self-esteem."

When Dwayne said "Okay," LaVeronica's thoughts turned to Millicent again.

She was torn between turning the other cheek and driving to her house to slap her face.

20.

Garden Party

There was once a Ricky Nelson song about a performance at Madison Square Garden - released in 1972 - with the leit-motif: *you can't please everyone so you ought to please yourself.* It was a good leitmotif, but it irked Cornelius to remember it - backwards, no less - when setting up his own garden party for Ruthie's son and his wife. 'Backwards' because he was no longer trying to please himself, but everyone else.

More than a month had passed since his walk with Don-nie. During that time, though he hadn't gone for another long walk, he considered his physical condition to be near-ly back to what it was before he took his tumble: fit, but grouchy; grouchy, but fairly fit.

He had purchased three plastic tables, each with four chairs, white paper tablecloths and disposable place settings, arranged equidistantly around his sloping backyard. Donnie and Emi and Phoebe would sit at one table, Yehudi and Bess at another, with LaVeronica and Dwayne - if he came - at table number three with Cornelius. If anyone else showed up they could bloody well stand.

They had had to wait until late August to have this final adoption meeting, this final "gunfight at the Ok Corral," as Emi called it, because Phoebe called off an earlier meeting, using the excuse that she had an appointment with Mrs. Dr.

Russo, and Cornelius cancelled another - his current good condition notwithstanding - because of a terrible summer cold.

So, okay, those were two good reasons, but they put him out of sorts. Something else that put him out of sorts was that he'd tried to cut his lawn that morning and ran out of energy halfway through. So the grass under two of his tables was mowed as flat as a Marine's haircut, while the grass under one looked like the top of a hippie's head. He mowed a path between the tables and his deck stairs, as well as one to his side gate, but the grass in the rest of his yard rose-up to above his ankles. He still might have finished mowing if Phoebe hadn't called him twice, first wanting his assurance that his cold was truly gone, and next to ask if anyone had arrived yet, though the party was set from three to four-thirty and it was noon at the time of her call.

By two o'clock, when the sun moved far enough east so that it wasn't shining brightly on his two Marine haircut tables, Cornelius brought out ice buckets, water and soda, and sauvignon blanc. He brought pigs in a blanket, too - once Phoebe's favorite - with half of the pigs made of tofurkey for any vegetarians. He ate two of the pigs while carrying them outside, so he had to rearrange them on their plates.

At two-thirty he cracked open a bottle of wine, poured himself a glass, and sat down. He liked this recent ability to 'crack' open wine bottles, though when screw caps first came on the scene he had called himself a ritualist and stuck to bottles with corks.

It was two forty-five when Phoebe called again, from up in his kitchen where she could glare out the window at him.

"How many times do I have to tell you that you shouldn't

drink?" she asked.

He looked around and found her and waved.

"Come on down here, Phoebs. I've got pigs in a blanket," he said.

He hoped she had come alone, though he didn't see how. Emi and Donnie rarely let her out of their sight these days. Phoebe opened the deck door, navigated the stairs, and walked toward him on the Marine haircut path.

"Why didn't you mow the rest? When I called before you said you were almost done."

"Precisely because you kept calling," he said, then he nodded to the chair beside his. He had lived a long time and seen them often, but she was as big as any pregnant woman he had ever run across.

"Dad brought me over and went back for Mom. I know I'm early but I didn't want to walk down those stupid stairs with everyone watching me."

"You could have come around the side," he said. "I did manage to mow a path."

"Yeah, but that would make me look like a debutante."

She took his wineglass, raised it like she was going to drink, then rolled its ice-cold side across her forehead. "Why did you pick such a hot day, and how come we didn't just cancel-cancel, instead of rescheduling?" she asked.

He took his wineglass back, filling another one with ice for her.

"She who asks such questions should be able to answer them," he said.

"Yeah, yeah," said Phoebe, but she ate a pig in a blanket. "You heard that Mrs. Williams knows this Bess lady from church, but I bet you didn't know that Mrs. Williams had her over to their house. Don't you think that's cheating, Grandpa? Like a congressman taking a bribe or a radio guy taking payola?"

'Payola' no less. What fourteen-year-old knew such a term, except one who spent too much time with her grandpa?

"I do think it's cheating," he said. "Who told you about it?"

"Well, duh...Roselyn, of course. She calls Dwayne every night and then she calls me. Except there's something going on between D and his Mom that Roselyn can't find out."

"'Duh' Phoebs? How am I supposed to know that Roselyn calls you? And why not let Dwayne and his mom have a little privacy? I know I'd like that."

"You're supposed to know because I told you eighteen times! I don't think you had a summer cold, Grandpa, but a sneaky version of Alzheimer's. Anyway, Roselyn's turned over another new leaf, while Dwayne's still the same old toad."

She rolled the glass of ice around her face, then ate another pig-in-a-blanket.

"Well, today let's focus on Bess and Yehudi. You and your mom and dad have a big decision to make."

"Only me and Mom and Dad? You get a vote, too. So would Grandma if she was alive."

She might not tell him her mother's secret but she would never leave him out of anything.

"I don't want a vote. I didn't meet the Moodys or the Browns or any of the others you interviewed... Unless I met them and forgot about it already."

He pointed up at one of the holes that Dr. Russo drilled in his head.

"Touché, but you still have to tell me what you think," said Phoebe.

Donnie and Emi came around the side yard just as she raised her glass again.

"That better just be water," Donnie said.

"What can I do? Is there something else I can bring outside, Dad?" asked Emi.

"There's veggies and dip in the fridge and a few more pigs in the oven."

When he pointed at the basket, Emi hauled Donnie off to help her, thus giving Cornelius a last few minutes to sit there quietly with Phoebe.

*****

Yehudi and Bess came around that same outside path at 3:05. They'd been parked nearby since 2:39, watching others arrive, with Bess saying they should show themselves at precisely 3:00, while Yehudi argued for 3:10. So 3:05 was their compromise. They didn't want to be early and show anxiety, nor late, with the built-in worry that people might think they were blasé.

"I mean," Bess said that morning, "We go to doctor after doctor, adoption agency after adoption agency, and end up at a stranger's house because your Mom has a fling with a man whose daughter happens to be a pregnant teenager's OB/GYN. Who finds a child that way?"

"It's not a fling. I've known Dr. Russo since I was ten years old," said Yehudi. "He used to be friends with my dad."

"How does that make it not a fling?" Bess had asked.

What Yehudi didn't say, what he never had told anyone,

was that Dr. Russo's daughter, Rhoda Russo, was the girl he lost his virginity to in that front seat of his father's Chrysler when he was seventeen years old. In about three seconds flat. Twice.

"She's not showing up here, is she, your Mom?" Bess asked now. "I know you said she wasn't, but tell me again."

"She's not, but Bess, let's cross our fingers and put smiles on our faces, okay?"

They got out of their car, crossed the street, went through the side gate as they'd been asked to, and started along a well-mowed, path. When Cornelius saw them he stood, his smile broad and his fingers crossed, too, figuratively, at least, behind his back. He wanted this to work as much as they did, never mind his nonchalance with Phoebe.

"Hi, I'm the grandpa. Come meet Phoebe and her parents," he said. "It's a beautiful day, even if this horrible virus does pirouette around us."

He regretted his effusiveness. He should have simply said hello.

"It is," said Bess. "Mrs. Williams isn't here yet?"

She hoped he could see what she believed to be true; that they had LaVeronica's support.

"Not yet," Cornelius said.

Donnie and Emi stood to meet the arriving couple, while Phoebe used her enormous girth as an excuse to stay where she was. She smiled, but she also put a hand under the table to pat the spot on her abdomen that she figured was nearest Mary Alice's head. "No worries, we get rid of these two and it's you and me," she said.

Yehudi bumped elbows with Donnie, while Bess walked directly to Phoebe, sat down beside her, and pulled a bottle of water from the ice bucket.

"Do you want one, too?" she asked.

Phoebe said she did. "My doctor says I should stay hydrated. You know her, right?"

"No, but I've met her dad. Don't let on I told you this, but he and my husband's mother have a thing going on."

Despite herself, Phoebe liked Bess for that.

"Yeah, my grandpa already clued me in. She's one of his Mopesters."

Bess had no idea what that meant, so she tried a different tact. "I'm only ten years older than you, but when I was fourteen I didn't know shit from Shinola," she said.

Phoebe liked that, too, and laughed. She knew the expression from her grandpa.

Over by the other Marine table, Donnie and Emi and Yehudi heard the laugh and took heart. "She hasn't laughed like that since this all started," Donnie said.

He looked at Emi, but Emi was watching Yehudi.

"Bess hasn't, either, she's had three miscarriages," he said.

When the side gate opened next, LaVeronica and Dwayne traipsed in, she carrying flowers and he with a shirt and tie on. Both of them were wearing masks.

"I told Dwayne, you can't be too careful, didn't I, Dwayne?" LaVeronica said.

Dwayne's eyes were on Phoebe, but he managed to agree with his mom.

Phoebe drank water while Bess went to greet the new arrivals.

"That table is for us, and I'm sorry about the unmowed grass," Cornelius told LaVeronica. "But please, everyone sit down, have something to eat and drink. This might be our last social gathering for a very long while."

LaVeronica didn't want to sit with Cornelius or Dwayne. She wanted to sit with Bess and Phoebe and Emi, relegating Dwayne and Cornelius and Yehudi to the table assigned to her. Donnie Cassavetes could hang himself from that willow tree, for all she cared. So she spoke, not of hating Donnie, but about the seating arrangements.

"Listen, Cornelius, let's do this the old-fashioned way, with boys at one table, girls at another. You can think of this as a social gathering if you want to, but we all know why we're here and it's mostly a female thing. So let's get down to it, shall we?"

She smiled, but everyone knew the die was cast, and they sat where she told them to. Some drank water, no one drank wine, and no one seemed inclined to eat, irritating Cornelius. He looked at Dwayne, who seemed as grouchy as he was.

"What's up, Dwayne? Are you sorry or glad that school won't be starting again?"

Yehudi cranked his head around in order to hear Dwayne's answer. Donnie did the same, though what he really wanted was to strangle the kid.

"I wish school was on so I could see my friends," Dwayne said.

"Phoebe would like that, too, if her friends were really her friends," said Donnie.

He had promised Emi that if Dwayne showed up he would not berate him - not today and not at her father's house. Yet he broke that promise right away.

"Come on, Donnie, Phoebe's got friends," Cornelius said.

He hoped that Donnie wouldn't ask him to name one, for he could only think of Roselyn Wilkinson.

"I still have friends from when I was your age," Yehudi told Dwayne. "I don't see them much, but when I do it's always great."

He couldn't have named one, either, except for Rhoda Russo, Phoebe's OB/GYN.

Dwayne was trying not to slide off his chair. If he got out of here alive he was going to kill his mother for making him come in the first place.

Meanwhile, over at the girls' table, Phoebe listened to her mother telling Mrs. Williams and Bess how fantastic her OB/GYN had been.

"That's good to know," said Bess. "I've been looking for a new one, would you recommend her, Phoebe?"

"She's okay," said Phoebe. "She talks a lot about birth control. She said she wished she'd used it when she was my age."

Bess was about to say she sounded wonderful, when Emi said, "She did? She told you that directly?" unable to keep incredulousness out of her voice.

"Yes, Mom, directly," Phoebe said. "What do you think? When I go to my appointments she speaks to me through her nurse?"

She pulled the saran wrap off their new plate of pigs-in-a-blanket and ate three. Bess, who didn't eat pork, ate two, after making sure to choose tofurkey. She wanted to support this girl, she wanted her to like her, but not at the expense of eating meat. LaVeronica ate one and poured herself a small glass of wine. When she asked, "Did you know that Phoebe's due in a week?" Bess said she did, and smiled.

Over at the boys table, the boys were openly looking at the girls again. Yehudi thought how beautiful his wife was, and hoped that the other women could see her inordinate goodness.

When Emi said, "Will you please stop staring at us!" he was sure she was talking to him, while everyone else understood that Donnie was her target.

"We can't. We don't like it over here. We feel left out," Donnie said.

Though he spoke for them without permission, the others nodded, even Dwayne, who loved being left out. His mother would ground him forever, though, if he asked to go wait in the car. So he asked Yehudi, out of the quiet desperation that every teenager knows, "Are you naming her Mary Alice if we give her to you? Did you guys talk about that?"

"Mary Alice?" said Yehudi. "No. We're naming her Sarah."

Bess called over from the other table. "I agreed to Mary Alice, honey, since it seemed important to them."

"But those aren't Jewish names," Yehudi said.

"They're not African American names, either. I was hoping for Ayotunde or Folake, something with a bit of traction to it for a change," said LaVeronica.

That perked Dwayne up. She'd refused to tell him those names at home, no matter how many times he asked.

"Mary and Alice were my mom and grandma. Everyone agreed already," Donnie said.

LaVeronica figured that if she threw her wine in his face, it wouldn't help. Plus, he was sitting too far away. "Maybe *you* agreed, but you aren't everyone!" she said.

"Wait, Mrs. Williams, it's not Dad's fault," said Phoebe. "We came up with a lot of names, but when I heard 'Mary Alice,' I knew it was the one. So if you want to be mad at someone, be mad at me."

Phoebe had been terrified of LaVeronica since the day she pulled her out of the apple tree. But just now, when her Dad said Mary Alice's name, her baby wiggled and jiggled and kicked inside of her, like she knew who they were talking about. So she settled down and stared at LaVeronica. Until her mother said, "'Cassavetes' is in the running for her last name. These days family names can come from either side."

She didn't look at Donnie, but hoped he heard her loyalty to him.

"Mary Alice Williams. Mary Alice Cassavetes... May I ask why Yehudi and I are here, if not to discuss the possibility that she might become our baby?"

This was Bess at her best, perfectly postured and brave, despite how much this meant to her. Or so Yehudi thought. When he said something like that to his father once, however, not long before he died, his father told him that he shouldn't objectify his wife, as he had, to his chagrin, Yehudi's mother. But was it objectifying Bess to believe she was dignified and brave, or had his father not known what he was talking about?

"You're right, and we're sorry," Donnie said, "We invited you here so that Phoebe could see that you'd be excellent parents for Mary Alice."

Phoebe looked from Bess to Yehudi and back to Bess again. "Do you promise to be nice to Mary Alice, and not to give her too many sweets?" she asked.

"We do. We promise both those things," said Bess.

"Do you promise not to let her go online or have a phone until she's fifteen, and do you swear to never let her get slut-shamed?"

"Yes, and yes, and absolutely yes," Yehudi said.

"And do I have to be 100% out of her life, or will you let me babysit sometimes?"

That was a tougher question. Most of what Bess and Yehudi had read said that cutting off ties with their baby's birth mother was an absolute must. Most, but not all. One book argued that with these new adoption arrangements all the old truisms were out the window. Bess looked at Yehudi, who gave her no sign, and then at LaVeronica, who was still staring daggers at Donnie. She feared that anything less than a full endorsement of Phoebe's babysitting idea might be fatal, but said, "To be honest, we'd have to give that a bit more thought."

To her great relief, Phoebe only nodded. "I would have to give it more thought, too," she said. "But I'm telling you right now if it does ever happen I'll babysit for free."

She ate another pig-in-a-blanket, then looked at all the sober faces. "That was a joke!" she said. "Someone's got to say something to lighten things up around here *OR...*"

The loudness of her *OR,* plus a sharp intake of breath right after it, made LaVeronica and Yehudi and Cornelius and Emi stand out of their chairs. Bess, who was closest, knelt by Phoebe to put her hands where Phoebe's had been, on top of Mary Alice's head. When Phoebe said *"YIKES!"* and then, *"OH!"* again, Donnie pulled out his phone and called Mrs. Dr. Russo's cell.

"Too many pigs-in-a-blanket," said Phoebe, just as Bess tried to lift her to the ground.

"Hi Dr. Russo, it's Donnie Cassavetes, Phoebe's Dad... Contractions? I don't know! What do you mean Braxton Hicks? All right, yes..."

He held the phone away and asked Phoebe if she just had a contraction. "If so Dr. Russo says that it ought to be easing up by now."

"It is!" said Phoebe, but then she bellowed, *"OUCH!"*

Emi took the phone to say, "She's in pain, Dr. Russo!" then she listened for a second, hung up, and knelt on the opposite side of Phoebe from Bess.

"Dr. Russo's on her way... She said she doesn't live far, that she'll decide when she gets here if it's time to go to the hospital."

"Of course it's time to go to the hospital!" said Donnie. "I'll go start my car!"

"No Dad!" said Phoebe, a half a second before her water broke.

"Oh boy!" said Emi. "How long since that first contraction?"

No one knew, so LaVeronica told Dwayne to open his phone and tell them how long between Phoebe's next two contractions.

"Huh?" Dwayne said, but he pulled out his phone.

"Someone go get clean towels," said Bess. "And can the rest of you put a barrier up, so she can have a little privacy?"

Her words sprang them into action. Cornelius went for the towels with Donnie right behind him, while Yehudi upended the tables and used them to build a fence around Phoebe and Bess and Emi.

As quickly as that they had a fort, with three women inside of it and no room at all for Braxton Hicks, since Phoebe's next contraction came just four minutes later, according to the stopwatch on Dwayne's phone.

"Someone go wait for the doctor on the street! Yehudi,

would you do that?" asked Emi.

Yehudi managed to hurry along Cornelius's freshly mowed path to the front of the house, without saying, "Who, me?" But should he call Dr. Russo, Rhoda? He hadn't seen her in decades.

LaVeronica and Dwayne stood outside the fort with Donnie.

When Cornelius tried herding them toward his deck, only LaVeronica went with him. Dwayne started to, but when another moan came from Phoebe he fell down into the taller grass. LaVeronica turned to get him, but stopped when Donnie lay down beside her son, put an arm around him, and spoke into his ear. Cornelius saw her watching them and said of Donnie, "He's a good dad and he wants to be a better human being."

"It's too late for that last part," LaVeronica told him, but she left them alone.

Inside the fort, Emi moved to Phoebe's head while Bess did her best to bend Phoebe's knees, slip one of the paper tablecloths under her, and pull off her panties. She'd been using her body to obscure the view of the gawking men, and was now glad to find them sequestered across the yard. Good! But where were Yehudi and the doctor?

"Mrs. Williams, could you please go see what's keeping my husband?" she called.

When LaVeronica heard her name she took off like a bull out of a chute, getting to the street in time to find Yehudi looking the wrong way, just as a green Volvo station wagon pulled up. Mrs. Dr. Russo waved to her before Yehudi turned around. He might deny it later, but there was no mistaking the disappointment he felt by having his job of greeter taken by someone else.

"Dr. Russo, please…" LaVeronica said.

"Rhoda!" Yehudi called, but Dr. Russo followed LaVeronica at a half-run.

"Hi Phoebe, what a nice place for Mary Alice to be born," she said when she saw the fort.

"Or Ayotunde," LaVeronica told Dwayne, who had stood again and joined her.

Dr. Russo wore shorts and a t-shirt with the slogan *"Yo Semite!"* written across its front. Yehudi had had one like it once, bought as a sort of Jewish in-joke on a visit to Yosemite National Park. What happened to that shirt? Surely he didn't give it to Rhoda Russo?

"Okay then, let's see what's what," she said.

She stepped into the fort by the towels and washcloths, stacked like people no doubt thought they should be from seeing such scenes in movies. She splashed her hands with antiseptic, pulled a packet of surgical gloves from her bag, and bent to check Phoebe's cervical effacement and dilation. If there was time, she would put her in her Volvo and race her up to T.G. faster than they could get there in an ambulance. To be born here or in a Volvo, though… Which would make the better story for Mary Alice to tell as she grew up?

"You're seven centimeters dilated," she told Phoebe, "You should have gone to the hospital when your water broke. Called me back and said you were on your way."

She looked around at the gathered people. "Mr. Cassavetes? Can you get my phone from my bag and call Jason Kim? He's my best nurse. Tell him to get over here now!"

Much like LaVeronica before him, Donnie shot across the lawn when he heard his name, found Dr. Russo's phone, and ran off to call Jason Kim, who answered on the first ring.

"I hope you know it's Sunday, Dr. Russo," he said.

"This is Donnie Cassavetes. She wants you to come to Cornelius MacLeish's house now!" Donnie said.

"Phoebe Cassavetes is it?" Jason asked, but Donnie was barely able to give him the address before he hung up and Phoebe howled again.

Donnie tried to give Dr. Russo her phone back, but she was down between his daughter's legs. Phoebe fixed her eyes on him, and when she reached out he leapt the walls of the fort to fall down beside her and grasp that hand.

"You'll be fine, baby," he said. "I'm here and Mom is here and…"

"Where is Grandpa? And where is…."

But a contraction made her clamp her mouth shut before she could say what Donnie and Emi told each other later she was about to, which was, "Where is Grandma?"

When Dr. Russo asked about Jason Kim, Donnie looked toward the side gate. What if he was standing on Cornelius's porch, pounding on his front door? When he yelled "Dwayne! Go wait for him!" Dwayne ran out of the yard.

Now the fort held Phoebe and Dr. Russo and Bess and Emi and Donnie, while Cornelius and LaVeronica stood outside of it with Yehudi, all of them sure that something was about to go wrong.

But when Dr. Russo said, "Phoebe, do you know what I think?" Phoebe craned her neck around, and even smiled.

"I think that Mary Alice has a mind of her own. We say September first, she says… What's the date today?… August 23?"

"August 23? Really?" said Dwayne, back almost instantly with Jason Kim. "Phoebe! August 23 is Kobe Bryant's birthday! Seth Curry's, too!"

Though it took Jason Kim less time to get there than it had Dr. Russo, he wore scrubs.

"How's it going, Phoebe?" he asked, "And folks, how about letting me set up this nifty tent I brought along? It's meant for rural births, but I think a backyard qualifies, don't you?"

He glared at Donnie and Emi and Bess when they failed to understand that he wanted them to vacate the fort. "Hurry up now, scoot on out of here!" he said.

All three of them stepped over the fort walls, while Jason Kim pulled a lever on the side of his 'tent' until a four-walled enclosure blew up to float above them like a huge balloon with most of its helium gone. Dwayne and Yehudi pulled it down when Jason told them to, then he settled it onto an unmowed part of the yard a few feet away.

He looked at Dr. Russo. "It's sterile, light, and its instruments are ready to use," he said.

When he unzipped the near side of the tent to reveal a yellow-lit interior with a thick white mattress, oxygen masks hanging down, and with enough room for a doctor, a nurse, and a woman about to give birth, Phoebe said, "I'm not getting in that thing." When Dr. Russo ordered Jason Kim to move her into it, though, another contraction started and she decided not to argue.

Dr. Russo slipped into a sterile paper gown and booties. When she crawled into the room beside Phoebe they looked to the outsiders like figures in a diorama, in an installation by Marcel Duchamp, or in a nativity scene - Mary arrived after the too-long journey down from Nazareth, with a Jewish doctor and a Korean nurse, but with no manger animals, no wise men, and no baby Jesus arrived yet to change the world. Seeing it so moved Donnie that he might have started singing *Silent Night*, were the sun not still shining high above them.

When an equally moved LaVeronica came up next to him, the others crowded in; Dwayne beside his mother; Emi and Cornelius on Donnie's other side; with Bess and Yehudi kneeling in the foreground. It was like the photo of the members of a family that had never met each other before a sly photographer lined them up. They smiled and spoke encouraging words to Phoebe, who called her baby forth using the voices of the missing manger animals. She brayed and mooed and baaed like a score of wounded lambs. The others believed that such sounds could not have been made at any other moment, for, despite Phoebe's pain, they were the sounds of hope, of knowing that life was a spiritual thing, eternally watched by all the deities; the dead, the living, and the unborn.

When Mary Alice, or Sarah, or Ayotunde, slipped from her world into this one, and added her voice to her mother's, it made those arranged for the sly family photo crumple against each other in what felt like free-fall. Everyone touched and all was forgiven. They simply laughed and cried, for those were the purest of emotions.

Inside the manger Jason Kim cried, too, when Phoebe took the swaddled newborn from her doctor to say through tears of her own - "Hello my love. Hello my darling. Hello my baby girl."

That she didn't use her baby's name was lost on everyone

but Bess, who inched forward like a supplicant. "May I say hello, too?" she asked.

The grandmothers came next, bright and smiling, then one grandfather and one great-grandfather, their hands down low in front of them as if they'd just doffed hats. It was only when Phoebe looked for him that Dwayne found the strength to go to her, for strength had been lacking in him since his mother told him what his own father did to her. When he saw his infant daughter a new strength came, however, for the face that looked back at him was his own.

Yehudi, meanwhile, knelt beside Bess to gaze at the newborn, before chancing a glance at his old paramour, who had stepped from the portable delivery room and was ridding herself of her surgical gown.

She caught his glance and winked. "Yo Semite," she said.

21.

Mary Alice Sarah Ayotunde

After a day of tests and a night of rest at the Tacoma General Hospital's neonatal ICU, this infant whom so many people waited for got a birth certificate with the following names: Mary Alice Sarah Ayotunde Segal. Her mother was listed as Bessie Jackson Segal, her father as Yehudi Benjamin Segal, and her birthmother as Phoebe Yuki Cassavetes. Her birth father's name was not in evidence.

The newborn's paternal grandmother, Ruthie Segal - Ruth Stern her nom du jour - was so pleased to have come up with the idea of Yehudi and Bess adopting Phoebe's baby, that she mentioned it to the elder Dr. Russo during every meal and couch cuddle, as well as to the younger Dr. Russo, who had delivered the child.

"I mean, there are so many angles to it, so many coincidences and places where things could go wrong if I wasn't in the right place at the right time," she said.

The younger Dr. Russo - Rhoda - wanted nothing more than to finish the steak her father grilled for her, on his deck at American Lake. Nevertheless she admitted that that was true.

"It really is," said Ruthie. "All the stars were just aligned. Cornelius's wife died when Ben did, so I met him in my grievers' group, and then he fell and broke his crown and who should his surgeon be but your papa, whom I hadn't seen in months. Not only that, but Yehudi and Bess were at their wit's end regarding parenthood just when Phoebe got pregnant."

"Sounds like it had as much to do with Mr. MacLeish as it did with you. But I'm glad it happened," said the senior Dr. Russo. "Not that he broke his crown, but everything else."

"Oh good grief," said Rhoda Russo.

She wanted to say that Ruthie's son, the "wit's end" guy, had nearly knocked *her* up when they were not much older than Phoebe. She also wanted to say that he had kept his horny eyes on her all during that bizarre birthing. She still had hope that her dad would end his foolishness with this woman on his own, however, so she kept all that to herself.

"How's your steak?" asked her father.

"Can't wait to finish it," said Rhoda.

"And, you know, baby Sarah is just so cute! I think she looks like Bess but I'm afraid to say so, for fear that Bess will make a racist thing out of it," Ruthie said.

"I don't think they call her 'Sarah,'" Dr. Russo said. "When Mr. MacLeish was in the other day he told me that his granddaughter got stuck on "Mary Alice," but relented just before signing the adoption papers."

"So they *are* calling her Sarah," said Ruthie.

"No, 'Ayotunde' won the day. I heard that from Phoebe," Rhoda said.

Now Ruthie said, "Good grief!" followed by, "Why?"

"Because Bess wanted to honor her African heritage ahead of her Catholic one, and Phoebe decided that it was a good idea as long as 'Mary Alice' was in there somewhere," said Rhoda. "Anyway, Dad, I've got to go. Long day tomorrow."

"Hold on, I brought rhubarb pie. Tart, like you like it. Made by a friend of mine."

Ruthie came down hard on 'tart,' to let this sassy young woman know that she would not be pushed around.

"How about I take a piece with me?" asked Rhoda.

"When I saw the baby I called her Sarah and no one corrected me," Ruthie said. "And sure, take the whole pie."

Just then, out of the clear blue sky, old Dr. Russo had a memory of Rhoda coming home years earlier, all googly-eyed after a date with Yehudi Segal. It was true that he operated on people's heads, but he had no idea how the mind worked, what brought that memory back now.

Rhoda took her plate to the sink, rinsed it, and put it in the dishwasher. Then she cut herself a huge piece of pie, not the whole pie, but a quarter of it. And somehow that cut deeply into Ruthie, for it told her that she would have to make a big cut, too, by ending whatever this was with Rudy Russo. She would she never be accepted by his daughter, and Ben had been dead for far too short a time. What had she been thinking?

"Thanks dad, and see you around, Mrs. Segal," Rhoda said.

This time Ruthie didn't ask to be called Ruth Stern, for she was cutting that name, too.

22.

Þórdís

Against all odds, just when COVID was killing more Americans daily than heart disease or cancer, Þórdís Jakobsdóttir returned to Tacoma. She hadn't exactly finished her degree at the Andersen Institute, but her courses were now online, and after her short-lived and mostly unfortunate flirtation with Annegrete Christophersen-Hemmingsen, where else did she have to go? - only Iceland, which suddenly seemed like a bad idea. Plus, she found she missed her Tacoma grievers, and even, a bit, the man who introduced her to the place. Not that she would call him after their mixed-message lunch at Doyle's.... but if she happened to run into him she would stop her negative signaling and let the chips fall where they might. Or may. However chips fell in that odd English expression.

Þórdís filled the week after her return, from sunup until sundown, dusting and mopping every room of her house, even to the point of washing all the windows inside and out. When she finished, she bought scrapers and primer, and enough paint to give her big front porch new life. It was the first thing people saw when they came for sessions, after all, so it ought to make a good impression. Not that people would be coming to her physically anytime soon. They'd be meeting online where a newly painted porch meant nothing. Still, she did not put off the work. She'd been reborn in

Copenhagen, and hoped, from here on out, to make Josefine Christophersen-Hemmingsen proud. Or, at least, to take some of the sting out of that Annegrete business. Ugh, poor Einar! Pórdís absolutely *knew* that Annegrete was in bed now with Ingeborg Ingeborgsen. She liked the expression "in bed with" with its myriad meanings; business, politics, sex. It blew the one about chips falling different places out of the water.

After her house and porch were in order, Pórdís emailed her grief group members to set up online meetings. People said they didn't like those meetings, but she did, since the moment a session ended, poof, she was alone again, without all the previously necessary social formalities. Still, there was too much small talk in the emails, and occasional phone conversations. She couldn't get rid of Ruthie Segal or Millicent Fleming, and even LaVeronica Williams talked her ear off before dropping the bomb that she hadn't changed her mind about quitting group therapy. Why she didn't say so in an email, why she had to call, Pórdís didn't know, but at least she left the door open to meeting privately - to talk about her husband.

Jane - whose last name escaped Pórdís at the moment - spoke more reluctantly, but that may have been because she was in double mourning, for the long-dead Giancarlo and the hospice-bound Sam, whom Pórdís had rather liked. She felt sorry for Jane, but sorrier for Sam. Some people were born under, lived under, and died under storm clouds. That was something she learned at the Anderson Institute. Aesop knew it, and so did the Brothers Grimm. Just ask Hansel and Gretel.

Cornelius MacLeish, the person she was most drawn to,

was the only group member who simply said yes, he would continue. He also presented Pórdís with the news - that she'd already heard - that his granddaughter had given birth. He said his granddaughter was "in recovery," and asked if Pórdís might recommend a therapist for her. She decided not to be offended that he hadn't asked her see the girl, supposing that he thought such a thing to be unethical.

The only other client who quit therapy outright was Frank Blessing. If someone had asked Pórdís before Frank quit, who among all her clients she would most happily lose, Frank would have been at the top of the list. But now - she hadn't talked to Frank, she'd received a letter - she wished to know what storm had come along to wipe out the imbecile in him. After she got Frank's letter she called him, but he didn't picked up or call back. And though she was sorely tempted, she refrained from asking one of the others about him. Still, as time went by, she grew curiouser and curiouser, and read Frank's letter many times.

Here is what his letter said:

My dear Pórdís,

I trust your hiatus served you well and that you have returned refreshed. A group like ours - indeed, all who come to you adrift upon the swells of heartache, whether from the loss of a loved one, from some heinous addiction, or from fear of the thoughts that come, unbidden, to take up residence in the gray matter between their ears - must bring on a weariness that can only be lifted by leaving for a while.

I am writing to say that I have been refreshed, too, and am therefore resigning my seat at the North End grievers' group table. It was a seat that served, if you'll excuse the extended metaphor, as a life preserver for me, because all of you were caring enough and kind enough to keep me afloat, to keep me from drowning, though I nearly drowned a couple of times anyway. So please thank Millicent, Jane, Ruthie, LaVeronica, and Cornelius for me, and bid them my adieu. They put up with a lot from me.

Your humble servant,

Francis S. Blessing

No matter how many times she read the letter, Þórdís came away with two thoughts: First, that the old Frank was hiding in it somewhere, ready to pop up guffawing like a jack-in-the-box; and second, that it was the most miraculous thing imaginable, one she would have taken straight to Josefine were Josefine alive, and *would* take to her new thesis director once she could wholly believe that she hadn't been fooled. She twice picked up her phone to call her thesis director and twice hung up before he answered.

The word "impunity" came into Þórdís's mind. If her first thought was correct, did Frank think that he could get away with such a trick with impunity? And if he was now a man she believed that Frank could never be, did he expect to get away without a detailed account of how it happened...yes, also with impunity? To say that they had "put up with a lot" from him was a mammoth understatement! She had shown great forbearance in not throwing him out of the group, and some of the others had had cause to take restraining orders out on him.

But, in fact, whichever it was, he did seem to think that impunity was something he had a right to. His unwillingness to call her back made that clear. What was more, though the letter was polite, its subtext "leave me alone now, for this is all you're going to get," had to be respected. So she wouldn't call him again.

Pórdís did finally call Cornelius to ask if he could shed light on either the miraculous metamorphosis or the astounding hoodwinking. But then, as with her thesis advisor, she hung up before he answered, for didn't the course she just completed - "Dangling Strings in the Well-lived Life" - teach that messy endings, unresolved issues, even friendships lost due to inevitable change, were far more common than happy endings? What made a well-lived life wasn't chasing after tying things up, but staying within oneself. *That* was the Fabulists' manifesto.

Pórdís read Frank's letter one last time before filing it away. She then picked up her phone yet again and called Lars Larson, a man so obsessed with finding himself that he looked in Iceland. And this time she didn't hang up.

"Pórdís?" Lars said after four long rings.

"Hi there, Lars," said Pórdís.

23.

Cornelius's Two Discoveries

His first discovery was that Phoebe soon went back to being fourteen years old, and therefore had less and less time for him. And Emi, too, though she called him daily, was busy with Donnie in couples' therapy.

So here was his dilemma: What was he going to do with his time?

Should he take up gardening or, God help him, golf?

Should he find another woman with whom to share the waning years of his life?

No, on all counts, and emphatically no on that last one.

He'd promised Þórdís he would continue with the grievers, so that would take up three evenings a week, but only online, and only for ninety minutes. He had also told Þórdís, and everyone else who would listen, that he was done with writing. Yet he'd started a memoir, so he could fill some of the slowly passing days and weeks working on that, he supposed. He needed to take Yuki's ashes across the Pacific, too, but that was for a future date. And, if his physical condition didn't allow it, maybe Emi would go.

He walked into his kitchen to find Agatha standing by the deck door. Agatha was fine now, not only free of grief, but fond of him. He opened that door for her, then looked across the kitchen to the one that led to his basement. When

Þórdís said that LaVeronica and Frank had quit her group he was sorry about both, yet lately had been thinking more about Frank. He remembered what Frank said regarding Kenji Okada's drawings when Cornelius admitted that he didn't know where to put them - *They're headed to your basement, maybe up over the dryer or next to where you keep your firewood...* Something like that. And after Frank left, that was where he put them, not only the two Frank spoke of, but all seven. He leaned them against the wall on either side of his workbench, in the order he'd found them in on the night of his fall. He knew the artist placed them that way for some intrinsic reason, because when he lined them up chronologically, from the youngest Yuki to the oldest, for example, things went haywire. And if he took one away it was like skipping a chapter in a book.

After he put the drawings in the basement, he went down several times to sit on his stairs and look from one to the next to the next; Yuki looking out their kitchen window, her sadness evident in the way she blew across the steaming surface of her tea; Yuki beneath the willow with Agatha, both in yellow, and with himself, out of view but in their upstairs window; Yuki with her shoulders bared and loving him, as she had in Hokkaido; Yuki with her father in his military uniform; and Yuki among the Mount Rainier wildflowers, in love with someone else.

In each, save the one with her father, she was alone, in each a mystery. In the penultimate drawing she was about to touch the nearest blossoms on the cherry tree she stood beneath, with cranes in flight on her kimono and on the inside of her open parasol. That drawing seemed to say as clearly as words might, *'I am staying but I want to fly away.'*

In the final drawing there was no Yuki, only that continually falling man. Himself? The artist? An amalgam? It should be called *Blindness*, or *Ignorance*, or *Naïveté*.

At times like this, alone in his kitchen, he was consoled by the thought that he *hadn't* continually fallen. He had slammed into his hallway floor. And what saved him in the aftermath had not only been his grandmother in her tracksuit, but those six Yuki drawings, keeping him warm until Emi came to rescue him some days later.

Was he a fool to think that was the case? Maybe no and maybe yes.

24.

The Lowdown on Frank

It was true that Franklin Blessing believed cold fusion could save the planet. It was also true that, even before Doris's death, he talked too much, often boorishly.

So in those ways Jane's report regarding seeing him at the opera had been spot on.

Frank's bad grammar, chronic lying, and his obsequious behavior with women, however, weren't caused by Doris's death, but harkened back to his rocky youth, which had been almost identical to Doris's.

Frank met Doris at a party that his then-fiancée, Lucille, threw for him on the eve of him receiving his PHD in electrochemistry. Lucille was doing post-doc work with Frank's advisor, having received her own degree the year before, though she was five years younger than Frank, who came to chemistry late. When the Utah scientists, Fleischmann and Pons, claimed to have made cold fusion a reality back in 1989, Lucille announced that she would try to replicate their experiments, thus gaining some concomitant fame herself. Frank loved the idea of fame but mistook it for love of Lucille, which she felt, too, only without mistake. So they worked together on cold fusion, breaking only for late-night sex on the chemistry lab floor, and for Frank to complete his exams.

Then, however, on the night of Frank's party, Doris

walked in wearing hot pink short shorts, white high heels, and speaking a language that Frank knew fluently from his childhood.

That marked the end of Frank's collaboration with Lucille, and though he didn't revert to speaking like Doris in academic circles, he did so immediately when they were alone. So the truth that his fellow grievers never quite discovered was that Frank was not a fake. He simply lived without duplicity, in homage to the woman he loved.

One last thing. Frank wrote *"Farewell, Doris, Love of my Life,"* in the steam on the door of his shower every morning. He believed it to be the one bit of fabulist exorcism that had put him back on track with cold fusion, and that it would continue to do just as long as he didn't clean his shower door.

That would have delighted Pórdís.

Yet he had quit her group so she would never find that out.

25.

The Replacements

As if recruited specifically to replace Frank, Alberto had been a chemistry professor at U.C. Berkeley before his retirement and move to Tacoma, his late wife's hometown. When Jane heard his name she sat up straighter in her chair, though it only served to make her nose look big, for she also leaned closer to her computer.

"Thank you for including me," Alberto said, after Pórdís introduced him. "But please, call me Bert."

"Not on your life," said Jane. "I can already tell that 'Alberto' suits you better."

"Scoot back a little, Jane," Millicent said. "We want to see your whole face."

"Welcome, Bert, I'm Ruthie," said Ruthie. "And I think we should be called whatever we ask to be called, don't you, Cornelius?"

"I do," Cornelius said. "Welcome Bert. And welcome Hortense, too."

"Thanks, but if that's the deal then call me Betty," said the other new member. "Can you imagine what I went through in school with 'Hortense,' hanging around my neck? I wanted to kill my mother for saddling me with such a name."

"Me, too, actually," said Millicent, "so Betty and Bert, you might as well call me 'Mills.' Ruthie asked us to call her 'Ruth' for a while, and we sometimes call Cornelius 'Corny.' It's funny about names, how the most suitable seem to rise to the top."

"I agree," laughed Bert. "I think I may have come to the right place."

His laugh was like a roll of thunder, making Cornelius turn down his volume.

"This is our first pandemic session, and I want to thank Bert and Betty for joining us," Þórdís said. "It's not easy getting down to things over the internet, but we'll give it our best try."

"You're right, there's better non-verbal communication in person," said Betty. "I learned that from Bobert, my late husband. He was a communications expert."

"Your late husband's name was Bobert?" Ruthie asked.

"That's what we called him. His real name was Bob."

"Not Robert? Most of the Bobs that I've known had their names boiled down from Robert," Jane said.

"Well, yes, 'Robert.' Then 'Bob.' Then 'Bobert,'" said Betty.

"My wife's name was Mary so I called her 'Mary,'" Bert said. "We were only married in 2011, but oh how I miss her. She was *far* too beautiful for me. No one could figure it out."

"First new to marriage. Now new to grief," Millicent said.

"Oh no, I've known grief for ages. My brother, Angelo, gave me daily doses of it before I met Mary," said Bert.

"You miss my point. *Giving* someone grief is worlds away from the grief we feel in here," Millicent told him.

"Well, I wanted these first few minutes to be a 'getting to know you' kind of thing. But could we lean in a little now?" Þórdís asked, since Bert quite bravely offered to be 'up.'"

"That doesn't mean you should lean closer to your camera, Jane," Millicent said.

"Bert and Betty, Millicent's sarcasm takes some getting used," said Ruthie.

"I thought we were supposed to call her 'Mills,'" Betty said.

"And you don't have to worry about me getting used to it. I know sarcasm from dealing with Angelo all my life."

"Are we going to talk about Angelo or Mary?" asked Jane.

That made Bert begin a long 'love at first sight' story - first sight for him. but not for Mary. He told them about their initial date, what a fool he'd been to recite the chemical formula for yogurt, and how he redeemed himself when Mary discovered he had a painting by the linear artist, Agnes Martin, sitting on the couch at his home.

"*On* my couch, not over it," he said. "Mary thought that was quaint."

While Bert droned on, Cornelius snuck looks at the newest pages of his memoir, Millicent rubbed her feet together under her desk - they would *never* know that she was naked from the waist down! Jane checked her phone for word on Sam from a North Tacoma hospice, and Ruthie ate pretzels. Even Pórdís, though she listened carefully, paged through *Fables for Therapeutic Situations,* a book she brought back from Copenhagen. She didn't want to rely on *The Ugly Duckling* when telling Bert to free himself of that "far too beautiful" thing, and came upon a fable Annegrete liked - *The Two-Way Mirror,* by Satyajit Ray. Good. Weird was better than wholesome for a wholesome guy like Bert.

After about fifteen minutes and under Ruthie's influence, Cornelius logged off in a way he hoped would make the others think he was having technical difficulties, and went down to his kitchen to see if he had any pretzels in the house. He was sure he didn't, but found a box in the back of his cupboard, and pulled it out to check its "best by" date. September 1, 2020. That certainly rang a bell.

He ate ten pretzels sitting at his kitchen table and reading over his newest memoir passages again. If he completed the memoir would he discover what the drawings in his basement refused to tell him no matter how many times he looked at them?

He ate five more pretzels, then three after that. As with his original ten, each time he pulled them from the box he told himself that they would be his last. Just when he was about to go back up to the grievers' meeting, he heard his front door open and Phoebe come in. She was babysitting today and had said she would visit him, but he'd thought it would be earlier and assumed she'd changed her mind. When he shouted her name, she came into the kitchen carrying his infant great-granddaughter, whose coal black eyes, small wet mouth, and too much hair sticking up, seemed all to be aimed at piercing his heart.

"What are you doing with pretzels?" Phoebe demanded. "Don't you know they've got a ton of salt? Anyway, take Ayo into the living room while I make a sandwich. Put one of your Gene Kelly movies on, like the one where he dances with the mouse, because dancing movies are gonna be as rare as diamonds at Yehudi and Bess's house. They don't even have a TV."

Cornelius sang a snippet of a song he remembered from the scene Phoebe mentioned - *"if you worry, if you worry, if you bother your head…"* until Phoebe told him not to forget to put his mask back on.

Upstairs in that online netherworld, meanwhile, Þórdís was saying, "Okay, any last words for Bert, or are we able to keep our powder dry till next time?"

She tried not to look at a watch she now wore, given to her by Lars when she got back from Denmark. She didn't like the watch but until their relationship made itself clear she would use it to time their sessions, as well as the limits of her affection.

Downstairs again, Phoebe came into the living room to sit beside her grandpa and the beautiful infant sweetheart she was babysitting. Babysitting *for free,* though maybe not always for free, since it was a lot more work than she expected.

She had cut her sandwich in half in the kitchen so she could share it with her grandpa if he was hungry. Or even if he wasn't, since he needed more than anything to put on weight.

Suddenly, on the television screen in front of them, Gene Kelly climbed through a window in an otherwise cartoon world, to sing to a gloomy mouse-king. When he got to the lyric that Cornelius sang a moment earlier, Ayo's head came up off his chest and she looked at the screen on her own. She was too young to be able to do that, but that was what she did. Cornelius saw it and Phoebe saw it, both of them knowing it would be a great first story for them to tell her as she grew up.

If they knew her as she grew up; a thing that seemed unlikely for Cornelius because of his age, and somewhat unlikely for Phoebe, too, if she couldn't come to some new accommodation regarding babysitting, a thing she'd offered gratis in the heat of a passion she didn't have anymore, but wanted to feel again when she was, like, twenty-four years old.

For the moment, though, while Gene Kelly taught that mouse to dance, she put half a sandwich in her grandfather's hand, even lifted his hand toward his mouth. It was a tuna fish sandwich with onions and pickles on whole grain bread.

Worlds better for him than pretzels.

Acknowledgments

Thanks to my friend of nearly sixty years, Dr. Barrie Raik, of New York City, for reading and commenting on the medical sections of the novel, and for seeing to it that my ignorance of such things wasn't too obvious.

Much appreciation and thanks to Dusty Sang of Stay Thirsty Press for recognizing both the seriousness and humor with which I hoped to tackle the subject of grief, and for making invaluable suggestions.

Thanks to my friends in Tacoma, Washington, for their continued generosity toward me; for loving the rain and the low-hanging clouds; and for cherishing the most beautiful mountain in all the world, Mount Rainier. It's a happy day when they can say emphatically, "Look! The mountain is out!"

Thanks to John Cushing, Nancy Loncke, and Pilar Wiley for their excellent and wonderfully helpful proofreading skills.

Lastly I would like to thank my wife, Virginia Wiley, for reading draft after draft of this book, in all its iterations - she always gives me great advice - and to my children and grandchildren, for making my life so precious.

About the Author

Richard Wiley won the PEN/Faulkner Award and the Washington State Governor's Writers Award for *Soldiers in Hiding* and the Maria Thomas Fiction Award for *Ahmed's Revenge*. He is also the recipient of the Silver Pen Award from the State of Nevada. He is the author of nine novels and a collection of short stories. A graduate of the Iowa Writers' Workshop and Professor Emeritus of the University of Nevada, Las Vegas, he now lives in Los Angeles, California.

Made in the USA
Las Vegas, NV
07 April 2023

70312414R00225